PULP AND PAPERMAKERS FICTION

greenhill
https://greenhillpublishing.com.au/

Nelson, Craig (author)
Pulp and Papermakers Fiction
ISBN 978-1-923214-11-8
FICTION

Typesetting Calluna Regular 11/16
Cover Image by Adobe Stock
Cover and book design by Green Hill Publishing

PULP AND PAPERMAKERS FICTION

CRAIG NELSON

DISCLAIMER

'Pulp and Papermakers Fiction' is purely that "Fiction!" This novels characters and stories are as such fictitious and a product of the Author's imagination. In saying that although all the three Paper Machines described within this book are now out of operation, Bowater was, and in form still is (under a new name and new ownership) a real company producing tissue paper in Australia.

Written in Autobiographical form my character (Craig Nelson) runs fluent with the Authors time at Bowater but is purely fictitious in its content and storyline. We must all remember that memory is imperfect and has its own story to tell.

The Author has made every effort to identify and contact copyright holders of pictures reproduced in this book. The author would be pleased to hear from any copyright holders who have not yet been acknowledged and will rectify any omissions.

AUTHOR'S NOTE

There are a number of people that have come into my life over the years and I would like to thank them all. Whether they were a positive or negative experience is of little concern to me now as they all helped form who and where I am at today.

In saying that there are two stand outs whose positivity and support are extremely important to me and I have to thank individually.

The first is Tamara (Tee) my partner in life who just totally gets me.

Then my Nanu (grandfather) Joseph, who is my Spiritual Father and taught me most of my life skills. He still guides me through life today with the numerous proverbs he entrusted me with as a young fella.

Then lastly and most pertinently to this book I would like to thank all the Larrikins of Bowater in the 80's and 90's as they are the ones who made this story possible and taught me the valuable lesson of not taking myself too seriously.

Contribution Thank You

A big Thanks to George Aston, Daniel Nolan and John Heagney for their fantastic photography as it greatly assists the readers who have never seen the inside of a Paper Mill before, and floods the memories of those who have.

Thanks George, Dan and John!

A Special Thanks to Albert and Judi for their participation in the story and more importantly over 40 years of loyal friendship.

Love You Guys!

INTRODUCTION

Life in Australia today is so far removed from the Australia of my youth. All through those years (from the 60's through to not so long ago) I really did not notice it that much as it was very gradual and as such we all adapt. But after giving away mainstream working I gained time to reflect and ponder the past. When you do that you soon see that the changes are truly amazing. As I penned this novel I realized that simpler times are truly fabulous times and I just had to share my story.

I trust my simple writing style lends itself to flow with the fun and simplicity of my time at Bowater. Further I hope that you all enjoy the shenanigans of the boys who made my story possible "The Pulp and Papermakers!"

HERE WE GO!!!!!!!!!!!!!!

Pre – Pulped

GROWING UP IN MELBOURNE in the 70's was fantastic but eventually everyone has to get real and do that dreaded task "WORK". As a seventeen-year-old my first foray into this ugly field was as a tyre fitter in the inner Melbourne suburb of North Melbourne. Lothian Street to be exact and a very ugly foray it was. This was because as an industrial tyre fitter, being filthy all the time is "part of the course." Still it paid the "BILLS", another ugly four-letter word that I had avoided thus far in my short but eventful life. (Five letters if you have a lot of them.)

Another bullet that I dodged in my childhood was the wrath of the Marist and Christian Brothers during my Catholic education, who are both well documented for their love of children – 'for all the wrong reasons!' I was fortunate to escape this and I am not sure if it was because I wasn't pretty enough or too strong willed. I would like to think the later, although if I am known as not being pretty I can live with that. I didn't escape entirely unscathed though as in my primary years I was flogged with a cane by a frustrated old cow of a nun, and could not put my legs into a bath for many days after. Getting the cane in those days was not uncommon and throughout my secondary years I copped a number of floggings by the crazy old Bastards who claimed it was for my own good.

Well as a tyre fitter in the late 70's and early 80's I hoped that I had not yet reached the pinnacle of my success, but as everyone knows you get stuck in the groove. You have bills to pay and you look at doing all the things that 'grown ups' do, and it was not long before I was looking to tick all the boxes. I had myself a girl and a hot car, in a Canary Yellow 1977 SS Torana Hatchback, how cool was that! Not sure which I preferred more but it turned out that the Torana was much more reliable. (See picture of me and my Torana in the "About the Author" section.)

Back on the work front I remember as a young fella, driving the work Ute (a HX Holden one-tonner) through the quiet streets of Melbourne central with my workmate and turning the ignition off and back on while still travelling to let off a big backfire. Boy oh Boy did people shit themselves when we did this as it certainly sounded like a gunshot in those cavernous streets. Fortunately it was during the day, as if we had of done it at night I am sure we would have seen return fire. It was fun at the time but looking back it was very juvenile especially with the company logo plastered on three sides of the vehicle.

The tyre fitting was hard and dangerous in those days as the truck tyres all had split rims with some even being the three-piece collapsible type that were renowned for blowing up, or in to be more precise. Of course, we were supposed to use safety cages when pumping them up, but we never did. In fact, most of the time we sat on the side of the tyre until the bead popped up and then we knew 'all was good'. We had one really horrible incident in my time at the North Melbourne shop, and that was when Peter (the service fitter) picked up a small forklift tyre and wheel that went off in his chest. It threw him six feet into the air and stopped his heart. Fortunately, the Store Manager was up to the task and got Peter's heart going again. There was an investigation into the incident and it changed how our company, and the owner of the wheels company, did business. Turns out that these wheels (that were two piece and bolted together) had had the bolts that held them together welded to the wheel, so that when being removed from the forklift the wrong nuts could not be removed. This caused the nuts to strip the thread off the bolts over time, as they were almost always removed and retightened with a rattle gun that eventually stripped them. Add to this that these little wheels held 90 PSI of air and you had a bomb waiting to go off, with Peter being the poor bastard at the end of it. It was not until the early eighties that the tubeless truck tyres came in, (in decent numbers that is) making the game a bit safer in general.

While working at this job I started to get more responsible and settled down a bit – career wise that is – and when a position came up as a storeman at the tyre depot I threw my hat into the ring, as it was more money and I would get a chance to better myself by using other skills. I was the frontrunner for the job as many of the other tyre fitters were both older, and liked working on the road, or others who were more my age but not too sharp. So it was easy for me to stand out as the better option. But bugger me if I was not sideswiped by some dumb prick who got his missus pregnant and got the boss to feel sorry for him. I remember the day he got the job and came out to the workshop spruiking like a f***ing rooster how he got the job, I turned to him and said, "Hope you have twins you Bastard". And sure as shit four months later his partner gave birth to twins – "there is a God!"

Not long after that I watched a fellow come over from WA and walk into the assistant manager's job. This was another kick in the guts, as even though I was not in direct line for the job it would have meant a progress through the ranks, where the then third in charge would have stepped up. Turned out this fella could kick a footy and with the Dunlop boys being a major Hawthorn sponsor, "say no more!" That's how shit went down in the eighties and we all knew it. Turns out Gary was a good bloke though and I learnt a few life skills from him, even though I was jealous as shit of the brand new SL/E Commodore that he got for his signature.

I was growing up in the school of hard knocks but boy was life good, as even though we worked hard we could play even harder – a product of a young liver – fat wallet and shitloads of willing ladies. One of these was a lass called Fran who had a bit of an eye on me, not that I knew it at the time as she was the girlfriend of Peter, one of my co-workers. She was a tiny little lass with an Aussie dad and an Indian mum making her a yummy tanned chick who had a hot presence.

Peter was a service fitter on the road most of the time and I was stuck in the depot fitting mostly passenger stuff for booked in clients. This did mean though at home time (4-00pm) I was able to get away on time, nine times out of ten. This suited Fran who came to the depot every day around knock off time (that's "work" knock off time). As Peter was mostly still out, Fran always hit me up for a lift and our journeys home were very flirtations and a good laugh. But being a good Aussie mate I never acted on her advance as it was not the done thing, to cut your mate's grass – "as green and lush as that grass was!" Turned out Peter caught her out some months later with another of his friends, not that he was much of a friend.

During my time at the North Melbourne Tyre store I decided that it was a good idea to start looking for a house to buy, and although just turned nineteen it was on my "Grown-up List." Add to this, that in 1982 it was so cheap to buy a home in Melbourne "why wouldn't you!" The smart thing to do was to look on the North side of Melbourne as my family were all over that side of town and I was kind of use to it. My girl at the time also worked on that side of town so it all made sense. She worked at a shoe manufacturer called Julius Marlow, and as you can see in the early eighties a large number of us worked in manufacturing, unlike today where retail and service seem to dominate our workforce.

We tried to get a loan for our first place but the Banks were very conservative and as we were so young, they were not so keen. My Plan "B" was to sell my beloved Torana and buy a home with a personal loan. It was devastating to me as I loved that car but keeping it was not on my "Grown-up List" so it went up for sale. This was only the first stage in the process as we would still struggle to get a home unless we moved way out in the sticks.

A way of helping the pain and reducing the drive that we would need to make was for me to get a transfer from my North Melbourne location to one in the then outer suburb of Preston. That secured we were on the hunt for a new first home, and when we found one, it was in the country town of Flowerdale not far from Yea. Had to take a hit on the Torana though as it was worth about six thousand at the time, I ended up taking four and a half thousand for it. That same Torana today would easily be worth more than a house in Flowerdale, Wow! Well it all worked out, and after securing a 5 year personal loan of $19,000 and $4,000 from the Torana sale we secured our home in Long Gully Road for the grand sum total of $23,000. Then came the misery of buying and driving an old HK Holden that we bought with the balance of the funds from the house purchase.

The tyre fitting job in Preston turned out OK and with my Girl working a few suburbs away in Brunswick we started to settle into life on the treadmill. The travelling to and from work took us around an hour each way in those days, and although not too far, in the old HK Holden it was a bit rough as it was quite basic compared to my Torana – shit I missed that vehicle. We also got a bit isolated moving out there, with our best friends Judi and Albert (The ones from my book "One Simple Journey" who live in Yarrawonga – now Wodonga) who lived in Brunswick being the only ones who were regular visitors to our new place. Judi and Albert also worked at Julius Marlow.

We had good times with this pair and Albie still had his pride and joy (not Judi – his other pride and joy) a Nissan (Datsun) 200B SX – and did I mention I really miss my 1977 Torana SS hatchback! I spoke to Albie the other day on the phone and he reminded me of a couple of our adventures.

The first was, one time late at night after a big night at the Glenburn Hotel (Burnt down in the January 2009 Bushfires), while we were driving back to Flowerdale on the back roads. Albie was at the wheel of his Datsun and I at that stage still had my Banana Torana, with both of us hooning around a bit. We turned into Long Gully Road to have a look at our new place (which we hadn't settled yet) and I floored it with Albie in hot pursuit. The road was pretty long (thus the name) and we were at quite a speed on this dirt road (track really) when I slipped down a narrow side road that dropped off to the left of Long Gully Road. Down this side road (which I knew very well) there were three or four homes and the side road came back onto Long Gully Road after about 150 metres. Add to this that as I dropped off Long Gully Road I switched off my headlights and I knew Albie would be in a bit of a panic. I saw Albie's headlights stop in the middle of the road and I later learned that he thought I had crashed into the bushes. I know this because when we stopped at our, soon to be, new home he called me a F***en Idiot about 27 times.

SS 154

The second event was after we took possession of my lovely HK Holden (did I tell you how much I really miss my 1977 Torana SS hatchback) and we decided to go for a country drive. All four of us were in the HK as we wanted to go down some pretty wild roads and Albie's car was a bit too pretty for that. It was out back of Kinglake somewhere, not sure where, (even at the time I had no idea) and we descended down this steep thick gravel road. I remember the road distinctly as at the time Albie said; for f**k's sake you aren't going down there are you? To which I replied; yeah why and proceeded to descend. Turned out that going down was the easy part as when we reached the bottom, the way out was even steeper – oh shit! To add to the plot, we could not turn around as the road was narrow and the edges were wet and muddy. Only one way out and that was up! Made sense to get Judi into the driver's seat while we all pushed, and with Albie beside me saying; you Idiot – you Idiot over and over we pushed while Judi gave it to the old girl. With Rocks and shit flying everywhere we started to get up the hill and then when Judi got the HK well ahead of us and she started to ease off the accelerator I yelled out GO GO GO – DON'T STOP!!!! Judi did a great job and even though the rest of us had a steep walk we were all relieved that the car was now at the top of this amazingly crazy road. To this day Albie still says we could have died in that place. I think he is being a bit of a drama queen, but don't tell him that I said that!

Not long after this adventure we settled into our new home and the daily grind of a fairly long drive each day. It was not the distance that was so bad it was more the winding roads and treacherous conditions, with heaps of wildlife, and in winter, very slippery conditions. In fact winter was the worst time to travel as the days got shorter and for a number of months we would leave home before sunrise and arrive home after dark. Add to this the freezing conditions where the pipes under our home would freeze and we couldn't even shower some mornings. Our hot water system was a wood burning type and we never seemed to have enough time to get it going in the morning, no surprise really as we left around 5-30am. It also got so cold that the windscreen of our car would ice up and even the radiator froze solid on many occasions.

The windscreen required warm water to rectify, and Bernie (our neighbour from a few doors up) had a ritual of standing on his bonnet and pissing on his windscreen to get himself sorted on these days. Not a pretty sight if you knew Bernie, although the frost prevented us witnessing what would have been an even uglier sight. I remember one time I had defrosted the radiator and was about three kilometres into my drive to work when the temperature light came on and I had to pull over. It was still dark when I did, and although I had water in the boot that was not frozen, I thought I would wait until the heat of the engine thawed out whatever was still frozen in the cooling system. I was standing at the front of the HK next to the pitch-black bush on the side of the road when I heard something charging towards me from the darkness. I shit myself and jumped into the driver's seat as something or someone crashed into the front passenger side of my car. With no further activity after the thud I went to investigate and found a huge black wombat, who looked dazed, turning around and scampering back into the bush. He must have been drawn in by the headlights – WOW that put the wind up me.

Another time I was well on my way to work (in the suburb of Bundoora) and coming up to a set of lights on the corner of Plenty and Settlement Rd when I heard a huge bang under my bonnet. I stopped the HK and lifted the bonnet to see a hole in the side of the engine block with oil sprayed everywhere. What surprised me even more is that on attempting to restart it the old girl fired up and got me up the Plenty Rd hill, past Mario's Pizza Shop, to a Service Station where she died completely. I got into a phone box (no mobile phones obviously in those days) and made some calls to get us both to work and have a tow truck pick her up and take her to a mechanics shop in Bundoora. In those days we had Repco Exchange Engines that were both cheap and reliable and it wasn't long before the HK had a new engine and was navigating us back and forth to work. What is totally amazing is that it cost a grand total of $383.50, I still have the receipt. While the HK was off the road my boss at the Preston Beaurepaires was kind enough to lend me a work Ute with the only condition being that I did a few stock transfers for him after work without charge or claiming overtime. I was happy to do this as I was in a pickle and was very grateful of his offer.

Life went on like this for a couple of months and we were happy with our lot but it was now time to do the "Grown Up Thing" and consider getting married and having kids. Looking back on this I was far too young and I think we did a lot of things because "that's what you do!" The only way we could possibly do this was for me to get a better paying job as my now future wife would have to stay at home if we had kids because "that's what you do!" The best way that we saw for this to happen was for me to enter into a tradition that was in my future wife's family for many years, and that was for me to become a 'Papermaker.' I had no idea before this point as to what a Papermaker did or even where they did it. Although my future father in law did work at a place in Fairfield Melbourne that made cardboard, in the 'Junker Section' which I knew better for the porn magazines that he got rather than what he did for a living. (Well shit I was only twenty years old).

Turns out though that my future wife's Uncle (Uncle Fozzie as he would be referred to as later) knew how to pull a few strings at the Bowater Paper Mill. Always a mover and shaker that fellow, and never short of a joke. But I think the fact that my future parents in law were friends with one of the head honcho's at the mill was the main reason I got a look in.

The Interview (screening stage)

WELL IT ALL STARTED with a job interview and that was a daunting task for me, as I basically fell into the job as a Tyre Fitter. Let's face it they are not a group that are known for their superior intelligence, so landing a job like that was not too difficult.

I dressed up for the interview with the best clothes that I had, which consisted of a newish pair of black jeans and a nice white shirt that I purchased specially to wear for this occasion. My shoes were a bit daggy but I think I looked OK in general, and hey "that's all that matters". I drove my old HK to Box Hill and turned off Middleborough Road and into Ailsa Street where at the end of the road I was confronted with a gatehouse similar to what you would see on Hogan's Hero's at the entrance to the prison camp, complete with boom gates and Sargent Schultz in the little gatehouse. The only difference between this fellow and Sargent Schultz was that he knew I was coming and "I knew Nothing!" Turns out I was on the list of authorized entries so he pointed me to where I should park my car and then told me to follow the signs to the administration building.

I was seriously shitting myself as I walked up to this place as it was massive and I had never in my life done anything like this, "I was only 20 years of age". Truth be known they generally didn't employ people my age as they preferred older men, who were seen as more reliable and mostly had a family to support. The other factor that came into play was that it was rotating shift work (no social life), and some of the young fellows just couldn't handle this. But I had bought a home and I had some good references so I was hopeful that they would see me as an asset. Another point that also probably helped was that they had just introduced a 38- hour week and had to put a completely new additional shift on to cover the 24/7 operation. The current shifts they had were GREEN – BLUE - RED & BLACK and now they were going to have a GOLD shift. I was greeted by the young lady in reception, asked to sign the 'sign in register', and then directed to wait in the interview room that was located close to the reception area.

The room was quite stark with only a few product posters that were framed hanging on the walls. There was a large table with about 6 chairs around it and two chairs against the wall near where I had entered the room. I sat down at a chair that was near where I entered and waited.

A minute or so later the girl from reception came in and asked if I would like a glass of water, she also advised me that the chief papermaker would be here soon for the interview. I declined the water as I was so nervous, I thought I may piss my pants with too much water in me, even though my mouth was dry. I reckoned a dry mouth was a better option than pissing my pants! A few minutes later an older gentleman came through the door, I stood up and as I did, he introduced himself as Mr Cogers the chief Papermaker. I replied in an almost squeaky voice (as I was so nervous); hello sir my name is Craig Nelson.

He gave me a bit of a funny look as I think the 'Sir' bit was foreign to him, but he didn't comment and asked me to take a seat at the table. As he moved to the table, he made a funny gesture with his two hands. "No!" more than funny actually, it was weird. He raised his two palms as to catch a football at his stomach and using his wrists gestured to pull up his pants at the waist. What an odd thing to do I thought, but obviously when going for a job you don't say – "what the heck was that!" He sat down, and started to ask me a few questions about myself and my family. I later found out that the hand gesture was a habit that he had developed when on the factory floor as a Machineman. I was told that he always wore baggy pants, and when they got a bit wet they would slide down. To prevent this, he would tie a bit of string around the waist of his pants to hold them up. But when they got really wet his pants would still creep down, and as he always had dirty hands (usually covered in pulp) he would use his wrists to prop them up. (The gesture that I had just witnessed). Mr Cogers was a straight shooter and grilled me a bit about why I wanted to work in a Paper Mill, he even told me how the shift work side of the job could be quite taxing on a person. I could tell he was a man that had worked hard all his life and seemed like a fish out of water in the business clothes that he was wearing. I liked him and I think that side of the interview went quite well. After about twenty minutes or so he told me that Mr Vardy would drop in to say hello and may have a few questions for me. Then he said; after Mr Vardy had a chat to me that the HR lady would give me an application form to fill in and I was to leave it with the receptionist on my way out. Now Mr Vardy was a friend of my future in-laws so I hoped that he would be light on me, as I was still nervous and as I had been here for a while now, I felt like I needed some fresh air.

Mr Vardy came into the room and immediately I thought to myself, he was not what I expected. He looked quite at ease in a suit and he fitted my brains perception of what an office dude would look like. I say this as I had been given a rundown from Uncle Fozzie on the roles that Mr Cogers, Mr Vardy and Mr Blueberry played in the establishment of the Box Hill Paper Mill. Uncle Fozzie told me that the three of them came to Australia for England as the machine operators for the new plant. Cogers was the Machineman, Vardy was First Boy and Blueberry was Second Boy. Not what you would call politically correct names but that was the traditional names of the particular roles.

The Machineman was in charge of the main papermaking process basically from the wet stock tanks through to the reel area. (My knowledge of this process is fair but not highly technical). For those who may be interested I will go over some of the processes in coming chapters – (Site layout described in the Induction / Introduction Chapter and Site Plan at the rear of this book). Cogers was the main man in those days and into the future I have been told that he spent a lot of his time with the Machinemen on the factory/mill floor well after he put on a suit. Vardy was the 1st Boy and this job entailed assisting the Machineman whenever required, but most of his time was spent at the reel section transferring the reel from one Corebar to the next and monitoring quality at the dry end for the Machineman. Blueberry's job as 2nd Boy was to assist the 1st Boy in the reel changeover, then remove the Corebar – clean up the reel – mark its details and then load the new Corebar into the machine for the next reel. When I talk of this process I am not describing the size in great detail, but to understand its scale the reels are approximately 3.4 metres across and approximately 2 metres high. The Corebars and reels are all moved by overhead cranes that are located on roller tracks just below the roof some 12 metres or so above. It is an amazing process that I will describe in more detail in coming chapters. You will also see photos of this machinery in coming chapters to assist those who cannot otherwise visualize.

Back to Mr Vardy who had just entered the Interview room!

Mr Vardy did not add much more, and his questions were more about my future in-laws and 'my plans' for the future, so I was quite relieved. We spoke for about ten minutes before Pam the HR manager came in, and with that Mr Vardy wished me luck and departed. Now Pam also spoke to me briefly before handing me an application form and giving me the same instructions that Mr Cogers had done. From all that had gone on during my interview stage it seems as though my application would be checked by HR and if I met the criteria then it would be passed on to Mr Cogers who appeared to be the main decision maker. It seemed to me from all accounts that this Paper Mill was his baby and he decided "who" worked in it. I stayed in the Interview room filling out the application form and when I completed it I walked out to Reception. I handed in the completed application form to the girl at the reception desk, she wished me luck and I was on my way. Out to my old HK and past Sgt Schultz, who opened the boom gate for me, and I was off home hoping that I would be successful.

Getting this job would be a significant change for me and my future wife as our plans hinged a fair bit on me being successful. Although we could survive on one wage and get by, this job would double my income and make life much better for us both. The main reason why this job paid so well was that it was shift work that included night shift and weekend penalties. In fact, on public holidays I would earn double time and a half, which I thought was amazing.

Day after day went by and I had not heard if I had been successful or not, so after the fourth day I gave Uncle Fozzie a call to see what the protocol was. Fozzie said that I had been unsuccessful as I was too young and lived too far away, "I was devastated" (and he could tell!), so he didn't keep his stupid little joke going any longer and told me that he believed I had the job but was awaiting confirmation. "Great joke – I was gutted!"

Turned out he was right as that afternoon I received a call from Pam (the HR manager) to say that my application had been successful and that I was to start day shift in two weeks for all the induction and safety training. I was over the moon and let my future wife (who was at work that day) know the good news. I considered ringing Uncle Fozzie to say that I missed out, but I thought he may ring the Paper Mill and get up them or something, so I decided against it. Even though I wanted to get him back for his little joke I was so happy that I decided to ring him nicely and give him the good news. He was very happy for me and after we chatted for a bit I rang my manager from the Tyre depot to give my notice. Mr Hurren was happy for me also as he knew of my plans, and said if it helped I could take another week off on holidays and not have to come back. He meant this in the nicest possible way (I think!) as I was already on two weeks leave and was owed about another five weeks in holidays anyway. A couple of days before I was due to start at the Paper Mill I dropped in to see Mr Hurren and the boys to say my goodbyes. Although not the best of jobs, the guys I have worked with have been fantastic and I will genuinely miss the laughs and good times that we have had.

As a side thought I must add that while working at this Preston site I reclaimed a large hammer head that I spotted on a scrap pile in the Sims Metal Yard that was next door at the time. I fixed a new handle to it and used it for many tasks around my homes at the time. I even used it in the 2000's while working as a Real Estate Agent to bang in For Sale signs.

I still have it today!

The Induction / Introduction

FOR THE SECOND TIME I have turned off Middleborough Road and onto Ailsa Street and was heading towards the Gatehouse at the entrance to the Paper Mill. That was the good news, the bad news was that I still had my old HK, did I tell you how much I really miss my 1977 Torana SS hatchback?

As I approached, I noticed that it was not Sargent Schultz this time but an English fellow named Harry, who had very yellow crooked teeth. A product of smoking and breeding I would say. A helpful fellow though and he directed me to the Paper Mill carpark that was inside the gate (known as the Northern Carpark), off to the right and all the way down the right boundary of the property. He told me to park my vehicle anywhere in the carpark and walk towards the big building, then turn right and travel along the safety barriers next to the reel storage warehouse. Then follow it all the way to the assembly area where a group of us will meet for an Induction tour of the facility. As I travelled I was amazed at the sheer scale of the place, it seemed the size of a mini city to me, it was enormous.

When I arrived at the assembly area I was only the second newbie there, and we waited quietly for a staff member to collect us and hopefully more newbie's to join us. We were soon joined by two other newbie's and then Mr Blueberry who was to give us the tour of the mill section. We were all given ear plugs (the little white cylindrical ones that you rolled in your fingers then shoved in your earholes) and after a role call we were on our way. Mr Blueberry (Charles) told us to stay close as we needed to keep clear of the workers and machinery and that it was quite a noisy and dusty place.

The tour went like this – (and this will give you an idea of the layout of the facility at the time). (***SITE PLAN AT REAR OF THIS BOOK)*** We had entered from the Northern side and Charles explained that from the carpark we had walked along the Northern Reel Store which was now to the left of us directly opposite Number 3 Paper Mill. We would now walk down the alleyway between No 3 Mill and the Northern Reel Store, which was the biggest Reel Store on site at the time, and be heading towards the Pulp Yard.

This place in general was tidy and well organized but due to the nature of the product there was a lot of wet and dry pulp with paper dust in every nook and cranny.

Pulp Yard viewed looking North

We looked through the pulp yard and viewed all the raw materials that, in the most part, came from the Pulp Mill in Myrtleford (Country Victoria) with some coming from oversees. I believe it was the highly bleached product that came from overseas but I did not ask the question of Charles at the time as I was still awestruck at the sheer size of the place. We then toured, via the wet area, through No 3 Mill *(below is a Photo of No 3 Mill from the Wet End to the Rewinder in the distance)* which was the newest of the three Mills. The first thing that hits you in this place is the noise, and I checked my ear plugs a number of times, as it was so loud that I thought they must have been loose or fallen out. As we moved along the Machine, the size and speed of the machinery was amazing, with water running everywhere and the vibrations went right through you.

Fortunately the workers had huts that were located on the wall of the building and strategically placed to allow the operators a good view of their particular work area. The first hut we encountered was the Machinemans hut, as the hut for stock prep was upstairs and the Pulp Yard boys had a smoko room near the stock conveyors. But I later learned that this was not the main reason that these huts had been installed as they were "designated smoking areas" – Now that was the 80's for you! We continued our tour past the reel section of the machine, where the 1st and 2nd boy had a hut and on towards Number 3 Rewinder. As we moved towards the Rewinder area the air got dustier and dustier. The Rewinder crew also had a hut and because this area was more labour intensive this hut was crowded. Apparently the machine had had some issues and the boys on the winder crew were awaiting a second reel to ply up the product. It was bloody amazing that they could breathe in there as all four of them were smoking. Then when one opened the door to check the Rewinder, it was like the car scene in the Cheech and Chong Movie – 'Up In Smoke'. What an upside-down world it was back then, going inside to smoke – crazy!

We continued out into the covered roadway behind No 3 Winder that was close to the Assembly Point where we started the tour. We travelled South on the designated pathway that ran alongside the internal roadway with Charles pointing out the areas and giving a brief overview of their functions. Straight across from the back of No 3 Winder was a smaller reel store and behind that, the Store itself where supplies were obtained for all areas of the facility via a chit. (A **chit** is a short official note, such as a receipt, an order, or a memo, usually signed by someone in authority). I thought I would put the official meaning of this word in as I had never heard of it before. In fact I have never heard of it used anywhere before or after I worked in the Paper Mill. We did not deviate to view the store area but kept walking along the designated pathway beside the internal roadway. This roadway was mainly used by forklifts that had different attachments at the front to obviously suit their main function. In this area the forklift was fitted with what was called a grab, and as the name suggests it was used to "grab" the produced reels that were either taken to one of the reel stores for storage, or to 'Conversion' (sadly nicknamed 'The Veggie Patch') that I will describe to you soon.

Back to the tour and Charles then pointed to the right where behind a cyclone wire fence sat masses of machine rolls, machine blades and other equipment that was being repaired or maintained by 'Fitters' who worked mainly on day shift. In addition there were also two Fitters per shift who worked on a 24 hour basis, looking after Breakdowns and did General Maintenance. These two fitters had a hut also, and worked with Paper Mill and Conversion shift crews, Black – Green -Red – Blue – Gold (the new shift). We continued our tour and past where the reels came out of the back of No 3 Paper Mill. This was also where the pallets of slit paper were loaded after being plied and cut by No 3 Rewinder (I will go over this process in coming chapters as this is where I spent a number of years working). The slit paper that came off the back of the Rewinder were called biscuit's, and at a minimum of 20 kilograms each not the type you would dunk in your tea or coffee. Funny name but I did get use to the terminology after a period of time working there.

Charles was giving us a rundown on many of the functions of the areas, but as it was so long ago I am relying on my memories of working there rather than memories of the tour commentary. It was around forty years ago! The next left is where we turned into the Broke Room, and Charles asked us to stay at the entrance while he requested the Broke Room attendant to stay off his forklift and ensure that other vehicles did not enter while we were on tour in his area. I remember the operator as John, an older fellow who had a serious limp and it looked almost painful for him to dismount the vehicle. I later learnt that John, who ended up on the same shift as me and was a ripper bloke, had been in a very serious motor cycle accident some time ago and was very lucky to still have his leg.

The Broke Room, as the name suggests, was used to recycle the paper that had been rejected or discarded during the manufacturing or conversion stage. The word "Broke" is the name given to paper that is of no commercial use and is to be re-introduced into the Papermaking cycle. The Broke Room is the point of entry for that "Broke". The Broke Room Attendants job is to gather the Broke and load it onto the Broke Conveyor, that when loaded, (which happens on a continuous basis) travels up and into a Hydro Pulper. When Paper is re-used like this the fibre content of the paper is broken down significantly and can only be introduced back into the Papermaking process in small quantities. The Job of the Broke

Room attendant is to ensure supply of this product so that the Stock Prep guys can draw on it within the parameters of the particular paper being made. With three Paper Machines running 24 hours a day though the demand is quite significant which is fortunate as there seems to be shitloads of Broke all over the place! Also running into the Broke Room are "trim shoots" – these are pipes that have air pumped through them that come from all areas of the Factory forcing the edge waste of Biscuits (paper reels) into a cavernous skip area in the Broke Room, that is extremely dusty and messy. In fact, we watched John empty this area while on tour and he came out looking more like a Lamington than an ex-biker!

The Broke Room attendant also had his own Hut, and as he was by himself most of the shift it was well documented as a place for depression among many who worked there. I was told a story not long after I started work on shift, of a Broke Room Attendant who went missing while at work. There was a search that went on for many hours and at the shift change, with the Attendant still not accounted for, there was fears that he may have had an accident. With still no sign of him many hours after the shift change (this is the time when one shift is taken over by another eg; Green to Gold), the decision was made to test the paper. What a horrible thought – but even worse the results of the test showed traces of human tissue. Although not conclusive in many of the staffs mind, the findings of an investigation stated suicide. It was believed that the poor fellow was very depressed and had simply walked up the Broke Conveyor and into the Hydro Pulper. As a result, a huge quantity of paper reels and converted goods were later destroyed, for obvious reasons. It also made staff more aware of the risks in the Broke Room and checks were made on their welfare at regular intervals by the leading hand or supervisor.

Back to the tour

Out the Eastern door of the Broke Room and to the left was Paper Mill 2 and to the right Paper Mill 1. Charles took us to the left and we were now facing No 2 Rewinder which was much older looking than No 3 Mill Rewinder. It had a less sophisticated system for cutting the paper into biscuits and there was no conveyor system to get the biscuits off the machine. I later discovered (in my time working here) that this was because it was not used nearly as often or consistently as No 3 Rewinder. In fact, there was a second winder crew who operated both the No 1 Mill Rewinder and this one, and they rotated their time between the two. We followed Charles past the CR lab (where they did paper quality testing) and started to walk from the dry end of the Paper Mill to the Wet end. The TC department was located above the CR lab and they also did testing there, but I believe (as I never really had much to do with this area) it was the wet product prior to hitting the Mills that they tested. At the reel section and opposite the paper running onto a new reel was another one of these huts. This hut housed the First and Second Boy, along with the visiting Rewinder crew. But if we thought that the number 3 Mill hut was crowded then this hut was overflowing. As we walked past, one of the boys from the Rewinder crew had his body outside the door and his head in the hut having a cigarette. He was trying to push in a bit further as Mr Blueberry went past as I believe he thought he may get in strife. There were six guys in this hut and by the size of it I think five would have been its maximum capacity.

At this point I should describe the huts as they were not factory-built units and they seemed to be tailor made for this application. They consisted of a timber floor that was raised slightly off the ground, (I would say to allow it to be moved with a forklift) with the back, top and lower front of three sides assembled in Plywood (probably marine ply).

The upper three sides (front and two sides) above waist height was Perspex, and there was a door at either end made of the same materials. Inside was a bench seat which ran the full length of the back of the hut (some 2 – 3 metres) and was covered in on old pick up felt, part of the wet area Paper Machine. There was a shelf near the ceiling of the hut that also ran the full length of the back of the hut and one along the front of the hut that was for cups, ashtrays etc. The shelf at the front of the hut seemed to be a very convenient height for the boys to put their feet up onto, but funnily enough I didn't see any feet up as Mr Blueberry was going past!

We continued along the No 2 Paper Machine which was very similar to No 3 Paper Machine but on a slightly smaller scale. This is coming from a guy who had never seen a Paper Machine in his life before, but fundamentally they were very similar. The back end of these creatures are amazing to see for the first time as they have an eerie look to them.

Hard to describe, but you see a lot of this industrial look in movies where the baddies hang out after a factory had closed down for many years. Difference was that these were still running. Not to say that the machinery wasn't fully functional and well maintained but it just looked really old, especially No 1 and 2 Paper Mills.

We continued our tour to the very end of No 2 Paper Mill and then across to No 1 Paper Mill, which kind of shared the same massive space. The only separation to these two Paper Machines was at the Dry end where the TC and CR Departments labs were. They were in a fully sealed brick building about the size of a two-storey suburban home. Actually, they even had a balcony, perhaps to take in the scenery and the fresh air (not). As we travelled along Paper

Mill 1 it was like a mirror image of Paper Mill 2 and again this is to the untrained eye. We continued to the Dry end of Paper Mill 1 and onto Rewinder 1 which was smaller than the other two Rewinders and was only for single ply. This was because Paper Mill 1 was for more industrial paper. You know the stuff, Industrial Roll Towel that they have at Service Stations to check your oil and in the toilet block to dry your hands. It even made that toilet paper that you don't see any more – you know the stuff, rough and ready stuff you could use to sand your timber with! One thing that was noticeable though, in No 1 compared to No 2, was the tighter space at the Dry end, it was significantly different. I would learn more about this when I started work there, as when the machine had trouble most of the Broke (waste paper) had to be manually removed from the area unlike No 2 where a forklift could access.

We left the Paper Mill area now and as we re-joined the covered roadway, we turned left into the area called Conversion (The Veggie Patch). Now as the name suggests this area's primary function was converting the reels of paper into finished product and in most cases ready for the supermarket shelf (not growing veggies for that Supermarket). As we went through the doorway into Conversion not only were we going from one type of manufacturing to another but we were also changing from one type of Australian to another. Now this is a very sensitive subject to many people but I am not trying to divide or discriminate. I am just trying to paint the picture of "the way it was", and that was that the majority of employee's in the Paper Mill were Anglo-Saxon's and all male, while in conversion the majority were ethnic. There were Italians, Greeks, Yugoslavs, Maltese, Chinese and the list went on. With the majority of the Conversion staff being Male and 100% of them that did rotating shift work being male, women did work in the conversion area but they were mainly on day shift. Although there were some who did the afternoon shift in one section I believe. This is not an opinion, this is 'just how it was'. I did hear a story one time that Ronald Biggs's (the Great Train Robber) wife once worked in Conversion or the Warehouse.

Back to our tour

Now this place was also massive, but the individual machines in the most part were much smaller than anything in the Paper Mill, as they all had more specific products to produce. There were printing machines that printed patterns on the toilet paper and roll towels. Embossing machines and a raft of other processes that made a huge variety of product. One amazing thing was that although there was automation all over the place most of the finished product was packed by hand into Cardboard boxes. What a job that was, you had to be able to switch your brain almost completely off to do this sort of work for a full eight-hour shift, or sometimes longer.

Hand packing of Toilet Rolls - Into Hand folded boxes and pushed onto a conveyor belt when filled.

Charles did a great job explaining all the processes to us, but again I reiterate, that this was about 40 years ago now (and maybe more by the time you read this) so I am not just using his tour speech but memories of working there also to paint this picture. The whole Factory, Paper Mill included, was like a small self-contained town as not only was there production and maintenance but other things like a kitchen/cafeteria, lunch rooms, nurses quarters with visiting doctor and the list goes on. This was a fair dinkum serious establishment with a unique culture that you will discover in the coming chapters!

Charles explained the other areas in light detail, which included the Despatch Warehouse, Administration building, Effluent area (nicknamed the Elephant Plant – which had water tanks big enough to wash a herd of Elephants) and various others. But for us Newbie's we had seen the areas that would encompass the majority of our working hour's onsite. Charles then said that he would escort us to the cafeteria as it was now lunchtime and that after lunch he would collect us for the in-room training. He also explained that we would do the in-room training for the rest of the day today and for the whole of tomorrow. I had brought my lunch which was in my car in an Esky, and I considered asking Charles if I could retrieve it. But as we got closer to the Cafeteria the smells were amazing and I quickly ditched that idea in favour of a hot pie and chips served on a hot plate with a chocolate Big M.

Life was good at the Paper Mill!

For the next day and a half we were seated in a training room and the only bit I remember was the lunch break as I repeated my order of a Pie and Chips, which you should be able to gather by now was Sensational! Come to think of it, it also explains the body shape of many of the staff who looked like they had been grazing in a pretty good paddock for a while! With all the formalities completed I was now ready (apparently) to be a Papermaker at the Bowater Paper Mill!

Now I was very fortunate that Mr Hurren my boss from Beaurepairs Preston had let me have some extra time off as I had a bit of organizing to do, and in addition, I would not have been able to attend the Induction /Introduction tour that I had just completed. Now this would not have stopped me from getting the job but I would have had to wait another shift rotation before joining my new work mates on Gold Shift. It all worked out great and I gave Mr Hurren a call to advise him of my new job and to thank him so much for the lovely reference that he had written for me.

10.01.84

To whom it may concern,

Craig Mahon has worked for Beaurepaires for Tyres for three years working at two of our branches. Craig has always proved to be a hard, willing worker.

I personally have known Craig for ten months. In this time, he has proved to me to be trustworthy, intelligent and with a mind of his own. Craig works well with those around him. I have no hesitation in recommending Craig for whatever job he applies for, and wish him success in the new job.

John Hurren
Manager.
7 Bell St, Preston.
443828.

Baptism of Fire

HERE WE GO!

DAY 1.

I ARRIVED AT THE Paper Mill carpark and as I was a Newbie the Leading Hand met me at the Assembly area where I had started my Induction Tour at, some four days prior. Larry was his name and he was a friendly fellow who had been with the company about 20 years. One thing that I found out early on was that many of the staff who worked in the Paper Mill were lifers. He had just become a Leading Hand with the inception of the new shift (Gold Shift) and had been a Machineman in No 1 Paper Mill for almost that entire 20 years – Wow!

Larry led me to the centre of the Mill, close to Rewinder 2, as this was where the Supervisors / Leading Hands office was, right near the timeclock. I had never used a timeclock before but it is quite basic.

Larry located my timecard and showed me how to clock in. Now it may seem like timecards are just for your hours to be paid but the simple system that they had here where you had an in and out column meant that the Supervisor could see at a glance who was in and who was out. Very handy especially on the occasions when a tragedy like that of the Broke Room attendant who committed suicide occurred.

After showing me how to clock on Larry took me over to the area where I was to be working for the day. He introduced me to all the Rewinder crew and said to me that I should take instructions from Rex the Winderman and just observe for the first four hours. As with all new workers I started my new position in training mode. You may as well have put a big red hat with a white flower on my head as I stood out so obviously! The main reason for this was that I didn't have a uniform yet and I was like a fifth wheel at the back of Rewinder No 3. They started all Newbie's on Day shift as there were more Supervisory staff around which was a great idea. This occurred even though Day Shift was the middle shift of the rotation - now let me explain the rotation.

We worked five days of Afternoon shift (3-00pm – 11-00pm), a day off, then five days of Day shift (7-00am – 3-00pm), a day off, then five nights of Night shift (11-00pm – 7-00am) then either three days or eight days off depending on the rotation. Night Shift is referred to in many industries, who do it, as the Graveyard shift. With the old shift roster (that these guys worked before the 38 hour week came in) they worked a similar roster with the main difference being that they worked seven days of each type of shift.

On starting today I was given 'a starters pack' let's call it, which included hearing protection (ear muffs this time), steel capped boots and a shift roster. Now the boots and the ear muffs I could understand but the shift roster was another story. My goodness what a complicated piece of hard paper this was. Folded into 3 sections and printed on both front and back, it was a full five shift roster for the next five years. Apparently it told us what days to work and what days to stay home! Wow it looked complicated, but with a new job in a new place and with people I didn't yet know it was the least of my worries.

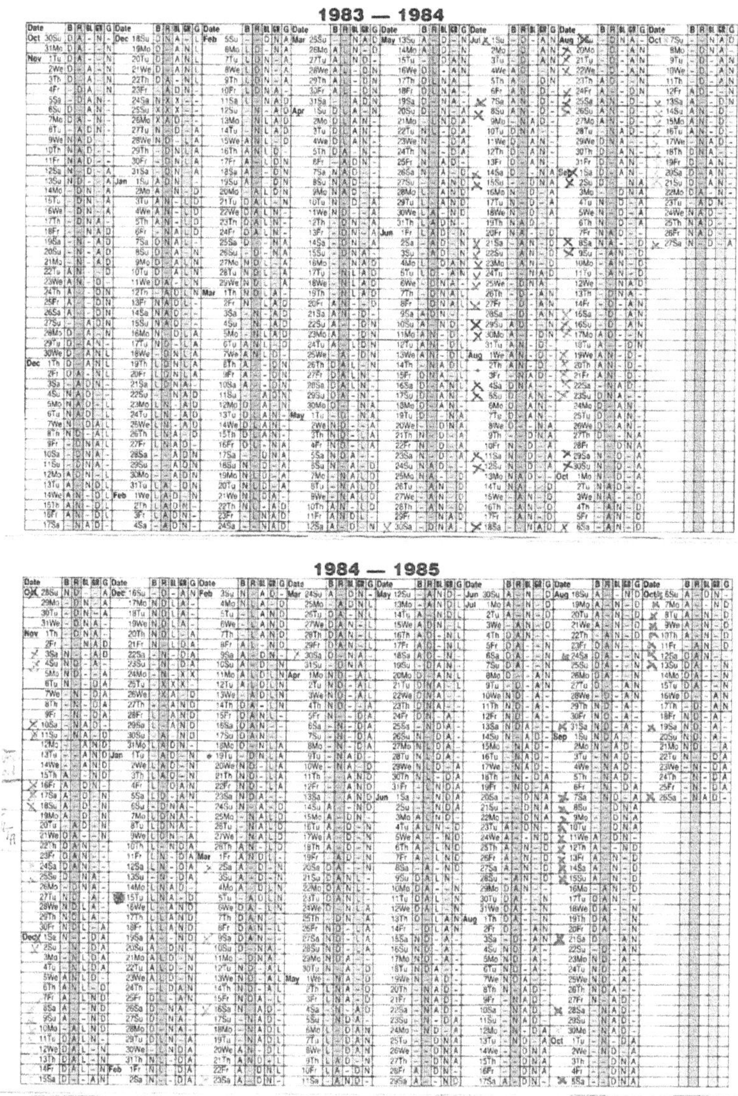

1983 — 1984

1984 — 1985

This was the first shift Roster I received (could only fit 2 of the 3 sections in – it came in 3 sections and was double sided). A masterpiece created by one of the boys from the floor after none of the suits could produce. I write about the author of this masterpiece later in this book and you will hear a few words from the man himself.

All Newbie's start on the back of the Rewinder as it is deemed as the least skilled area of the Mill. It was reasonably hard physical labour and I learnt in time that this was mainly because of the odd hours that we worked, rather than the purely physical side of things.

Now it was the start of the shift and it was a tradition on the Rewinder that the newest team member went to the hot water urn and fill the teapot. Bloody teapot, are we at an 'afternoon high tea' for the royal family or working in a Paper Mill? But I had forgotten that this place was full of Poms (English Folk) and that's what they do! – From filthy industrial tyre fitter to Tea lady in two weeks! Not only that but I hate tea and have only had one cup in my entire life, and that was only to try and impress my future in-laws. As I had no idea where this urn was I asked Rex who said in a gravelly voice – it's up in the computer room of the Machine area. Not a big communicator Rex but I headed up towards the Machine with my bloody teapot. Well as I got closer to the Machine all I could concentrate on was the noise – it was deafening even with my earmuffs on. I later was told that it was extra loud because there was a bearing going on one of the press rollers or something. Wow! With this place you are either in a wet area (in steam and water) or covered in paper dust, and that was only within 50 metres or so. If you worked a bit in each area like the 2nd Boy did, you end up looking like a sweaty lamington.

Back with the teapot and Rex introduced me to the crew, there was Kev who was a smaller fellow wearing a baseball cap and was the Assistant Winderman (Rex's offsider). Fred and Greg who were reasonably new to the job and doing the same task as I would be doing. Fred was on Gold shift but Greg was doing overtime as he was staying back off night shift to cover my training. Fred Van-alphabet was a fellow in his early twenties who didn't say much but was a pretty nice guy. (I called him Van- alphabet here as I have no bloody idea how to spell his surname!) We all had a bit of a chat in the hut for about five or ten minutes as Greg was on a meal break and the Rewinder had not been fully loaded with paper yet by the 2nd and 1st Boy of the Machine crew. While the fellows had their tea in the hut I stood watching the Machine crew as I was fascinated and in awe of the size of the machinery.

I asked Rex if I could get a bit closer to the machine to watch – he said; that's fine but stay near the back wall as it was safer and I would not get in the crew's way. I watched as the 1st Boy moved a series of levers on his control panel and the huge paper reel moved away from the Reel Drum as the new Corebar touched the Reel Drum and the paper sheet looped until it broke free of the old reel and wrapped onto the new Corebar. As easy as that! Then the freshly made reel was guided along two rails (some 4 metres apart) and a brake was then applied to stop it spinning. The Crew then stripped the reel of the loose paper on the top and as it was going into the Rewinder to be plied and split, a tail was made by spinning and peeling the reel from one end to the other of a few more sheets. Then the 2nd Boy kicked the Overhead Crane into action. The crane consisted of a large winching motor that raised and lowered a metal cable that in turn was attached to a 4 metre piece of H-iron. At either end of this large hunk of H-iron was a chain with a large hook for picking up the Corebar, with the reel of paper just produced. As the paper was to be twin ply it was required for one of the reels going into the Rewinder to be spun 180 degrees. This enabled the rough side of the paper to be on the inside of the finished product – otherwise you poor bastards would be blowing your noses into sandpaper. The paper is rough on one side and smooth on the other as I believe the fibres are able to penetrate the surface of the sheet when on the wet roll felts causing them to be rough, and smooth on the other side as they pass over the metal

Yankee Roll which acts like a hot iron. This process has the added bonus of helping 2 ply product (like Tissue) bind via the touching rough surfaces, similar to Velcro.

As the first Reel was already in the Rewinder it was this one that had already been spun and located into its cradle. The Corebar is what holds the paper reel in this cradle and allows the paper to be driven by the Rewinders drive belts and through a series of rollers and cutters and onto a much smaller Corebar at the business end of the Rewinder, all while free spinning it the Rewinder cradle. The 2nd Boy with the assistance of the 1st Boy locate the reel into the second cradle and the Rewinder is ready to go. The Rewinder has three cradles to allow for 3 ply paper, usually used for napkin production.

And they are off! Not exactly flying out the gates as Rex must be in his 60's although he looks about 100 to me. He is a funny character who served in the Australian Navy in the occupation forces of Japan sometime after World War 2. He was a slight fellow with a very ruddy face that looked even ruddier when he wore his ear muffs as they seemed to squash all the loose skin into his drooping bulbous nose. As he reached the first Reel in the Rewinder he barked out to Kev to get going, in the gravelly voice that I mentioned before. He let out a few more expletives under his breath as he seemed to be pissed off that he had to leave his cuppa. His body was crouched over and he had no arse, as his pants struggled to stay on at the back, even with a belt in place. He had a protruding little tummy that seemed to have stolen its mass from his arse, which was all but non-existent and disproportionate to the rest of his body.

I said to Fred; what's the go with Rex?

Fred replied; Craig, believe me, you have got him on a good day, wait until he gets into full flight.

I said; why is that?

Fred replied; well first thing is he doesn't know you yet so he is probably being a bit cautious. But the main reason is that it is day shift and with all the bosses around he is not pissed.

I said; he sounds angry to me.

Fred replied; NO pissed drunk – which is his normal state.

I was shocked how he could do this with all the high-speed machinery around. But I later learnt that Rex staggered more when he was sober than when he was pissed. He had been doing it for so long, apparently, that he functioned better half-drunk than he did sober, and they tell me that he is a lot more pleasant half pissed also.

Kev was a funny fellow whose brother was a Union Boy in the Paper Mill and I think that Kev wanted to do the same. Kev was quite short, shorter than Rex, (even with Rex losing a good 3 inches to his serious stoop) and he always walked like he had a crook back and wore a baseball cap. The baseball cap, I was to soon find out, was to shield his hair from the vegetable oil that was used to "Oil the Slitters".

Rex yelled out again with a look of disgust on his face, and Kev went flying out of the hut and up to the second reel ready to thread the paper through the Rewinder. Rex engaged the drive belts from the side of the cradle, as did Kev, and they joined the tails of paper from each of the Reels. Rex then hit the crawl button and they threaded the paper through and between a series of rollers which eventually ended up at the small Corebar that would become the papers new home.

Today we were running "Scotties" which are the start of the process for making tissues. This was supposed to be a physically demanding job equal to or harder than any other that happens in the Paper Mill. The Reels of paper that come off the paper machine are wide enough to produce 16 rewound Biscuits that are 195mm each wide, about 800mm in height and weighing around 20 - 25 kilograms each. Here I should explain that all Corebars are cylindrical steel bars (fibreglass on some winders) with bearings at either end. They all get cores put onto them to allow for the Corebar to be extracted from the paper. These cores are all made of cardboard, and to get idea of what they look like, examine your toilet roll at home as they are the same – just the scale is different, much thicker.

The job descriptions of the Rewinder Crew went something like this;

Winderman; (Rex)

- Running of the Rewinder
- Communicating with Machine crew on any paper quality issues
- General supervision of Rewinder Crew
- Recording of Reel weights and breaks in paper
- Quality of finished product

Assistant Winderman; (Kev)

- Assisting Winderman
- Oiling – Cleaning – Changing and sharpening of the Slitters
- Core loading onto the Corebar

Winder Crew; (Fred, Greg and the fifth wheel - Craig)

This is normally a one or two man operation depending on the product being run – but I am a trainee.

- Assist Winderman as directed
- Communicating quality issues to Winderman or Assistant
- Separating of biscuits
- Stacking or rolling Biscuits in preparation for forklift removal
- Identification labels to product

It was not long before I saw why Kev wore a cap, as immediately the paper was set onto its new Corebar (or just before actually) the Slitters were engaged. The Slitters were located in a narrow walkway at about knee height (waist height for Kev). It was a narrow walkway as it had a metal bridge above it that the new reels of paper would have to cross when lowered on the unloading stage that I will describe shortly. These Slitters had oil containers (holding about 250mls of vegetable oil) that fed oil onto the slitter blades to keep them lubricated and sharp. As we were cutting 16 Biscuits (and 2 edge trims) we needed 17 Slitters. The edge trims were part of the new reel as there was no Broke Room trim chute from No 3 Rewinder – only No 1 & 2 Rewinder. Kev's main job was to keep these Slitters sharp and to do that he needed to keep them oiled, sharpened and clean – all while the paper sheet was running between them and the Slitter Barrel in excess of 200 metres per minute. Remember that there was 17 of them and the oil was filled in a slot that was the size of a jelly bean via an oil can. The slot had to be small to keep the dust out, and shit was there some dust – even with dust extractors all over the place.

Number 3 Rewinder – slitter (one of 17 when cutting Scotties) can just be seen bottom right.

Poor Kev what a tough job – the poor bugger was run off his feet as he also had to load the next Corebar with the 16 cores – two trim cores, and spacers where required. If the core cutter, who cut the cores ready for production, had a bad day then it was a nightmare for the Assistant Winderman. Fortunately the Core cutter (who was Fred's father-in-law) was pretty accurate as I believe he had done the job at one time and understood how difficult it could be. Fred did tell me a story of his Father in Law's rather unfortunate time when he did have a really bad day in the form of Priapism. I had no idea what the heck Priapism was as I am sure most of you will not either, so I asked. Fred told me and of course I could not help laughing and said; so what was the problem? He went on to tell me the full story of how his father-in-law tried to get rid of it with ice packs, exercising and just trying to ignore it. But after 6 hours it was still there and the pain he said was excruciating. In the end, as embarrassing as it was, his mother-in-law had to take him to the hospital where a doctor numbed it with medicine, and a needle was inserted, to drain the accumulated blood. By this stage I was buckled over and squeezing my upper legs together, as even the thought of it was excruciating. Even now writing about it I am cringing! (For those readers who still don't follow what I am talking about please look up Priapism and prepare to cringe with me).

Now back to the Papermaking

Kev came out of that tunnel most of the time covered in oil and paper dust and a look of disgust on his face as he tried to shield his mouth and eyes from the mess. Add to this that each pair of machine reels made about 7 subsets (Rewinder sets) all in around an hour or slightly less – a pretty frantic pace with all the tasks required to be performed.

Kev's height was an advantage to him in this environment as he was a little closer to the action than most, but the biggest advantage to his height was that he did not have as far to duck when Rex dropped the metal bridge at the wrong time. A reasonably regular occurrence I was told. I was also told that Rex's response was nearly always; "What the f**k are you doing there when I was dropping the bridge f**khead!"

I watched as the first reel of 16 biscuits was "running up" and the boys moved into position when Rex slowed the Rewinder down, as the reel had reached it designated height. I never timed it but I would estimate from memory that the process for each reel to "run up" took between 5 and 6 minutes. After the Winder stopped and Kev cut the twin paper sheets, the boys unwound the clamp pin from either end of the Corebar. Then Rex enabled the ejection bar to push the Reel with Corebar inside onto the conveyor belt (with built in weighing scales), over the metal bridge that crossed the Slitter area. From the Rewinder side the process started again while the boys on the back (Fred and Greg) grabbed an iron bar each and started to whack the biscuits as they travelled along and removed themselves from the Corebar. What a primitive operation it looked like – but even with great thought I could not see how else they could do it. As well as whacking with the iron bar they had to tuck in the tails on each biscuit and remove the trims for the rubbish pallet. The trims (ends of reels) were tucked in as loose tails would be a fire hazard on the stored goods. (Loose paper is easier to ignite than tightly wound paper reels). Then they had to drop the biscuits off the lowered conveyor and stack onto pallets, 24 to a pallet. The first four of each stack were pushed from the side onto the pallet and straightened, with four of these stacks per pallet. Then the last two biscuits were manually lifted one by one on top of each stack of four until all 24 biscuits were in place. Add a layer of paper top and bottom to protect the sides of the biscuits and an ID card to each pallet and the job was done – "Until the next reel was ready five minutes later that is!" Then it was all done again until the Machine reels were depleted and removed and reloaded by the Machine 1st and 2nd Boy.

Reel after reel for the entire shift of eight hours was quite a day but fortunately as a member of the Winder crew we received a half hour meal break where Fred and I took off to the Canteen/Cafeteria. I bet you can't guess what I had? How did you guess – that's right – Pie and Chips. I like it when my readers are intuitive!

Larry (the Shift Leading Hand) came to see me at the end of the shift and asked me how I went. I told him good, and he then asked; Do you think you will be right on your own tomorrow? I said; I would be fine as the boys had shown me the ropes well and I was aware of the dangers. Larry was happy with this and said that he would keep an eye on me, and that if I fell behind a bit, he could pull somebody over to help catch up if required. I was happy with this as I was keen to get into it as I felt more comfortable working with just the two of us. Normally I would have to wait for my Relief (that is the guy from the next shift who takes over your job to maintain the flow of the 24/7 operation), but as I was a trainee I got to go home on-time. After clocking off I headed to the carpark and my trusty HK and home I went to Flowerdale.

DAY ONE COMPLETE!

Here Come the Larrikins!

YES IT WAS STEADY and there was a fair degree of manual labour involved but it was more the mindless repetitiveness of it that wore you down. Fortunately the place was full of fair dinkum larrikins, the unfortunate part is that today I will have to put in a description of what a larrikin is as in the most part they do not exist – (Larrikin is an Australian English term meaning "a mischievous young person, an uncultivated, rowdy but good hearted person", or "a person who acts with apparent disregard for social or political conventions"). Thank God they did in this place as it kept us sane on the rotating shift work and I believe warded off the black dog that some in this line of work fell victim too.

I had spent the whole of Dayshift doing "Scotties" on the back of No 3 Rewinder and after a day off, (well sort of, as we finished at 3-00pm on Saturday and started at 11-00pm on Sunday) I was back at the Paper Mill and feeling a bit foggy in the head. I think this was because I had a sleep this afternoon for a couple of hours and my body clock was telling me to now go back to sleep again. Anyway, stacking Scotties on night shift will sort me out quite quickly I thought. Turned out though that that screaming bearing that we had been listening to all week had shit itself this morning and it was still being repaired. This meant that the Paper Machine had to be shut down while repairs happened and they decided to do more repairs and maintenance while it was down and to re-start the Paper Machine on Tuesday morning. A bit of a reprieve for me as I was still finding my feet and doing my first Nightshift was going to be a task in itself. We still assembled in the No 3 Rewinder hut as that was what you did until the leading hand instructed you as to what to do next. Also you still relieved your co-worker from the previous shift. After arriving I thought I would get in first with the teapot shit and it would give me a chance to fill my coffee cup also as I seriously needed one! Fred and Kev were already there but Rex was still not, as he was chatting to the Green shift Rewinderman over by the clock cards or in the locker-room where we all had a locker.

I had the tea ready and poured, just how Rex liked it, while Kev and Fred chatted about some Union shit that I hadn't got into yet. As Rex approached Fred said: Here you go Craig – let the games begin.

I said; what do you mean Fred?

Kev butted in and said; well it is night shift – the Rewinder isn't running and Rex is walking straight!

What the heck did that mean – I was soon to find out!

Rex arrived at the hut took three swipes to find the door handle, gingerly climbed into the hut (all of six inches which Rex made look like half a metre) took off his ear muffs with a grin on his face – missed the hook that his earmuffs usually went onto – his earmuffs fell onto the cup of tea that I had just made him – all over the crouch of his pants – he fell back onto the hut bench in the corner and past out asleep.

Wow what a show! And all by 11-05pm!

A few minutes later Larry came over – looked at me – looked at Rex, said for us three to come over to the office when we had finished our cuppa and he would allocate us some tasks for the evening.

Sounded like a plan with Kev going to work in the Pulp Yard as he told Larry he liked it there – truth was he could nick off for a few hours kip as the boys in the yard were pretty cool. Fred loved the Machine area so Larry allocated him to No 2 Paper Machine and I was to go and help the second Winder crew on No 1 Rewinder.

"Little did I know what I was in for!"

Larry introduced me to the crew which consisted of Gerry Gee and Spider. He also introduced me to the Machine crew, there was Ralph, the Machineman, who must have been in his early 60's and quite a nice fellow. There was Bruce, the 1st Boy, now Bruce was a nugget of about average height but he was almost as wide as he was high and forearms that would give Schwarzenegger a run for his money. Turns out Bruce had been a solid plasterer most of his life, thus the enormous forearms. When Larry introduced me to him Bruce said some joke about fresh meat for night shift or something followed by a burst of laughter – What the hell was that laugh!!! It sounded like a hyena getting a kick in the ribcage and at serious volume also. It set Larry back a bit too so I wasn't the only one who reacted. Good family man was Bruce, and then there was Karl. Now Karl was into his 60's also and was quite feeble looking, even more so than Rex. Karl was the 2nd Boy, with the word Boy sounding stranger than ever with this individual. They were running a waxy napkin material that went into the Rewinder to be slit into six Biscuits for conversion into industrial and surgical drop sheets or something. The difference between this job and the one that I did on dayshift stacking Scotties was worlds apart, as this job was a doddle. The reels on the Machine took almost one and a half hours to run up and Gerry Gee boasted that he could run it off in less than forty minutes. I was an extra on this job as it was so easy that the 2nd Boy helped on the Rewinder. He had little else to do, and that allowed the company to crew the Rewinder without a man on the back. Now to Spider;

who was Gerry Gee's Assistant Winderman and quite a Larrikin, he once boasted "that if it wasn't bolted down it was his!" He was also a short fellow and one that looked to be the quite inactive type. Bruce told me that his missus was a stripper in Melbourne and they had a young daughter.

Gerry Gee — Has Arrived

NOW TO THE MAIN attraction of the Paper Mill, "for all the wrong reasons" – Gerry Gee! To describe Gerry – he was a little taller than Spider maybe 5'7 at a guess, with a grey motorcycle helmet for a head of hair, a pot belly that was so hard and well-formed that it looked as though he had just placed a basketball under his shirt. His back was straight and his legs were disproportionately short for his body. He was well documented for his antics as being a clown that was always trying to show off and act cool, even though he was obviously the total opposite. Now I say this but he wasn't nasty or anything, he was just a real oddball and Spider was his sidekick. The reel was still running up and as I had about 20 mins before anything was about to happen I asked the guys if it was alright for me to go over to No 2 Paper Mill and chat with Fred for a while. I wanted to do this mainly as the hut on No 1 Mill was full, with Bruce and Gerry Gee arguing over Gerry's smoking. Technically Gerry was allowed to but with Bruce and Karl both non-smokers they were used to an environment in the hut that was smoke free.

Gerry Gee — The Renovator

I WENT OVER TO see Fred Van-alphabet and I also got to meet Snoozy Winebars, Simon Bend and Little Legs who worked on No 2 Paper Machine. These guys were a bit more switched and the atmosphere was a lot quieter. They asked me where Larry had put me and I told them I was on the back of No 1 Rewinder with Gerry Gee and Spider. Then the stories started, and turns out Little Legs had them all as Gerry Gee had been at the Paper Mill for about 10 years and Little Legs considerably longer. With Gerry I believe he was Little Legs assistant prior to him getting a Machinemans job on Gold Shift and Gerry the Rewindermans job also on Gold Shift. The new five shift roster gave many of the guys in the Paper Mill their first opportunity of a promotion in quite a while, many years in most cases.

Little Legs told the story of Gerry when he and his wife bought their first new home, in Belgrave I believe. Gerry's wife who was quite attractive and not too bright was on Gerry's back to do some renovations to the home as the rooms were so pokey. It was an old 50's fibro home but in reasonably good condition for its age. She wanted Gerry to take down the wall between the living and dining rooms as they both had doors on them and were more like bedrooms than living areas. She was on Gerry's case for years and in the end, he decided he could put it off no longer. But when he went to move his trailer closer to the home to cart away the rubbish he could not as a sapling had grown through the A-frame of it and the trailer itself was still full of rubbish from when they moved in almost four years earlier. This again gave Gerry an excuse not to move forward until one fateful Saturday morning.

Gerry was in the middle of a night shift rotation and had been asleep for a couple of hours when he heard loud banging. He got up and went to investigate only to find his missus with an axe swinging it into the offending wall with dust and shit flying everywhere. Unfazed by the situation Gerry went and got a sledge hammer out of his shed and headed back into their home to help in the demolition of the offending wall. On his way back in, his neighbour spotted him and asked what all the banging was. Gerry told him what it was and the fellow, who was a carpenter, asked if he could have a look and maybe give Gerry a few tips. As they entered the home the fellow shouted to Gerry's missus, who was in mid swing, to stop as they were removing the main structural wall of the house. Gerry just picked up some of the broken bits of sheeting while his wife vacu-umed a bit and they slid a cabinet from one side of the room to the other to cover the hole and that was that!

Snoozy Winebars

TURNS OUT SNOOZY (NO 2 Paper Mill second boy) was quite a character. Over the time working in the Paper Mill I got to spend many hours on No 2 Paper Mill and we all got to know each other quite well. Snoozy was not his real name (obviously) and I believe he got the name from falling asleep on the job a lot, but this is unconfirmed. As we worked such odd hours a lot of us started to socialize together and what a funny bunch of guys, so it was always entertaining.

The particular story I would like to tell you about happened over a typical winter period in Melbourne and I am guessing it was about 1985. My then wife and I had just purchased a 1968 Valiant V8 VIP, which she proceeded to bend after spinning off the road not far from our Flowerdale home. The next day at work I was talking to the boys about what had happened and Snoozy said he was keen to buy the wreck as he wanted the engine and interior. This would work out well as the body was smashed front and back and the whole chassis was twisted. We made arrangements for him to come and pick it up in a week's time when we would both be on an eight day break.

Well Snoozy turned up at our home early in the morning and the plan was for me to travel with him so I could help him take the

Valiant off at his home. It was mid-week so the roads were quiet, (even quieter than normal for the mid 1980's) so we thought it would be a pleasant run. The old girl took a bit of coaxing to get onto the car trailer that Snoozy had on the back of his 1970 Valiant, as it was a bit twisted with the front panels pointing at 25 degrees to the line of the body. We got her 90% onto the trailer but she sat back a bit from the front of the trailer. Snoozy was happy though as she was hooked on underneath and the winch was locked – So off we went!

I Jumped into Snoozy's lovely 1970 Valiant and was suitably impressed with the lovely lush sheepskin seat covers and how nice he had the vehicle, especially the interior. Now I am not sure what the road from Flowerdale to Melbourne is like these days but I am pretty certain it is still a winding road from Flowerdale to Kinglake and a steep descent from Kinglake to Whittlesea.

The trip started well with Snoozy's V8 beast eating up the climb, even with a heavy V8 and trailer on the rear. Then as we topped the climb and the road levelled out the old girl on the back decided to start swinging her hips. Not just a light swing but a ferocious swing that gave Snoozy no option but to use the entire blacktop (North and South) and we even spent time in the gravel road edge on either side! I was shitting myself, gripping the lovely sheepskin seat covers like a baby bear on its mothers back in full flight. Snoozy was not responding to my cries of "are we OK - are we OK" and his eyes were lit up like the Hella's on the front chrome bumper of his Val. Wow what a ride, but fortunately Snoozy got her under control when the VIP on the back slid a bit sideways and seemed to centre herself on the car trailer. At this point two things happened, Snoozy spoke again and I began cleaning the lamb's wool from between my fingers.

Things settled down again on the trip and as we dropped altitude down the Kinglake range, so did our blood pressure as we cruised through Whittlesea without incident. In those days there were no traffic lights and the road ran continuously with the town of Whittlesea being bypassed. The only point at which we had to stop (or at the very least slow down) was at the town of Mernda. Mernda in those days was a bit of a stopover country town much smaller than Whittlesea and boasted a few historic buildings and a huge roundabout that graced Plenty Road (the road we were travelling on). In those days the roundabout was quite a feature and always planted out in lovely annual flowers, brightening the town which was otherwise quite drab.

As we approached the town of Mernda Snoozy had to stop at the roundabout while a tractor entered from the side road in front of us. As we began to take off into the roundabout the old VIP thought to herself "I have had enough of this, I am getting off" and proceeded to slide off the back of the trailer and onto the single lane roundabout.

Snoozy quickly pulled to the left shoulder of Plenty Road just beyond the roundabout and as we exited his Val to assess the retrieval, a huge semi-trailer coming the same route as us took evasive action to miss the VIP by going straight through the roundabout. When I say through – "I mean OVER!" – Over the centre strip, through the beautiful flower gardens, sending flowers and plants flying through the air in his wake.

He passed us with his air horns playing La Cucaracha and vigorously shaking his head.

Back to No 1 Paper Mill

The Gerry Gee story was a story that Fred had not heard either and we all had a bit of a laugh before I composed myself and went back to No 1 Rewinder. I was not sure how I would look Gerry in the eyes after that story but of course I wasn't even sure of its authenticity either.

When I arrived back the Reel on the Paper Machine was just about ready to come off. I was interested to watch this as I had not witnessed it yet on this machine. It went smoothly and was similar to what occurred on No 3 Paper Machine but as the area was more compact I was a lot closer to the action. The paper that was being produced was so much different and it was quite difficult to tear down the reel ready for the Rewinder. The 1st Boy had to use a Stanley Knife (brand of Box Knife) as it was almost impossible to rip with any more than a couple of sheets at a time. In addition Bruce had to do a test sample of this paper which would be delivered to the CR Lab, just behind us. Bruce showed me the process of cutting the sample and where he delivered it through a hole in the wall with a Perspex sliding flap. (Similar to the old Breakfast flaps you see in cheap Motels).

Now the CR Lab was where Uncle Fozzie worked and it was the first time that I was working close to where he was. Bruce said I could drop the test into him via the flap and say hello if he was there. Turned out he wasn't and Paul his offsider said he would tell him where I was working when he got back from Conversion (the Veggie Patch). Paul was a nice fellow, very tall with a beard similar to Captain Ahab (Moby Dick). He was well spoken and easy to talk to. I remember Uncle Fozzie always saying how pleasant he was to work with.

Back watching the guys doing their respective jobs and Karl was just loading the huge paper Reel into the Rewinder cradle. As I mentioned before this Rewinder was only a single ply winder with Slitters that were completely different to No 3 Rewinder. No 3 Rewinder was the only machine that used oil, as it was a Slitter on drum system, and all the others (No 1 & 2 Rewinder and later No4 - Jagenberg) cut the paper by the slitters sitting slightly into a groove of series of metal discs that were about six inches wide. The top of these metal discs had a series of grooves that resembled the shape of a castle wall – referred to as a Curtain or Parapet wall. Sorry hard to explain but if you look up the wall reference you will get the gist. The Slitters sat inside these groves at their pre-determined distance, and when running, created a cut in the paper at its correct biscuit width. There was a barrel that these discs were on that had an inflatable bladder in it to hold the discs in place and it was essential that this area of the Rewinder was well cared for and well maintained.

Gerry Gee in Full Flight

After sitting in the corner of the hut half asleep Spider came out and gave Gerry a prod as Gerry too was snoozing in a pile of paper that he had set up behind the Rewinder panel. They both kicked in and asked me to stand at the back end of the Rewinder, and to pull the paper through with Karl. Spider got into the narrow space between the huge Reel of paper and the Rewinder rolls then began to feed the paper over and under the series of rolls and the Slitter barrel before feeding it out to Karl and I but on Karl's side. It was a task that seemed a bit tricky but only because Spider was not too tall, and for Gerry his pot belly would have made it a tight squeeze. Normally Gerry would feed the sheet but as I was an extra, he was able to stay perched at the Control Panel and feed out his instructions. The tail came out and Gerry still had the Corebar raised so the paper did not wrap immediately without the Slitters engaged and the tension correct. If you get this wrong on any of the paper types then separating the biscuits can be very difficult. The lower the problem in the new reel running up, then the harder it is to separate the biscuits. Add to this when the paper type is harder, like this product, and the biscuits are larger like these are, then the separation can be near impossible. This means that if it can't be separated it must be rejected and used as Broke. So with the quality of this product that would be a very expensive error. Karl raised the sheet so that it would feed in the correct direction while Gerry lowered the Corebar. The process was new to me and when the Corebar sat onto the Bed Roller Drums I wasn't keeping the sheet tight enough and the paper grabbed into the nib and started wrapping prematurely.

Now if Gerry was pissed with me he wasn't showing it and he simply stopped the Rewinder and raised the Corebar to allow us to free the grabbed and wrongly wound paper that had only done a few rotations. As the Rewinder was now stopped and the sheet was feed through to its full Reel width Gerry said to just straighten the sheet at each end as he lowered the Corebar onto the Bed Roller Drums. Spider then cut the paper on the top of the cores the entire way across the sheet, while Karl grabbed some paper gum tape and taped down the paper ends to the Corebar and Gerry engaged the slitters. I apologized to Gerry, but he just said that this was really the way it should be done (apart from the bit of the paper running in prematurely), and that when more experienced you can break the sheet at one edge and let the paper feed itself in from one side to the other in a spiral motion. Now it was just a matter of running up the biscuit Reel until it was at its correct height.

As Gerry got the Rewinder started a big cradle at the back of the Rewinder that Karl and I had been standing on was raised into the air and created a safety barrier at the back of the Rewinder, so no-one would get caught on the high-speed Reel as it Ran Up. All good and Gerry got the Rewinder up to a reasonable speed (I was told this as I had no idea how fast or slow these things went), and in about 25 minutes or so the Reel was up to size and ready to be ejected. Now No 1 Rewinder was an old girl as was No 1 Machine and as the name suggests was the first of the Mills. Thus most of the work, especially at the back of the Rewinder, was done manually. The process went like this:

- Spider as Assistant Winderman got up onto the safety barrier (which had a walk platform and was shaped like a big scoop) and he cut the top sheet of paper from one side to the other before flicking the side of the sheet that was still attached to the Reel over the Ejection Bar.
- Gerry then engaged the Ejection Bar to push the Reel into the Safety Barrier/Basket.
- Then Karl undid the lock nuts and bearing wheel from the front side of the Corebar – and gave Spider the OK.
- Then Spider pulled the Corebar with my assistance and we placed the empty Corebar onto the stand that was back from the Rewinder.
- Then Gerry dropped the basket and the freshly made Biscuits rolled onto the floor scales – while Karl and I stopped them from rolling off the other side of the scales.
- Spider and I then took the new loaded Corebar back into the Rewinder and locked it into place.
- Then Spider cut and taped down the sheet that was still connected to the Reel and gave Gerry the Ok
- Gerry then started the Rewinder in crawl while the safety barrier went up and then he gradually brought it up to speed.
- ID tags were made and placed in the Biscuits – Deckle sizes (Biscuit widths) re-checked – then they were rolled by hand to where the Forklift with Grab would pick them up for stacking and storage.

Gerry checked the paper and said that it looked real good so he may go for a "Speed Record!" I had no idea what he was talking about and asked Karl what he was on about. Karl said; well he is going to get the Rewinder running at full speed and one of two things will happen.

I said; what is that?

Karl said; He will either get the Reel run off in no time and we will have a big break before the next one "OR" the sheet will break and there will be Broke everywhere before the Rewinder stops!

I said; that's crazy as it is a great job the way it is!

Well I must say that Rewinder was flying and even though I had no idea as to what was a good speed and what was a super speed, the fact was that the place was shaking and it seemed really quick to me.

All was going well until about 2/3rds thorough the Reel and then sheet broke. Wow "what a show", as paper was flying everywhere! Gerry had hit the emergency stop and disengaged the Slitters but it seemed to still take ages to stop. In the meantime the paper was wrapping around every Roll it could find as well a shooting bits of paper over 6 metres into the air. Some bits even went into the next Reel running up on the Machine - much to Bruce's disgust. All this while Gerry watched on laughing his head off. Unbelievable! The paper had wedged that hard into the main Drive Belt that it was smoking.

What a disaster! It took us 25 minutes to clean up all the paper and get it to the Broke Room. Then by the time we got going again - cleaning the break on the new Reel, marking up etc, the next Reel was almost ready to come off the Machine. Fortunately Bruce was able to run the Reel a touch oversize and we caught up. Ralph (the Machineman) came down and had a quiet word to Gerry, not sure what he said, but there were no return performances by Gerry for the rest of the night.

I was a bit annoyed with Gerry as I wanted to go and listen to a few of Little Legs (No 2 Mill Machineman) stories during the break. But as we got the next Reel going Uncle Fozzie came into the Hut from Bruce's end. Bruce made a bit of a comment about Gerry's little performance before Uncle Fozzie piped up with a "Wocka Wocka

Wocka, ya wanna hear a joke! (He actually didn't say Wocka Wocka Wocka but it makes a good story in line with the real Fozzie Bear). Bruce seemed genuinely excited and that was enough encouragement for Fozzie to get going. His joke was aimed at Bruce who was a bit Churchie and it went like this;

- How do you make holy water? You boil the hell out of it.
- I bought some shoes from a drug dealer. I don't know what he laced them with, but I was tripping all day!
- Did you know the first French fries weren't actually cooked in France? They were cooked in Greece.
- My daughter screeched, "Daaaaaad, you haven't listened to one word I've said, have you!?" What a strange way to start a conversation with me...

Now normally the jokes are the funny bit but in this case it was the noise that came out of Bruce that was the funniest. Every time Fozzie told one of his cornball daddy jokes Bruce made the sound of a Hyena being kicked in the guts, and as I mentioned before, the volume was way up there. His laugh though was infectious and even Ralph, who doesn't say too much was in stitches. Fozzie must have thought his jokes were amazing as we were all in fits of laughter and I had tears in my eyes I was laughing that hard. I think it may have a bit to do with the fact that I was also so tired that all my emotions were in overdrive.

But just as we were all enjoying ourselves so much the Paper broke on the Machine and the Machine crew bolted into action. A good thing about this morning was that, as I did not have a set job, I did not have to wait for my relief in the morning and got away bang on 7-00am. It was very fortunate in my case as it took me over an hour to get home to Flowerdale.

Night Shift — The Ups and Downs!

WELL THIS NIGHT SHIFT caper is not all that easy to get used to as I am not sure what is the best sleeping pattern to attempt. I spoke to a lot of the guys in the Mill and they do their sleeping in a number of different ways. Some go straight to Bed when they get home in the morning and then after waking, stay up until they go to work in the evening again. Others go to bed straight away but only sleep until around lunchtime, and then have a sleep in the late afternoon again before going to work in the evening. Some stay up when they get home and go to bed after lunch and sleep through until they go to work in the evening. For me on the first day I was so tired that I crashed straight away and was asleep by 8-30am, and I slept through until 5-00pm. But when I got to work that evening my head was foggy and I felt like I was in a bit of a dream state. I was OK but not fully clear in the head and I believe I was operating at 80%. At this point I felt sorry for the older guys who worked in the factory as it must get harder, the older you are. Add to this that we worked rotating shift work which never really allows you to set a sleeping pattern.

After my second night of night shift I was not too bad and was hoping that once set in a pattern I would be good for the full five nights of the rotation. Well it was different again for me as I could not seem to fall asleep in the morning and spent a number of hours tossing and turning until at lunchtime I decided to get up for a while and try to make myself a bit tired. This worked for a few hours but after going back to bed around 2-00pm I woke at 5-00pm and was wide awake again. I did a few odd jobs around the home and watched a bit of TV and again tried to go to sleep around 7-30pm hoping to get a couple of hours in. But again I was tossing and turning without sleeping and before I knew it I had to head back to work. At work I wasn't functioning at full capacity but I was coping and it all seemed like I was in a bit of a dream. But on the way home the following morning I was driving through Whittlesea when all of a sudden, a wave of tiredness come over me. I was okay though as I drove up the Kinglake range, but once on top of the mountain I could hardly keep my eyes open. I drifted in the old HK and the passenger side wheels went onto the side of the road that was loose gravel. Fortunately this woke me immediately and I corrected my line and tried to focus harder. I slowed down my speed and slapped my face a few times which helped but this was 'not good' and I decided to pull over and have a couple of minutes of walking around in the cold morning air. This helped immensely and with the passenger window down half way for the rest of the drive home, although cold, I was more awake and it got me home in one piece.

I had to find a better way to sleep and this near miss started a series of different ideas and attempts to improve my sleeping.

- I once was able to sleep with sunlight in the room – now I have to have complete darkness
- I once could sleep with a bit of noise around me – now it has to be completely silent

- I once could fall asleep easily after being woken or waking up – now if I wake up once I take a fair while to fall asleep, and if woken twice I cannot go back to sleep and have to get up.

This gave rise to heavy curtains and plugging every light gap in the bedroom. Zero noise or I was a cranky bugger and many other little things that I thought would help. These included soft background music, different temperatures in the room and essential oils that assist calming and sleeping. One thing I was determined to stay away from was sleeping pills or any type of medication as I felt that if I had to do this then the sacrifice was not worth the monetary reward.

I have not spoken of the monetary side as yet so I will touch on it a bit now. It was sensational as it allowed my future wife to stay at home and we could plan our future around living on one wage. Not only that but it was so good that in a few years we would be able to upgrade our home to one that was closer to my job.

The longer-term effects seemed peculiar also as after about six or so months of doing the shift rotations, I found myself falling asleep at extremely odd times. One time we had Judi and Albert over, and while having a few beers with Albie I fell asleep while he was talking. (Not that your story was boring Albie – Ha Ha!) It was weird, and I remember going to a party once and falling asleep with loud music playing near my ear, in fact my head was resting on the speaker! The night shift sleep issue proved to be the hardest hurdle for me in all my time in the Paper Mill, as I loved the work and the guys I worked with.

In recent years (some 30 odd years later) I have become more aware of the things that affect me, and it explains a lot of how I felt in those times. I now know that I have digestive issues and take digestive enzymes to address this issue. I am not sure if it was the shift work that brought it on, or if it was something that I always have had. But I do know that if I have this issue and don't have digestive enzymes then I have a terrible sleep even today.

They now even have a name for this Shift Work issue – it is called "shift work sleep disorder" not an overly inventive name but it shows that it is a recognized issue. Seems to me that we were far more unaware in the 80ies, or it may have been that youth was my issue!

Its findings state that; Shift work (including rotating Shift Work) disrupts the body's circadian rhythms and causes them to be out of sync with the external environment and/or behavioural cycles. This explains why I felt like I was in a dream state. Even more disturbing is the WHO's (World Health Organization) findings that inconsistent working hours can cut your life short. Its findings go further to say that it increases the risk of death from any cause by 11% for anyone who worked rotating shift work for at least five years – Scary!

Short-Term Health effects include;

- Gastrointestinal symptoms like – upset stomach, nausea, diarrhoea, constipation and heartburn
- Increased risk of injuries and accidents
- Insomnia
- Decreased quality of life
- General feeling of being unwell

Long term shift work is associated with an increased risk of certain cancers, as well as metabolic problems, heart disease, ulcers, gastrointestinal problems and obesity.

It is said in studies that Workers are at risk of;

- Sleep deprivation
- Lack of adequate time to recover from work
- Decline in mental function and physical ability, including emotional fatigue and a decline in the function of the body's immune system

- Higher rates of depression, occupational injury, and poor perceived health
- Higher prevalence of insomnia among shift workers with low social support.
- Increase risk of illness and injury
- Strain on personal relationships, such as marriage and family life

It is also said that these effects have a wider effect than just on the worker and that the Risks to the Employers include;

- Reduced productivity
- Increase in errors
- Absenteeism and Presenteeism (present at work but not fully functional because of health problems or personal issues)
- Increased health care and workers compensation costs
- Workforce attrition due to disability, death, or moving to jobs with less demanding schedules

Studies also mention the risk to the community; with potential increase in errors by workers - leading to Vehicle crashes, Industrial disasters and Medical errors. They also mentioned that the Serotonin levels differed greatly between day workers and rotating shift workers as the rotating shift workers serotonin levels were significantly lower. Low Serotonin levels are said to be associated with conditions like anger, depression and anxiety.

They also had some tips on how to stay awake and alert during a shift;

- Nap – take a 30 minute nap before your shift begins and, if possible, try to get in a few 10-20 minute naps in throughout the night

- Eat small portions throughout the shift
- Keep moving
- Chat with your co-workers
- Be careful of your caffeine intake.

Now all this info would have been very handy when I started working Rotating Shift Work back in 1984, as the tips on what to do would have been very useful. But if I had hindsight I may not even have gone for the job, or perhaps with my youth I would have ignored it all and still worked Rotating Shift work. But really all this is irrelevant as most of this information was not out there at the time and more to the point I did it and 'that was that!' I think the main reason I am adding in this chapter is for people to be aware, and loaded up with more current information. It also gives you, the reader, a better understanding of what I, and my fellow Rotating Shift Workers went through AND STILL GO THROUGH. It also helps give an insight into the behaviour of some of the individuals that I am writing about. (Fictitious or not)

Finding my Groove

NOW WITH THE FIRST shift rotation under my belt it was in my nature to work out a career path that I would like to follow. Over the coming months I would go in depth into the career paths available to me. I am also, as I am writing this, looking for someone who worked in the Conversion area so I can give you a more in-depth account of that area. If I am not successful at finding someone then you will soon notice, as the description of the area will be less in-depth and I am sure less accurate. What I can guarantee though is that it will be entertaining!

Some of the fellows that I am working closely with have clear career paths in mind, and Fred who I work with quite a bit, is keen on going through the Machine path. But if I can step back a little I will explain to you how the Career paths work in the Paper Mill, and I believe that the Conversion area also worked the same way or at least similar.

The whole process worked on the Seniority System.

To explain this in its basic form is quite simple as it means that the employee that has been there the longest and applies for a job will get it over another who hasn't been there as long. Now in saying that it was simple is correct, in broad terms, but to expand on that and be more correct I will explain further, as I think by today's standards it is extremely interesting.

Firstly an individual's Seniority started when he started in the Paper Mill, not when he started with the company. For example an employee who had worked in Conversion for ten years and then transferred to the Paper Mill was less senior to someone who started with the company, in the Paper Mill, one year ago. I won't go into the politics of it but say; that was just "the way it was". Now add to that the internal career paths and you have an entrenched system that for the most part was smooth running, but on occasions did cause a bit of friction amongst the fellows. The Machine path was reasonably straight forward as it went like this;

Most started stacking Scotties on the back of Rewinder

You apply to be 2nd Boy (or get asked to do it)

You progressed to 1st Boy (if you wanted to)

You progressed to Machineman

But this was at its purest sense as there was a twist and in addition to this twist there was Seniority and a low turnover of staff which meant that often guys would have to change shifts for a promotion (Red- Blue – Green – Gold and Black). The twist came as this line of promotion was intertwined with the career path of the Rewinders. The Rewinder career path went like this;

General worker on the back of the Rewinder (didn't have a formal name as it was where all employees started when they started in the Paper Mill).

Assistant Winderman

Winderman

Then the Winderman could move onto the Machineman's position.

Now this was where it annoyed some employees as the Winderman had limited experience on the Paper Machine (apart from dealing with quality / product issues created by the Paper

Machine that affected running and quality at Rewinder level). Yet the 1st Boy had spent all his time around the Paper Machine and directly assisting the Machineman, which gave them much more practical experience. A lot of them also felt that as it was their career path, that they should take priority over Winderman. But that was not the case as the system worked on Seniority and the Winderman with more years up would get the job. All that being said, in most cases the Winderman stayed on the Winder and did not progress further as a matter of choice.

The other Career paths were;

- Broke Room attendant who could progress to Stock Prep
- TC Department that was open to all employees but I recall that Seniority did not play a major role here as there was an aptitude test involved. (Ruling out many of the Guys!)
- The CR lab (who also did paper testing) was located in the Mill area but the staff were drawn from the Conversion area I believe and were classified as "Staff" as were the Paper Mill Shift Supervisors. As Staff members they were not part of the Union and paid no Union membership fees. They also were paid a salary which did not include any payment for overtime I believe.

Then there was the Leading Hand position, who worked directly with (or under) the shift supervisor. The Leading Hand position also worked off Seniority with mostly Machineman moving onto this position as it was necessary for them to understand the whole Paper Mill process. Although in my time there I believe one of the Leading Hands had come directly off the Rewinder. This was in the very early days of the Paper Mill as most Leading Hands had 20 plus years of service.

When it came to the Shift Supervisor this became a "Staff position" and meant that they were no longer union members and were paid monthly not weekly like the rest of the Paper Mill. In addition as Staff they were not paid overtime as they were told it was "calculated into their salary".

I remember in my time in the Paper Mill this created a situation where Leading Hands did not want to progress to Shift Supervisors and in the end Shift Supervisors jobs were offered to "Staff" members from other departments. In fact Uncle Fozzie who was in the CR Lab (paper quality testing) applied for and got the Black Shift Supervisors job when the then Supervisor retired. Now this was also a sticking point for many on the Paper Mill floor as it again restricted the natural flow of progression through the ranks. (ie; Leading Hands remained as Leading Hands and no opportunities for Machineman to climb to Leading Hand and down through the lines of promotion). It also meant that "Staff" who had no, or very little, experience on the Paper machines were now in charge of overseeing the members who were running them.

As I saw it, what choice did the company really have as I know that Mr Cogers and co put a lot of pressure on the Leading Hands to move up to Supervisor but without success. For a long time they did allow Leading Hands to temporarily fill the Supervisors position and prior to that the Leading Hands and Supervisors were covering it with overtime. But this situation was not sustainable as the Supervisors, as mentioned, were not paid for overtime and Leading Hands were paid double time for all their overtime. This was a fault in the system that was generated by Supervisors having to be "On Staff", but neither the Company nor the Union would back down so it stayed that way. To his credit Uncle Fozzie put a lot of time and effort into trying to blend in, and all in all he did to a degree.

Last but not least was the Pulp Yard that was classified as the unofficial retirement home for older papermakers.

Now that I have explained to you all the options available to me, I would have to eventually make a choice for myself from a number of career paths. Not that there was a hurry to do this as most of the guys stayed in their position for years and years. It was in my nature though to try and progress and better myself, so I looked at all the positions intently to ensure I made the right choice when I was able to. The Seniority system may seem a little antiquated to most of you but after my experiences in the Tyre game and being passed over twice in that job, it made me feel a little more secure.

Well as I am writing page 95 of this book I have been contacted by a Conversion Gentleman who has described the Conversion Seniority line in great detail. Now as I had no experience in this area (other than packing dunny rolls when the Paper Mill was down) I will assume its accuracy as the Gentleman providing the info was a straight up guy.

Thus I am inserting his description almost word for word with some further information added at the end by other members who have now come forward with their additions and descriptions. (Although interesting to me it may be hard for some who have no idea about the industry to follow. I apologize in advance for this.)

It goes like this;

> Hi Craig, Sorry I didn't get back to you sooner, I hurt my hand and have trouble typing at the minute. You are really testing my memory trying to think back 40 years with conversion seniority, but here we go.
>
> Unlike the mill, seniority never began until the mid-1980s, up until then it was basically up to the supervisor if you were promoted. For example when I started at Bowater in 1975 each shift in Conversion had 5 leading hands. On my shift, all were related by marriage.

Seniority in conversion as I remember it was part of Award Restructuring and Multiskilling program, that came out of the Hawke Government Prices and Income accord, which was supposed to supress wages and price increases. It also came out of the 35-hour week and associated job losses. The Multi-Skilling component basically removed the one position-one job. e.g A hayssen (wrapping machine) operator was required to run 2 Hayssens, the Senior operator concept also came into being on the converting lines which were combined in groups of two. I am not sure how familiar you were with what the machine lines were called, but they were numbers, the combined lines were known as, 106-112, 105-107, 108-109, they were grouped by proximity. The lines of seniority became Packer ▶ Wrapping Operator ▶ Machine Operator ▶ Senior Operator. Conversion was also divided - Conversion B had: Packer ▶ Machine Operator ▶ Leading Hand. To transfer from Conversion 'B' to Conversion 'A' you were required to start at the bottom and visa-versa. There was also a line which went Cleaner - Fork Lift Driver - Printer Operator. An interesting note to this and to the Chagrin of the Fork Lift Drivers, they basically went from the highest paid workers in Conversion to in the middle range. Mainly because while everyone got some sort of pay rise under the restructure, the Operator and Senior Operator got the bigger rises. There were also 2 other machines 257 and 110 which were towel machines, I can't recall where they fit into the system. Also day shift was a discreet group.

What may be of interest also is that the seniority system allowed us to better claim wage increases for increased skills and technology. For example when Machine 110 was upgraded with embossing and a printer, the operators were selected on

> seniority from the other machines, and the machine went to the top of the seniority system with an appropriate wage increase. When No 4 Paper Mill was built and the Perini convertor bought, it went to the top of seniority etc.

Now even though this may not be easy to follow for probably a lot of you readers, as well as myself, it has triggered my memory to questions I always had about why certain people were in certain jobs. A lot of Conversion employee's had been chasing the dollar and ended up in a job that had been sidelined by this new award. My friend's example of the Forklift Drivers stands out the most as a lot of these guys interacted with us in the Paper Mill as they transferred our product to Conversion and the Warehouses. I remember a lot of these guys being quite switched and with the Forklift driver's job being restricted in opportunity for promotion it seemed strange. (An Aha moment for myself).

One of these Forklift Operators was a fellow called Tex Bogan who was a real practical joker and was always stirring the pot – "only one of many in this fine establishment!" Some people are known for their intelligence and others for their own perception of their intelligence, Tex is one of these.

Being a large fellow he took a bit to swing up onto his Forklift and was very hesitant to dismount for this very reason. Unless of course it was home time or more importantly "lunchtime!" On one particular occasion while removing product from our Paper Mill, on overtime, he appeared more annoyed than was normal. I was not sure as to why this was until I got closer to his Forklift which had been embellished on all four sides with the slogan "Get Some Pork on Your Fork" an Australian Pork ad campaign from the 80's. It appeared that Tex had been tipped at his own game, "and he was not happy!"

As mentioned earlier I have now has input from other gentlemen who worked in Conversion in the 70's – 80's and beyond, and here is a few things that they had to say. For those who were working there it will fill in the gaps, for those who just want to hear the crazy antics bear with me, it won't be long!

Prior to the Award Restructuring and Multiskilling program of the mid 80's Conversion used what was called "The Box" for new employees/ Laborer's. They had to apply for spare operator positions in a specific line and wait for a permanent position to be advertised and that was given by Seniority within the spare operators.

More input came from another member who wrote; Conversions was a mess when I first started - then they added things and got to the point where you need to be a lawyer to work it out. It was near impossible to move from conversion to the mill it was like a "different town". Then there was the Warehouse (simple) you could move from Conversion to the Warehouse but not from the warehouse to Conversion – "Go Figure!"

This is an area which I haven't mentioned much (the Warehouse) where the follow process occurred;

The Warehouse was obviously for storing finished goods, as opposed to the Reel Stores where, funnily enough, Reels of paper were stored. The Warehouse also had an active crew who loaded Interstate Trucks during the dayshift then on the afternoon shift the Local and Rail Shipments were loaded for next day delivery. Amazingly all production came from conversion on the main line (a roller/conveyor system) and was stacked by two people and a Forklift driver. There was also a sorting area in this building where boxes of colored toilet paper arrived and then opened, mixed and re-sealed as assorted colored toilet paper. From there it was shipped to Retail or stored for future distribution. A labor intensive operation that drew labor from Conversion 'B' when in full swing.

Workers mixing the coloured Toilet Roll Packs then re-sealing for outlets.

Slippery Sam and the Spider...

AS I WAS STARTING to get a bit of experience under my belt on the Rewinders, Larry would put me on No 1 or No 2 Rewinder with Gerry and Spider as an extra to train on these winders and to get a bit more familiar with No 1 and 2 Paper machines and their crews. I enjoyed working with all these guys and in the most part you got to chat more with them than you did on No 3 Rewinder. There were two reasons for this, the first was the noise and the second was that it was almost always Scotties. Scotties was more fast-paced and physically harder than most product run on the other two Rewinders.

So it stood to reason that I would end up socializing with some of them outside work. Now it was not that these guys were the typical friends I would chose, but they were good blokes in the most part and the hours we worked also meant it was much easier. Add to this that Spider had just purchased a small farm in Yea. So you now have two people working the same hour, in the same company and living in the same distant region of Victoria. Apparently his Wife

Sam loved horses and had always wanted a paddock to keep them in. Ended up that that was not all she loved, as I later found out. Bruce had told me that Sam was a Stripper but I thought he was just talking shit and at the time paid no attention to his comment. So when I met her that thought was not on my mind.

As Yea was about 1.5 hours from Box Hill, Spider thought it would be a good idea if we drove in to work together. In those days it took me a bit under an hour to drive to work from Flowerdale and he said he would pay me petrol money. So I agreed and he would drive to my place and then we would travel together to work in my newly acquired HZ Ute.

Now at first the whole thing worked fine as Spider would be on time and the company on the drive was good. Sam also got along with my then wife, and my ex even looked after her daughter while Sam was at work. This gave my ex some extra pocket money and as we were trying for a family it may have been good practice also. We had BBQ's together at each other's place and it was going along fine. My first hint of Sam's profession came when my ex and I were sitting in their living room one evening while Spider was bathing his daughter and Sam was feeding the horses. Spider had finished bathing his daughter and yelled out that he was just getting a shower and would be out in a minute. His daughter came in and went straight to the TV cabinet and pulled out a Video. My ex and I presumed that it was Bugs Bunny or something so didn't think much of it until the picture came on with Velvet Curtains and loud rhythmic music starting up. Just as the curtains opened we spotted someone who looked very much like Sam in suspenders and hitting into a routine. But as quick as the curtains opened, Spider (with towel "almost" covering his plump stature) dived at the Video player and hit the stop button, all while yelling at his daughter that that was "daddy's special tape".

My ex and I just smirked at each other as Sam entered the room and asked what was going on seeing Spider half wrapped and wringing wet.

Awkward!!!! But the ex and I acted as though we hadn't seen anything so the presumption was, from Spider and Sam, that we hadn't and we all kept going as normal. Not sure how dumb they thought we were, as even Spiders show was enough for us to presume Sam was a Stripper even if we didn't see anything. And "Daddy's special tape!" – Spider didn't come across as a closet Ballet fan. But everyone was happy with the silence and we moved on.

Around this time Gerry decided to rent a Farm at Dixon Creek. I think all these moves came about because Spider had visited us and Sam must have started on him about buying a farm out that way. Then Gerry being Gerry thought it may be an opportunity to make a few dollars as Spider had mentioned how much Sam had been paying in agistment fees.

My Trusty 1978 HZ Ute – with our Flowerdale Home in the Background (top shot)

The Barbeque Table...

NOW I BELIEVE THAT I have mentioned that Gerry's wife was more attractive than she was intellectual and was part of the reason why Gerry got away with his harebrained schemes. Her love of animals is also documented and part of the why she was excited by this move to Dixons Creek with their three Children (two boys and young daughter). Gerry's plan was to lease the property (twenty odd acres) which was set up as a horse property for $350 per week if my memory serves me correct. Which in those days was a huge amount of money as most suburban homes rented for around $120 - $150 per week. But Gerry, the Entrepreneur that he was, had a brilliant plan of agisting 20 horses at $25 per week and not only living rent free but turning a profit. Sounds good "hay!" pardon the pun, and it was not long before Gerry had 15 horses onsite. Trouble was that after paying the first four weeks many of the owners never returned and Gerry soon realized that the average age of the horses on his property was well over the retirement age. Turns out that most were just dumping their old nags as getting them put down was far more expensive than the first four weeks of agistment. OMG! Gerry had Vet bills and debt coming out of his proverbial.

As this was all happening Spider was pissing me off by tuning up late, which made me late and sometimes not turning up at all without letting me know. No mobile phones in those days so I was late on those occasions also, as I felt guilty leaving without him. (Not sure why!) What pissed me off even more was that one day he didn't turn up and I was again late for work, this time though Larry, my leading hand, gave me a Verbal Warning as Spider had rung in sick. This went on my permanent record and even my relief who was waiting for me had a go at me. GRRRRRRRRRR!!!!!!

Fortunately though another, more positive twist was unfolding. As my then wife found out she was pregnant and we put our home in Flowerdale on the market. I was also working with a Vietnamese fellow named Bobby Dan and we struck up a good friendship. Bobby had transferred from Conversion, he was a very worldly and interesting fellow. Within weeks of putting our Flowerdale home on the market we had a buyer, a single fellow from Epping who wanted a tree change. We were so excited as we got close to the asking price and although $48,500 is not much these days it was good money back then, especially for Flowerdale.

Bobby Dan had invited us to a party at his home around the same time, and as fate would have it upon driving to his home in Seville East we spotted a for sale sign in Seville. Located next to a strawberry farm was a small estate and a new spec home that had just come onto the market.

We arranged a viewing for later that day, after our visit to Bobby and his young family. We bought it the next day after checking with the "State Bank of Victoria" (now Commonwealth Bank) that we could afford the loan, and a month later we moved in.

During this time Spider had decided to travel to Gerry's home and come to work with him as he could obviously sense I was not too happy with the current arrangements. It was a straighter run from Yea via Dixons Creek with less twists and turns. But I think the Glenburn Pub stop off was also a drawcard. I felt compelled to discuss my disappointment with Spider, but alas I refrained and life got better (That is Sarcasm – if you missed it).

Spider was not vindictive though, as he didn't hold grudges. Truth is he didn't give a shit about anything really and a few weeks later while having lunch in the Canteen he told me a ripper story about Gerry.

It went like this;

They arrived at Gerry's property around 11-45pm after our afternoon shift and as Gerry drove his falcon up his driveway he noticed one of the nags lying oddly in the paddock. Spider said "he is just sleeping Gerry" but Gerry knew this was not the case as this horse had not been eating for days and looked quite weak when he left for work that day. Gerry pulled up at the fence and got out of his car to investigate. The horse was definitely no longer with us and Gerry called out to Spider to come and see for himself.

Just as Spider was about to tell me more Little Legs and Snoozy turned up at our table in the canteen and sat with us. I said "what are you guys doing here? Simon running No2 Machine on his own?" Snoozy said, we are down for a roll change as the bearings had gone in some main roller. (When down for maintenance the Machine crew got a meal break, and as it didn't happen very often they always took advantage of it and came to the canteen for lunch). Spider then explained that we were just discussing Gerry's Ranch and the goings on a few days ago. Always telling Gerry Gee stories, Little Legs leaned forward in anticipation and Snoozy had a big smirk on his face – "They were ready!" Spider continued seamlessly from where he left off, only backtracking slightly to where they had pulled up to Gerry's place.

Gerry called again for Spider to come see, and casually Spider came over and said "Yep – its Dead!" Gerry said "what shall we do?" to which Spider responded "we!" Gerry said; oh Boooooody I can't move it on my own, what should I do? Spider said; we should just dig a hole right next to it and bury it. So at 12-00 midnight they started digging – and digging – and digging, and by 2-00am they had dug a huge hole. Then unable to push the horse into the hole by manpower Gerry took out three fence rails and moved the Falcon to sit against the poor animal's body. If he couldn't move the beast with manpower then he thought Horsepower was the go, and with a lot of revving and wheel spinning the beast dropped into it final resting place.

With all the commotion, on came the porch lights and Gerry's half naked wife appeared. She called to Gerry as to 'what was going on', to which Gerry replied "just pulling out a tree stump honey!" A quick OK with a puzzled look and off to bed she went. She was very use to Gerry's harebrained shenanigans so there were no further questions and off went the lights. Spider and Gerry then turned their attention to the next problem, and with Gerry Gee on the job there were always more problems. In their haste to get the hole big enough they did not get it deep enough. Although Spider said he thought the legs would fold back, it was obvious that rigor mortis would prevent this and the body was always going to fall with the heaviest part at the bottom. So what they ended up with was the horse's four legs facing the sky about two to three feet above ground level. At this point Little Legs interjected with the comment "You should have put a timber top on them and made a Barbeque table!" To which we all burst out laughing, and with relative silence in the canteen (due to the serious eating) and the area full of "suits" we were peppered with filthy looks and eye rolling. As if that would worry Spider, who wiped the tears from his eyes and meat pie from his shirt and carried on his story.

Gerry, with a look of horror, turned to Spider and said "Boooooody ah ah ah, what do we do now?" And as quick as the last time he said it Spider said "we!" Then a Lightning Bolt moment for Gerry and he took off to his shed and came back with his trusty chainsaw. At this point Spider said "for F**ks sake Gerry you can't use that it is 2-30am you will have all your neighbours over here!" Oh Boooooooody but how are we going to fit the horse in the hole. Spider said "get your Axe!" and they proceeded to remove the legs below ground level and lay them beside the poor beast in relative silence and under the cover of darkness.

The Postman never rings Twice...

NOW WITH THE JUICES flowing and the audience fully enthralled Little Legs could not help himself and chimed in with his own new Gerry Gee Story. This one was also at Dixons Creek and I can verify part of it as I had met the Bulldog in question.

Little Legs began by setting the scene and describing the crazy Bulldog in the story. Unlike Melbourne, in those days the postman rode a Honda Bike to deliver the mail as it would not be possible to cover the distances between properties on a pushbike and yet it didn't justify a four wheeled vehicle. I suppose the land in the area would be classified today as Lifestyle Acreage or hobby farms. That explained why the Postmen of the day hated these runs as there were always dogs and usually plenty of them. Gerry's property was no different, although the Postman's arch enemy on this property was not your typical troublesome dog but an overweight Bulldog named Winston. But Winston could move when he had too, and even with those stumpy fat legs could keep the Postman at full throttle.

Day after day the ritual would unfold with Winston jumping out of his slumber as the Postie put letters into the box and then it was on with Winston hitting top speed and his fat legs moving so fast that he looked more like a low flying Scud Missile than a household pet. When Winston did, on occasions, get close enough he would bite at the rear tyre with the Postie raising his legs forward to ensure that "he" was not confused for the tyre. Then alas one wet day disaster struck in that Winston actually caught the back tyre and got caught up in swing arm, drive sprocket and rear fender of the Postman's bike. This brought the Bike to such a stop that the Postie was flung off his Bike, through the air and into a Gumtree breaking his arm. Poor Winston was killed instantly and the whole scene was horrendous. Gerry's wife came running out of their home and immediately assisted the Postie to Hospital. Gerry came home some hour or so later and found the remaining carnage, with Winston infused into the bike, he could not believe what had unfolded on his driveway. But if it was going to happen to anyone, then it was going to happen to "Gerry Gee!"

Roll Change...

AFTER MANY MONTHS OF stacking Scotties on the back of number 3 Rewinder I was asked by Larry the Leading Hand if I would like to be 2nd Boy on Number One Paper Mill. I said to him that I would do it as long as I had the flexibility to still choose which career path I wished to take. Larry and Pat (the Gold Shift Supervisor) explained to me that the 2nd Boy position did not lock me into the Machine line, but in saying that said that I would be suited to that path. I said that I would think about it overnight if that was OK and let them know tomorrow. My real reason for asking for overnight was to check the facts of what they were telling me as I did not want to get locked into a Career Path at this stage.

I asked a few guys in the Paper Mill and they said I would be OK to do this as it was not a lock in position and my Seniority (as short as it currently was) would not be affected. In saying that I had not been there long, I had still been there long enough to see four or five new guys start after me, as with the new shift being created they were still employing a few people. So I thought it would be a good opportunity to meet the Union Rep as I was on Day shift and I should be able to catch up with him. Now Des Onion was an interesting fellow holding an interesting position. Des was employed by Bowater as a Union Representative that fought Bowater for the rights of its members (Us). How does that work?

Des originally worked on the Floor and I believe he came out of Conversion but I am not sure as I never asked this question, I just recall hearing it somewhere. Des was an average sized fellow with dark skin and possibly had some native Australian blood, but again I am not sure if this was the case. He was a little on the chunky side and I presume that this was a side effect of the 'good wicket" he was on, as he was paid a shift work rate but worked Monday to Friday on Day Shift. He had a small office onsite between the two Conversion sections and near the First Aid room and Nurses Station. As I was on the Rewinder for the day I was entitled to a 30-minute meal break and thought I would use this time to go and see Des and confirm what I had been told by my Leading Hand Larry.

I was fortunate enough to catch Des just as he was coming out of his office and asked him if I could talk to him for a minute. He seemed quite eager to get going as it was lunchtime, and that seemed to be his number one priority! But he opened his office door again and we entered. I told him what Larry had requested of me and that Larry had said that it would not lock me into the Machine line. Des assured me that this was correct and not to worry as he quickly shuffled me out of his office and darted towards the Canteen.

Little Legs had told me that Des Onion's Nick name in the old days was Gorilla Pits and can only guess that this was due to his chunky stature that had given him almost female sized breasts. But again I am only guessing as it was never confirmed. (Funny nickname all the same.)

Armed with this knowledge (not the Gorilla Pits bit) I went and saw Larry and Pat and told them I was happy to do 2nd Boy on Number One Machine. Larry asked if I still wanted to think about it overnight, to which I replied No and I was good to start when they wanted me to. They told me then that Karl was wanting to take up a position in the Pulp Yard on his old shift (Red shift), which had recently been advertised. As Karl was in his 60's it seemed appropriate for him to take up a position in the unofficial Retirement Village! Larry said to me that Karl was off in one more week so he needed to get me trained. This was good timing (or well planned) as Gold Shift had just started Day Shift today and it was the best time to learn a new position with many extra Day Shift people around. I asked Larry why Fred Van-Alphabet didn't want the position and Larry told me that a 2nd Boy position on Number 3 Machine was coming up and Fred really wanted to work there. He also said that he had offered Fred the Number 1 Mill position but Fred had been told by his Father-in-Law of the Number 3 Mill job. Barry (the day shift Core Cutter) heard a lot, as working where he did, he got to talk to all the shifts and let Fred know as soon as he heard. Fred was super keen to work in Number 3 Mill and for the life of me I don't know why, as personally I find it the noisiest - dirtiest and dustiest of all the Paper Mills. Although the Machine end is not so dusty it is definitely noisy and you can feel the vibration of the machine go through your whole body. But to each their own and soon Rex and Kev would have to adjust to a new bunch on the Back of the Rewinder.

The very next day I started on Training as 2nd Boy on No 1 Machine with Karl and Bruce. I must say it was a much more pleasant atmosphere as the guys here were more mature and the machine itself was cleaner and quieter. Also stacking Scotties on the back of the Rewinder was very dusty, mind numbing and on Night Shift was hard work. As new staff had not yet started in enough numbers to cover all the jobs there was a lot of overtime on offer, so when Fred took up the 2nd Boy position on No 3 Paper Machine a fellow called Sean was transferred from Blue shift onto Gold shift so that

Rex and Kev had at least one experienced guy on the back of the Rewinder. Scotties (tissues) were a big seller and the run of these on No 3 Rewinder / Machine seemed to go for extended periods of time. With two guys required on the Back of the Rewinder all the time, the Overtime was flowing and so were the dollars.

I explained to Larry that I was keen to get some of this overtime as my now Wife and I were planning to buy a new home closer to work. He told me that as I was on No 1 machine that he had to offer it to No 3 Mill workers first. This seemed a little unfair as I was asked to go to No 1 Mill by Pat and Larry and had worked on Scotties for a long time without getting much overtime. But Larry had his favourites, and I appeared not to be one of them, so I thought I would tell other Shift Leading hands of my eagerness to do Scotties overtime. Kev, who was an aspiring Union Rep put me onto this as he agreed that it was a little unfair what Larry was doing. It worked well as the next day I received a call from the Blue shift leading hand to come in 4 hours early on overtime. I did not even have to ask where I would be working as I knew it was to stack Scotties.

By this time though they had got a few more new blokes on and I was asked to come in to cover for a bloke who was on his first day and therefore training. Now Blue shift was quite a different shift to Gold Shift and to be honest all the Shifts had their characters, with this mob being no exception. The Winderman was a fellow of German extraction named Phil Yocker, and Yockers, as he was known, was a real character. He was a fellow in his late 50's who looked older than that to me and he was built like a knackwurst sausage only not as tight. He loved a yarn almost as much as a rumour, and was forever talking about the stupid things that other people in the Mill did. He was also a keen gambler with the ponies being his weapon of choice. On the weekends especially, the hut radio was always tuned to them and could not be touched or he would turn on you like a Cobra.

The similarities between Yockers and a Cobra were the vigour of his attacks and his distinct lack of teeth. In fact when he laughed, it was not only loud but dangerous, as you had to dodge the saliva that flew out the huge gaps in his teeth as he turned from red to purple in excitement. His Assistant was Daniel who was a youngish fellow in his mid 20's, who was married with a couple of kids. Just how the Mill liked its new workers "married and committed", as they were seen as stable employees. Daniel was tall and quite slim (although as the years rolled by I saw him fill out a bit), he was totally different from Yockers and they were quite the odd pair.

At the Back of the Rewinder was Henry who had started after me and Ricardo who was on his first day in the Paper Mill after transferring from conversion. When I met Ricardo it was 11-00am and he was already half way through his first day. I introduced myself as Craig and he said in a heavy Spanish or South American accent; "Hello – I am Ricardo – but you may call me Rick". Now this was a trigger for Yockers to flip into his Cobra stance and he belted out an enormous laugh that shook the dust off the hut we were in. Daniel and Henry soon chimed in with supportive laughter and I could see that Ricardo (or Rick) was not too impressed. He turned and stormed out of the Hut and headed off towards the clock card area. The good part about coming in early on Afternoon shift on the Rewinder was that it was around their lunchtime and you got their half hour break with them. Today was no different as I had only stacked two sets of Scotties before their break, which was when the Ricardo incident unfolded.

Nothing like a bit of excitement to start the day and the next thing we saw was Ricardo heading back with the Leading Hand in tow. He burst into the hut and started banging on about how Yockers was treating him like a fool and how he was being victimized. I knew this could not have just been from one burst of laughter at what he said, and that these boys had been winding him up. But if he thought by making Yockers apologize to him at the request of the Leading Hand, that all this would be over, then he was sadly mistaken. I worked with Henry and Ricardo for the rest of the day without incident as Yockers had somewhat pulled his head in a bit. I don't think that this occurred because of what Ricardo had done but more that the Horse Racing was on and the Rewinder was flying. No-one had time to stir shit!

I heard a week or so later that Ricardo had been fired, which was a shock to all of us in No 1 Mill as it was very hard to lose your job in this Unionized Paper Mill. So the next time we saw Des Onion, Bruce asked him what had happened to Ricardo. Des explained that Ricardo had pulled a knife on Henry at the back of No 3 Rewinder and threatened to harm him. I immediately knew that Yockers and his team had not let up on Ricardo and that with Ricardo's hot blooded attitude it would not be long before he snapped. I could have said something but I didn't, as I was not there and even though I had my theories (which were probably correct) I could not be 100% sure. Also I did not want to rock the boat as I was only new myself and needed to be working here with our new home not far away and our first child pending. Before going any further with the goings on in the Paper Mill I would like to tell you some stories from my first home in Flowerdale (country Victoria). Some linked to the boys at Bowater, some not – but all very entertaining yarns that must be told before my move to the outskirts of civilization (Seville Victoria).

Movin From the Country...

LIVING IN FLOWERDALE IN the 80's was quite an experience and one that was quite different from my life to that time. Before moving to Flowerdale my then wife and I had lived in a one bedroom unit in Reservoir. Prior to that I was in Bundoora – Preston – Regent and Reservoir with my Grandparents, so I was very much a Northern suburb boy. All these areas were fairly high density (by 1980's standard) and a huge change from where we bought our first home. People in the 80's in general were more family orientated and had a more genuine community spirit mentality. This was not too different than what we experienced in Flowerdale except that there were some very odd characters that called this place home. I would like to tell you of a few:

THE LOCAL

Our first night in our new home at Flowerdale, and after the heavy lifting while moving house and cleaning all day, my then wife and I decided to treat ourselves to a pub dinner. With the Flowerdale Hotel only a few minutes' drive away we set off around 7-00pm for a drink and a feed. This place was quaint but quite rundown and we were hoping that the food would be OK. When we arrived we were greeted by the publican's son Richard who introduced himself as Dick, to which stupid I, with a smirk on my face responded "really!" My then wife gave me a dirty look but Richard just responded with "I have never heard that one before".

To strike up a bit of a conversation I mentioned how handy it was for the Fire Brigade shed to be directly across the road from the pub. Richard agreed that it was in some ways and that the fire bell was located on the veranda of the pub. Then he proceeded to tell me a story of the last fire drill they had a few months ago where the bell was rung and the local volunteer fire fighters all came to assemble in readiness for despatch. One of the Volunteers was "on that very bar stool" (pointing to the stool closest to the dartboard) when the bell was rung, and as he proceeded to run to the fire station he was hit by a minibus that was travelling on the main road. The whole drill was then transformed from a Fire drill to an Ambulance run to the Yea hospital. Richard went on to say that even though he had flown twenty metres through the air he only received a broken arm and multiple abrasions. He added that this was probably because the fellow was pickled and landed in the paddock beside the pub which was sodden from recent rains.

The meal turned out to be very nice as it was quite home-style and hardy.

THE WILDLIFE

Over the time living in Flowerdale and the many Kilometres that we travelled, it was common to see wildlife on the roads (some living but most dead). The vast majority of these native creatures were

Wombats and it seemed that the higher you got into the Kinglake Ranges the bigger and Blacker these creatures got. My then wife came home one evening from her local job making Ugg type boots, and told me a story of the local school teacher. Apparently he had been travelling late one winters evening and struck one of these beasts, just on a bend at the start of the decent into Flowerdale. Driving a small Japanese car, he struck the poor creature that slid under his vehicle causing enormous damage to both. In fact the forty plus kilogram beast was written-off as was the Honda. A few weeks later and in a brand new Honda the poor schoolteacher, on the same stretch of road spotted another Beast in his path. In his horror he swerved to avoid a repeat of the prior incident only to lose control and end up kissing a tree and writing off another Honda. Fortunately he wasn't injured and lived to purchase a new Holden which was much more sensible under the circumstances.

DRUNK AND DISORDERLY

These poor Wombats seemed to litter the road at certain times of the year and there was perhaps a reason why there were more at certain times of year, but as a young bloke I really didn't give it much thought.

In fact there was a disrespectful act that occurred for a period of time that at first I thought amusing but later was a bit disgusted by. My first encounter of this was; I remember travelling home from a day shift one Sunday and noticing a Wombat that appeared to have landed against a road sign in an upright position. I was traveling North and he was facing North, on the opposite side of the road, so I slowed down to look at him in my rear-view mirror. I thought he had been hit and landed there after being struck but this was not the case. What my rear-view mirror revealed was that he had been propped up to the sign by a silly human being. How did I know this? Well the poor fellow had a VB Can (Beer) taped to his front paw, and with his stance he looked like a drunk leaning against a wall. To add insult to injury (so to speak) with the heat of the day he had a volley of flies circling him and his now odorous body.

To be perfectly honest as a young twenty something year old I thought it quite funny, but on reflection it got past being funny when copycats started doing it and these poor disrespected creatures were everywhere.

WOMBAT MAN

With the abundant resource of dead wombats grew the birth of a local legend known as Wombat Man. Now it is not the way you would expect a fable to read out these days, as today the story would read of a local wildlife carer who nurtured the sick and injured while respectfully burying the dead.

No No No!!!!!

This wombat man was an 80's wombat man and a Neanderthal one at that. The habits of this fellow was to stop at the fresh (or not so fresh) grave of one of these departed creatures and proceed to lift him onto the roof rack of his vehicle and head home. His home was a heavily populated side road in Flowerdale (Hazeldene) that traversed King Parrot Creek. In the 80's this area was transforming from a holiday shack area to a more permanent population of less fortunate Australians.

Once he arrived home, and with his three German Shepard dogs barking in anticipation, Wombat Man dropped the poor creature off his roof rack and retrieved his chainsaw from his shed (which I think was also his Lounge room). Yes you guessed it, believe it or not he then proceeded to chop up the poor fella and feed it to his now drooling dogs.

His neighbours were the ones who witnessed this and told stories at the local of how the fur and flesh would spray across his yard and jamb up his chainsaw. This practice went on for many months, and after a number of warnings from the local cop he ceased the practice and went back to Pal (canned dog food).

CRACKERS

One of the most well-known of all characters in the area was a fellow who lived near the end of our street (Long Gully Rd) on a 14 acre property, if my memory serves me correctly. They called him Crackers and he amazingly rode a 1950's Harley with sidecar. Over the years he adapted this vehicle to maximize the carrying capacity of the sidecar as he used it to carry produce that he grew on his property. Every week he would travel the area on his bike selling vegetable's mainly to the locals. He was no doubt an eccentric bloke and would have been in his 60's I guess, but he was quite ruddy and lived quite rough, (with no services at this property) so it is hard to say exactly how old he was at the time.

Crackers invited my then wife and I to his property to show us "his rock eating bugs". Yes they were his words and we agreed to visit, more out of politeness than any curiosity of his bugs. I have trouble recalling what his home looked like but I do recall it being very basic and Bushman like (probably – "no definitely" wouldn't pass Council Inspection today). He led us directly past all his sheds and towards the back of his property where he had discovered his bugs. I could not help notice the motors that he was using to cut his timber and pump water etc. I said to Crackers "what are those motor's fella?" and he answered that most of them were Harley motor cycle engines from the 40's and 50's. I was fixated on them and was staring at them while Crackers and my ex were off up the path to the bugs. Crackers turned and saw me way behind and yelled to me to catch up, which I did while my mind stayed with the machinery in his sheds. Up at the cave, which turned out to be about 30 X 30 centimetres in size, Crackers explained that he had had University professors and students out here who could not explain the phenomenon. All I could see was a hole and a few bugs crawling around, but apparently according to Crackers the hole is growing rapidly (about a centimetre a year). Sorry to sound unimpressed but at 22 years old this wasn't exactly riveting, and even today I would struggle. But those Harley Motors – WOW! – What would they be worth today!

I think Crackers sensed this and on the way down he showed me through his sheds in greater detail. I am still impressed as I recall the tour today. The people of Flowerdale were a bit harsh on Crackers I believe, as my memory of him is that he spoke well and must have come from an educated past. Perhaps the people of Flowerdale were intimidated by his intellectual capacity, which was not surprising after just finishing a chapter on Wombat Man!

*** Later I reflected on this visit and remembered that Crackers name was Les – not sure where the memory came from but there you go! *** (Perhaps a handy entry for your book of useless information)

NEIGHBOURS

What a diverse group of neighbours we had in those days and we knew them all. As I said earlier this area was changing from holiday shacks to permanent residents and our Road (Long Gully) was no exceptions.

The homes at the start of the street were very small but that was mainly because there was a small creek at their rear boundary and then the land went straight up a large hill at almost 90 degrees. But as you drove down the street the land mass to the left got wider and the homes had more room to grow. Not that many of them did as the further you went down Long Gully Rd the higher the fire risk, which was a real and ever present danger. In fact the first year we lived there we were evacuated in the Strath Creek fires of 1982, which they believe was triggered by the root of a tree that had burnt down the year prior and had smouldered to the surface and re-ignited. Apparently fire can smoulder underground and re-ignite when it hits open air again. These fires were scary but nowhere near as bad as the Ash Wednesday fires only months later in February 1983.

One home on the left was down in a ditch and it was tiny, made from old Tea Chests. No need to say that it deteriorated quite rapidly and to my knowledge was never used as a permanent home. Our home was fibro and split into two sections with a breezeway through the middle, which we later filled in as it was all under one roofline. It even had an outside toilet when we moved in, but fortunately it was shell only, as the toilet itself was brought inside a few years prior to us purchasing it. The neighbours on the left at the start of the street were friendly enough but they had their own little group and kept to that group. They all had “Slow Down – we have to live here” signs on their homes that appeared to be written and produced by the same Author, thus reinforcing the bond they had. The dust was shocking in summer and the front of their homes reflected this fact. One of these neighbours worked for Dragway Wheels and was also good friends with the Splatt family. I bought my Torana wheels from their West Heidelberg Factory as it was not far from where I worked in Preston, before Bowater (You can see the mag wheels in the picture of me and my Torana included in this book). Ironically they moved the factory to Kinglake West and it burned down in one of the big fires. The rest of the street was a mixed bags with most of the homes on the right being on acreage. One couple that we spoke to a lot were Brian and Gwen. They had an amazing parrot who would say "Just a Minute" whenever anyone knocked on the door. One time it kept an encyclopedia salesperson on the doorstep for over an hour. In the end and being told "Just a Minute" over 30 times he gave up and left. I know this as Brian was inside at the time, and in those days everyone knew how resilient these Salesmen could be. Sadly Gwen died in a car accident while we lived there, she was not wearing a seatbelt. The local policeman told us later that she would have only had minor injuries if she was wearing her seatbelt as the car held up well to rolling down an embankment.

Straight across the road from us was a 14 acre bush block that a fellow in his mid-20's owned. A nice bloke just a bit older than my ex and I. We would chat whenever he came up and he eventually built a log cabin style place on the land but never lived there permanently. Next door to him and diagonally across the road from us was an elderly couple on about the same amount of acres as their young neighbour, maybe a bit more. But their property was quite established and had grassed paddocks for horses and other farmyard animals. They were extremely permanent and had been there over twenty years when we first moved in. They lived in an old style weatherboard home while his son and his family, consisting of his wife, 2 young boys and a teenage daughter all lived in a caravan and large annex beside the main home.

The boys would play happily but the teenage girl was a bit of a loaner. She went out every day after school on a walk down the road and off into the bush, and always alone. Then I noticed that Tom, a young bloke in his late teens who lived two doors up from us would follow her and then return some ten minutes or so after she returned. Thinking that they were just sneaking off together I thought no more of it. But one day when I was off up the road to find my crazy dog that had escaped I startled her in the bushes 'mid-session'! Turns out that it was not a rendezvous of young Tom and herself but a Solo Show with Tom watching from behind the trees. Not sure who was more embarrassed but the walks ceased and Tom didn't say much again to myself, or anyone else for that matter.

Back to the "Roll Change"

WHEN WORKING IN NO 3 Mill we knew what was going on around the place, but it was different on No 1 Paper Machine. Not sure if that was because we were a bit away from the action or because the fellows on No 1 Paper Machine were more mature. I reckon it was the later as when on No 1 with the Rewinder going and with Gerry Gee and Spider there, we heard it all. In fact Gerry and Spider were regularly the main characters.

I have chopped about here and not focused on the "Roll Change" that has come about in my career, and "Roll Changing" was the greatest slice of my new position as 2nd Boy on No 1 Paper Machine.

Karl was a great teacher as he had been doing 2nd Boy here for many years and was well motivated with a vested interest in my learning the job quickly and well. He wanted the heck out of there so he could enjoy his early retirement (often referred to as the Pulp Yard). To explain the job in detail I will split it into two section – "wet side of the Reel" and "dry side of the Reel". With most of my new duties happening on the Dry side I will run through that first.

With Bruce at the controls of the 1st Boy panel, myself as the 2nd Boy would assist in the changing of the Reel. It goes like this:

- The Reel is run up to a specified size
- At that point with the next Corebar set and locked into its place above the Reel, that Corebar is brought down onto the Reel Drum while two 'y' shaped arms eject the Reel that is now at size (and the reel slitter, if on, is dropped away stopping its cutting process)
- The fresh Corebar at speed moves downwards with air shooting from below creating a loop in the paper between the old and the new Reels.
- As this loop of paper gets bigger it gets caught by the new Corebar (in the nib) and with the 'y' arms returned to the Reel Drum and the Slitter re-applied (if required) the new Corebar is bedded on the running rails and starts its growth into a new Reel.
- The brake is applied to the freshly completed Reel and the process of preparation for storage / Conversion or Rewinder begins.

Picture of the Dry end of No 1 Paper Machine - note: the workers hut to the front left covered in dust - the reel of new paper running up with the slitter cutting it into two (meaning; not for Rewinder but to be taken to Conversion or Storage). Wet end of the Machine in the distance and the top of the Rewinder (front right)

Also note that the next corebar is not sitting above the Reeldrum as it is being processed at the rear of the Rewinder, by the 2nd Boy out of view.

The process of preparation involves cleaning the loose winds of paper off the top of the Reel down to where the slitter came off (or if going into the Rewinder where the paper is level and clean). This is all done in a position where the running rails have been lowered. It ensures safety, as the Full Reel is unable to roll back into the New Reel that has just started to grow. After cleaning, the Reel has a tail made in the paper (if it is going into the Rewinder), or taped into position if going into storage or Conversion. On a pre-determined number of Reels a sample test is also taken by the 1st Boy and delivered to the CR Lab (Uncle Fozzie). The results are documented for quality control and conveyed to the Machineman for adjustments if required.

Then the major role of my new job as 2nd Boy kicks in;

- The overhead crane with the two hooks is brought over to the completed Reel and places onto the Corebar.
- If the paper is for Rewinding it is lifted into the cradles of the Rewinder and with the assistance of the 1st Boy secured into the cradles and locked in place. (that is the easier of the two processes and unfortunately the least common)
- If the Reel is slit then it is picked up by the Overhead Crane
- Lifted over the Rewinder and lowered onto the scales for weighing
- The weight is recorded on a sheet that also records the reel number and other details including - Machinemans name – shift – and other product details. These details are all transposed (or copied) onto the Reel prior to it being picked up by the Forklift driver. (who uses a Grab mechanism on his Forklift) It is written on the smooth cut side of the reel, close to core to ensure that the Conversion operator can see the details well into the running of the Reel if required.
- The Reel is then lifted again, ensuring that the rear hook is firmly secured around the Corebar at the rear – (front one you see easily as you are standing beside it) The rear hook is viewed via a rounded mirror but most good operators walk around to ensure it is place correctly and securely.

- The Reel is then positioned facing the Electric Winch and placed on the ground (or one side of the Reel on the spin plate if you are an experienced operator).
- Then the thread of the Corebar is undone in a clockwise direction (if memory serves me correct) and the horseshoe shaped Core holder is taken off using a special tool in preparation of the Corebar being extracted.
- The 2nd Boy then goes to the back of the Reel and hooks the Winch (via a metal gadget) to the Corebar and while the Winch starts extracting the Corebar, a sling attached to a vertical Winch, is placed around the Corebar to hold it above the ground. Experienced operators can do this while the Winch is running, but as I am a learner I had to stop the winch when the Corebar had been extracted just over half way and using the handmade mark on the Corebar, lift the Corebar until it was at the point of balance and level with the cores that it was coming out of.
- Then when the balance is just right I hit the Winch Go button again and extracted the Corebar completely. This was a bit of an art and took a bit of practice, and a high level of skill and timing was required to do this as the Winch was running. I eventually mastered this but it did take me a couple of months.

If you got this wrong the Corebar would drop at one end, and being so heavy (probably 500kgs or so from memory) it could be hard to handle. Or in extreme cases you would have to rest it on the ground with a block of wood holding up one end and re-align the strap so the point-of-balance was restored.

- Whatever method was used to get to this point the next stage was to push the suspended Corebar over the Corebar holder/stand in preparation for the new Cores to be placed on it and locked into place. (Cores are the cardboard cylinders similar to toilet roll cores on steroids!)
- It was important to ensure that the new Cores were the correct size as if not it would be hard to part the Reels when they had to be split (the next process). Most operators put a mark on the wall near the area so they could quickly check this before sliding the Cores on. There was a box of core spaces available (of various sizes) that allowed for required adjustments and to hold the Cores tight to the Corebar when locking the Cores on the front end.
- Then came the process of splitting the Reels in preparation for the Forklift/Grab to pick up. This was done by pushing the Reels onto the Spinning Plate (if not landed on with the Overhead Crane and split).

If done well this is a reasonably simple process but here is a list of issues that can occur. Reels will not separate when;

- Slitter on Machine not engaged early enough; letting many wraps of paper to build up prior to engagement
- Loose wrap; causing the paper that has been cut to weave into itself and become interwoven on the new Reel.
- Misaligned Cores; leaving one Core embedded onto the wrong side of the Slitting (if not too bad the Forklift / Grab can fix this.)
- If really bad then a huge Bowsaw type blade is required and the Core is sawn through like the hand log saws of the olden days.
- There were more technical causes but these were the most common

Presuming that this doesn't happen then the process continues like this;

- The Reels are pushed (one at a time) onto the spinning plate. This took more effort the less skilled you were.
- Then the Reel is spun 90 degrees to face the exit door into Conversion where the Forklift / Grab would eventually pick it up from. Again this took some effort especially if not well centred on the spinning plate.
- Then the Reels had the info transposed onto them as described before near the core (in Crayon).
- After that the new Cores were put onto the Corebar and locked into place (as described earlier).
- Then the Winch was re-extended for the next use – the strap and Vertical Winch re-set and then the Overhead Crane was used to pick up the New Corebar for return to the Machine. (Noting that the rear hook was replaced in a different /wider position on the Corebar to allow for the change in weight distribution caused by the Paper Reel being removed).
- If the Reels of paper were different sizes (which often happened with Industrial Roll Towel) then an added piece to this process was that the smaller Reel had to be pushed back onto the scales and reweighed. This was because the total weight could not be split 50/50 due to the size disparity.

Now a good operator could do all this process in 10 -12 mins but it took me about 15 – 17 mins for quite a few months. When doing some types of paper this was not a problem as the Reels could take up to 90 mins to run up. But when running industrial Roll Towel the Reels ran up in about 18 mins. And I remember many a time having to write up Reels after the next Reel had come out just to get the New Corebar back in time.

The biggest issue was the high level of manual labour required, and when we were running this product and other areas were stopped we would sometimes be fortunate enough to get extra help. But mostly the 2nd Boy was "it" and on Nightshift it was not fun at all. To add to this for the first few months of doing the job on my own I got a number of night shifts in a row doing it on my own. I recall dreading coming around the corner of the machine at the start of a shift and seeing Roll Towel being run on the machine. This process caused numerous back injuries as it could be hard physically (especially if you were inexperienced) and many times you did it from a "Cold Start"! Not too good on the body especially on Night Shift. I fell prey to this when I had only been in the job for about six months, which was surprising to me as I had been an Industrial Tyre Fitter for three years where the physical labour was much more intense. But I think the twisting of the Reels on the turning plate was what got me. I was not fluent with this movement and was inexperienced on the job, so my technique was still undeveloped.

Now with this injury came a lot of extra hassle for me as I seemed to be the icing on the cake in a long running list of back injuries in the area. First I had to visit a specialist doctor in Melbourne who was affiliated with the company somehow and then some Investigator interviewed me about the incident and tried to get me to sign a declaration form. Fortunately Des Onion had informed me that this may occur and that, as my Union Representative, he suggested that I signed nothing.

I was off work for a couple of weeks and after getting a release by the Doctor I was back at work. Still doing the same job, I was more conscious of my back and took my time with the job and Bruce (my 1st Boy) helped me when I got a bit behind. But this injury had stuck in my head and I decided there and then that the continuous change of pace of the job was not good for me as it was either too much work or not enough. I would look at other areas harder as I was not keen to do this job long term.

As a note; about six months later construction (or I probably should say de-construction) started on the brick wall at the end of No 1 Paper Mill where the task of removing the Corebar and spinning the Reels to face the original exit doorway occurred. This process would allow the Reel to be just pushed out and no spinning the Reels would be required. It would make the job much easier physically and cut a couple of minutes off the turnaround of each unload. I later found out that a few years back they always had two 2nd Boys on the job when running Industrial Roll Towel as it was a constant problem. That made me feel a bit better (as I felt that I was underperforming), but it did not change my resolve of not wanting to pursue the Machine line of promotion. In hindsight this decision was a bit hasty as both No 2 Mill and No 3 Mill had automated Corebar extraction that made the job less physical, with No 3 Mill being the most advanced system.

THE WALL REMOVAL...

NOW THIS JOB TOOK a while as it had to be fully engineered and physically done in a 24 hour a day operating / busy factory. The red brick wall was very thick and the opening needed to be about 4 metres wide. This required a massive Concrete Lintel Beam to be constructed to support the opening. Now this amount of work and effort commanded a lot of attention and became the target a character named Derek Sorters who would perform his mastery on this prime target.

As normal I came into my Day Shift – clocked on and went to my 2nd Boy position on Number 1 Machine to relieve my mate who had now completed his night shift there. I came in early (around 6-30am) as this fellow always relieved me early and it was so exciting to see your relief early when you had worked all the night. It was my first Day of Day shift and was a Monday morning which meant two things; Plenty of bosses around and a Monday to Friday Day Shift. It also meant no penalties for this week's pay and a lot of extra Bullshit as the Bosses always made sure you were busy as they pissed around on the Machines trying different things. But today would be payback day for the workers as Jeff, the fellow I was relieving, showed me the crack that had appeared in the Concrete Lintel Beam of the new opening. Now this would have been scary if we had been using this opening, but as it was still apparently curing it was not in use yet and flagged off. We were running a wax based paper which was the best to run as it took about 90 mins to run up. I lived in hope that the run would last a while as when running this on night shift you could get a bit of shut eye in the hut between Reels. Not so on day shift as you had Bosses around all the time who would always spoil your fun. But as I said earlier today would be different, and at about 8-30am Mr Cogers (the Chief Papermaker) arrived with the Night Shift and Day Shift Supervisors to inspect the crack. Prior to this Larry had warned me of the problem and everyone was informed to stay clear of the area. The Union even wanted to shut down the Machine – sighting that it was an OH&S issue and endangered their members. But it was allowed to continue until assessed and this occurred, as I mentioned before, at around 8-30am. Well at least that was the start of the assessment, as it was when Mr Cogers and the Supervisors arrived. As time went by between 8-30am and 9-00am the place filled up with Bosses, and I was surprised as I didn't know that there was so many of them. There was a heap of head scratching, whole face rubbing and swearing going on until it was decided to call the Engineering firm in for assessment. Mr Cogers even made me store the Reels in the Rewinder and away from the area of the Concrete Lintel Beam until I ran out of room. Fortunately as I said we were running Wax based paper and the Reels took 90 mins to complete, so by 11-00am I only had 2 Reels stacked. If it was Industrial Roll Towel being run then we would have had to shut the machine down a long time before that.

At about 11-00am the head engineer from the engineering firm arrived and at first glance he looked extremely concerned, asking the crowd of Bosses to move back as it looked serious. The boys on the Factory Floor joked that it was an ideal time to maximize profits and streamline production by having them move closer! He then propped a ladder on the wall above the Concrete Lintel Beam to allow closer inspection with a reasonable degree of safety. The minute he got his eyes closer to the crack he reached for his face – spat on his hand – and proceeded to rub the crack. Presto! And Derek Sorters carefully crafted pencil crack drawing was removed. What a cracker of a practical joke!!!!! All the Bosses looked on in disbelief as the news of the practical joke spread throughout the factory floor. Mr Cogers was enraged by it all and the rest of our week on Day Shift was like hell as he took out his frustration on us all. Not that many knew of it before the Bosses did, but Mr Cogers seemed to think that we were all in on it from the time it was done. It seriously was a Cracker of a Practical Joke! But such was the times that after a week or so no grudges were held and even Mr Cogers saw the funny side of it – or so he told us! Being a Larrikin in these times was an asset to the moral of the workers and an accepted part of life in the 80's, as long as it didn't go too far. By todays standard this would have been way too far but as I said in the 80's Larrikins were cool and accepted.

When I saw this Photo of No 1 and No 2 Paper Mill pulled down 35 years after I worked there I could not believe my eyes. Spotting the Concrete Lintel in the far distance that was the source of this amazing practical joke. Amazing!

Correction

While writing this chapter a colleague who worked in the Paper Mill at the same time I did has just contacted me and we had a great conversation on the telephone. Dean Quick who is now 79 years of age worked in the Stock Prep area of the Paper Mill and I hope to get some more yarns out of him in the coming months. He told me that he remembered the incident, but that my Fiction is Fictitious as Derek Sorters was not the perpetrator of the prank. The credit in fact needed to be directed to the Shift Electrician who was also well known for his masterful practical jokes. This flies in the face of the Factory Rumour Mill as it was widely believed at the time that Derek Sorters was in fact the perpetrator. It also proves that even Bullshit can be a lie.

Back to the Story

Now the job description of the 2nd Boys roll is close to complete as the majority of his role was done at the dry end of the machine. This was about 90% of his duties and the rest was performed at the Wet End of the machine, or more specifically the Drying Section. The requirement for the 2nd Boy to work in this area was triggered mainly by two events. The first and main cause was the paper breaking somewhere in the process (usually close to the dry end) or a blade mark appearing in the Paper Reel. The blade mark was caused by the Blade that touches the Yankee (or main drying Roll) to be worn or have a build-up under its cutting point of the Yankees surface. I am not technically knowledgeable in this area as I never made it to the Machinemans position, so those of you that have worked in the industry will easily pick holes in my descriptions. But for the average punter it will give you an idea of how the process works.

The paper breaks happened from a number of causes and could occur from something as simple as a piece of wet pulp falling in the wrong spot. It is quite an amazing process really as the machinery is so robust and yet the tissue paper is so delicate. I was always amazed that the paper did not break more often than it did, "but I was glad that it didn't"! On 99% of all breaks the Blade was changed as it was the only time that this process could be performed. The process went like this;

- The 1st Boy who was in charge of the blade changing also needed to ensure that he had a good stock of replacement blades at hand in the Blade Rack.

- The blades were maintained and kept in supply by the Maintenance Fitters on the Day Shift crew. But it was the 1st Boys responsibility to get them from the Maintenance Fitters Area.

Now when speaking of these blades we are not talking about the size of your shaving razor, these beauties were about 10 centimetres wide – roughly 2-3 millimetres thick and in excess of 3 metres in length. Gloves were always required when changing these, for obvious reasons.

- The 1st Boy would pick his blade (as they were always cleaned just prior to fitting) and he would have his chosen blade sitting in a position that was easy for the 2nd Boy to identify and retrieve when asked to.
- All three Machine crew would be present during a blade change and when ready the 1st Boy would signal for the sheet to be dropped. This occurred by the Machineman lifting a 'wet roll' away from the 'pick up roll' via a pneumatic lever and the sheet of paper would then fall away from the process and into a pit under the Wire section of the Machine.
- The Paper would then disappear from the Yankee and the existing blade that was trimming against the Yankee.
- When this paper had gone completely (taking only a few seconds) the 1st Boy would disengage the Blade Holder via a pneumatic lever and remove the old blade.
- He would then signal to the 2nd Boy for the New Blade and he would install this.

The area where the 1st Boy was performing this task was poorly lit – Hot – Dirty and very noisy. It was a bit like taking a Sauna in front of an aeroplane engine.

- Once the new blade was engaged he would signal the Machineman to re-engage the 'Pick up Roll' and the paper would run back on its course and back over the Yankee to hit the newly installed blade. At this point the full 3 metre sheet of paper was running into another pit just below where the 1st Boy had performed the Blade Change. (It is also where it was running when the sheet first breaks).

At the bottom centre of this picture you will see a staircase – this is where the 1st Boy would enter to do a Blade change with steam, dust and noise all around him. (See description of area in above paragraph) Above the Yankee is the Gas Fired Hoods.

On Number 1 Machine this pit is very small and it is vital that this process of changing the Blade is done swiftly. If it is not then after the pit is filled the paper must be allowed to run free onto the ground, and the huge task of removing it has to be done manually. In my time on the job this only happened a couple of times and it was a lot of work to keep on top of.

- After the Paper hits the Blade area the process of getting it to the Dry End and onto the Reel begins. Again this is a manual process and takes all hands on deck to perform.
- The first part of this is to have the Trim Cutter engaged – Now I am not sure if I have the terminology correct here but what I am calling the Trim Cutter is a jet of water that is sprayed at the nib of where the paper is hitting the newly installed Blade creating a cut it the half dry paper about 40 centimetres in width.
- This 40 cm width of paper is then grabbed by the 1st Boy and thrown into the After Dryer Section (which is a series of rollers covered in a felt that completes the drying process prior to the Reel Section)
- Then the 1st Boy and the Machineman use sticks or rods to flick the 40 cm wide Paper Tail through the series of After Dryer Rollers until it comes out just before the Reel Section at the Dry End. The 2nd Boy helps in this process once he is experienced, as it takes some skill.
- Then the 40cm Paper sheet gathers on the ground, as the Machine runs at speed, gathering quite quickly into big piles of what is called 'Broke' (loose Paper).
- The 2nd Boy is in charge of cleaning up all the Broke, and as this process can take a while, the job can be quite a big one.
- Once the paper reaches this point the Machineman will grab a bunch of this now dried paper, break it off the Broke and quickly pass it to the 1st Boy who is standing on the other side of some spreader rollers and the Slitter just near the Reel Drum.

- The 1st Boy will then throw it between the Reel Drum and the Corebar which has been lowered to create this 'Nib' and allow the paper to run in between the two. The loose sheet will then run onto the ground in front of the Reel Drum on the Rewinder side.
- Once the slack has been caught up and the 40cm sheet is taut with the speed of the machine, the Machineman will resume position near the Trim Cutter and the 1st Boy will bring the Corebar down the Reel Drum.
- With the 2nd Boy clearing the Broke away from under the Reel Drum and the Blower, the 1st Boy hits the Blower which in turn will blow the Tail into the Nib, wrapping the Corebar.

At this stage it is important to stop the Broke that is attached to run back into the Reel as this will create a mess inside the Reel at the Core, and could prevent the Reels from Splitting if the Paper Reels are not for the Rewinder. If this does occur then sometimes a new Corebar is loaded and the small Reel that has this fault is rejected, ejected and cut down.

- Once the Tail is wrapped the 1st Boy signals the Machineman to hit the Trim Cutter and as it moves across the Nib of the Blade / Yankee the sheet returns to its full width on the Corebar. (Slitter put up if Reel being cut).
- When all this is done the mess is cleaned up and the job gets back to normal.
- As mentioned earlier the Broke (loose paper) has to be removed by hand, as unlike Paper Machine 2 and 3 there is no forklift access.

Of course the 2nd Boy has other duties on the Wet End but these are normally done when the Machine is "Down" as he is mostly kept very busy at the Reel Section and the Back of the Rewinder.

Crack to the Rack...

As a footnote; Ralph told me a horrendous story that occurred when Number 1 Paper Machine was in its early days.

It went like this;

THE CREW HAD HAD a horrible run on the machine and they could not get the paper onto the end reel for many hours. With the Broke building up and the boys not able to remove it as fast as the build-up, there was Broke everywhere. Bearing in mind that the pit for the Broke was very small and the access restricted this created a situation where the Broke was six feet high in places and covering the machine from wet to dry end. Extra staff were brought across from other machines but still they could not get it out quick enough. Just removing this Broke was not the solution, as the best solution was to get the paper onto the reel – where it was meant to be. Eventually this occurred and there was a lot of celebration and a lot of mess.

Not thinking of the dangers one fellow decided that the piles of Broke were like a snow field full of fresh snow. He decided to climb the stairs to the TC lab and jump onto the fresh fluffy white Broke in an act of celebration at the paper now going where it was meant to. Without knowing what was under (as he worked in another section) this unfortunate individual landed on the Blade Carrying Rack. What was even more disastrous was that the bar that was used to pull the Rack was still attached and facing skyward. Not only was this a mess it had now turned into a medical emergency as the Rack Pulling Bar had penetrated this poor fellow's anus.

His screams were heard above the roar of the machinery and while the shift Supervisor called an Ambulance, two of his colleagues gently put a hand each under each knee's and under his armpits and lifted him off the offending Bar. They kept him in a type of foetal position until the Ambulance guys arrived. He was taken to hospital and made a full and fortunate recovery. The Ambulance officers involved came back a week later and told the two hero's that what they had done was amazing as the Bar had gone in a substantial way, and to lift him off without further damage was near on a miracle.

Wired For Overtime

NOW MOST OF THE fellows in the Factory loved overtime as it was attached to our normal hours of work and paid at "Double Time". In addition, if we were called in to do it we were given 30 minutes extra overtime called a "call in allowance". There were also free Taxi vouchers available if you spoke to your supervisor and could justify the need for one.

In my early days in the Job there was a lot of Overtime on offer as the 5 shift system had just started and many of the guys hated stacking Scotties on the back of No 3 Rewinder as they thought it was too hard. Some of the blokes that worked there were so old and lazy that they physically could not have done it anyway. I loved it as it was great money, and it was a lot easier than fitting industrial Tyres on the Wharves of Melbourne in the 80's. (The era of Snoopy and the Red Baron) Two huge Forklifts famous on the Melbourne docks in the late 70's.

So it was annoying to me when I got asked to do 2nd Boy on No 1 Machine as in most cases the only time I now got overtime was when my 'Relief' took a day off. With a Second child now on the way and a new home Mortgage to pay it was also a time that I could have used the money most. Larry sort of tricked me into this as I was

'Green' and didn't think of the ramifications of my move to Number 1 Machine. I asked for a share of the overtime but my request fell on deaf ears, even though most of the Rewinder Crews on the other shifts wanted me there. They wanted me there as I was young and fit and I worked hard, making their life easier. There were a number of lazy workers who worked harder at avoiding work than if they just mucked in and got it done. But 'it was what it was' and I just had to make the best of it. It did help me decide that I was not going to go through the "Machine" line of promotion and that I would have to look at other areas long term. Fortunately I got along with many of the guys and when other areas of overtime came up I was called in. One particular day stands out in my mind and it stood out, not for the job performed, but the stories that I was told about the now infamous Gerry Gee.

It was a cold winters mid-morning in Seville and I had just had an eight day break, which was marvellous as it allowed me to get stuck into the Garden that was all mud due to us purchasing a new-build home. It was 10-00am and because it was my first day back to work today I was on afternoon shift, a 3-00pm start. The phone rang and because I was relaxing before starting work today I was inside and answered it. It was the Shift Leading Hand from Day shift and he asked me if I would like to come in to do a Wire change on Number 2 Machine. I said I had never done one before but would love to. He explained that it just needed a lot of people on hand and I would be fine, just having to follow instructions. I was chuffed at being asked, and as I was about a 35 minute drive from work I told him that I may be a couple of minutes late. He was cool with that and I got ready to go. I was excited as it was a call-in so I got an extra 30 mins overtime, and the extra money would be very welcomed with all the Landscaping materials I had to still purchase for our new home.

Upon arrival I had to walk past Number 2 Paper Machine where a bunch of the guys had already formed in preparation of putting the Wire on. Luckily I had a good run into work and arrived a couple of minutes before 11-00am, I clocked on and joined the crew as they were waiting for the last two guys to get there before starting (I was one of them). The Wire section is the Wet End of the machine and it is a 3.2 metre wide sheet of woven plastic and roughly 20 metres in length formed into a continuous loop. I am not exactly sure of it's length but 20 metres would be a good guess – it could be longer. In the not too distant past these were made of Brass making them highly prized for scrap value once they had seen their life out on the machine. Many used ones went missing before the day shift Bosses could collect them, and I was told years earlier that they didn't even bother collecting them with opportunistic workers grabbing them out of the waste bin. In fact I believe that one Brass one was fitted onto Number 3 Paper Machine in my first few months with the company, meaning that they swapped to the Plastic type around 1984. (You can log that in your book of useless information if you like).

Back to the Job

I was happy that I got to work before the last guy as we were still waiting for Gerry Gee to turn up at 11-10am even though he lived less than 20 minutes from work. He got a big cheer and welcome when he arrived and Little Legs commented that he must have been combing his hair. (A dig at Gerry's hair that looked like a Brillo Pad that had been set in the shape of an Open Faced Motorcycle Helmet). Gerry's response – "Good One Booody!" A phrase that he used regularly and I had never heard before.

Finally ready to go and we proceeded to unroll the Plastic Wire (which I will refer to from now on as The Wire), ensuring that it was kept off the ground and not creased. Apparently creases, kinks, jams or ridges will shorten the life of the Wire and may make the process of Papermaking more difficult. I now began to see why so many people were needed for this task as the Wire was quite large and it seems quite delicate, or at least easily damaged. It was required to be maneuvered through narrow gaps and over rolls etc, so there were some protective sleeves that had been slid into place to protect it (the Wire) from the sharper metal items on the Paper Machine. All in all it went smoothly, mainly due to the fact that there were so many experienced operators on hand to ensure it was done correctly. The task was completed in about an hour and because it went so smoothly we were given a half hour meal break. A bonus when working on the Machine and a huge bonus when you had just arrived an hour earlier.

Now with such a big audience it was time for Little Legs to shine with his Gerry Gee stories and even though Gerry was there he did not hesitate to get into it. The first was a story about the Possum.

Gerry Gee — The Possum Whisperer

Note; these stories are older Stories – happening well before Gerry Gee and his family moved to Dixon's Creek.

WITH GUYS CRAMMED INTO the Machine hut and hanging out the sides Little Legs began his tale;

Gerry Gee and his wife were asleep this particular evening, as were their three children at the other end of their home. I have described their home in an earlier chapter – it was an old 50's home made of Fibro and located in the Belgrave area of Melbourne's outer east. Gerry's wife awoke to a rustling noise in the ceiling and was not sure what it was so quickly woke Gerry and said; there is someone on our Roof! Now Gerry who was fast asleep turned and tried to brush it off saying it must have been a tree branch scraping on the roof. His wife replied; But Gerry there is no wind! And even though there were trees all around their home she was right as there was not a breath of wind. But Gerry just turned over and went to sleep again. A few minutes later the rustling got louder but this time it woke Gerry who sat up, bolt upright, like a startled rabbit caught in the headlights. He jumped out of bed to try and trace the noise but it again stopped before he could definitively identify it.

Back to sleep again as the noise seemed to cease and Gerry, being the highly unmotivated character that he was, would rather shrug it off than investigate. Then after they had both drifted off to sleep again a louder rustle, then loud scratching, sliding, scraping and banging in the wall behind their old freestanding wardrobe. Gerry's wife became hysterical, yelling at Gerry to do something. Gerry then got out of bed and searched for the source of the noise, which seemed to be coming from the hallway adjoining their bedroom. But upon inspection of the hallway and the entire home, with a torch from the kitchen, Gerry could not find anything. The noises did not cease though and it soon became apparent to Gerry that it must have come from inside the wall of their bedroom. It was also apparent that it was coming from behind the freestanding Wardrobe, so together they moved it away from its position against their bedroom wall. Gerry then positioned his ear against the wall to pinpoint the exact location of the noise. He said to his wife; I think it is a rat! Again and again he positioned his ear against the wall in different spots trying to get its exact location and when he thought he had it, he smashed his fist through the wall and reached for the creature. Not a clever move as upon grabbing a fist full of fur and pulling out of the newly created hole in the wall Gerry was staring face to face with a pissed off possum. This Possum then reacted by scratching and biting Gerry, at which point Gerry dropped the creature and it scurried off into the lounge room.

In hot pursuit Gerry started after the crazed animal with his wife in tow as she was petrified by the ordeal. As Gerry scampered down the hallway of his home he reached out and turned on as many lights as he could reach at speed. With the house now lit up like a Christmas Tree their children awoke and started appearing from their respective bedrooms, rubbing their eyes and enquiring to what was happening. Gerry's wife shuffled them back to their rooms as Gerry searched the Lounge room for the now elusive creature. Fortunately Gerry's wife did put the children back to bed and closed their doors as when Gerry moved their sofa the frightened creature shot off between Gerry's legs past his screaming wife, back into their bedroom and disappeared back into the hole in the wall that Gerry had just created.

Not to be beaten Gerry put his bloodied arm back in the hole to try and capture the little rascal. But all Gerry's attempts to reach the Possum were not succeeding as he just could not reach it, even though the sounds were clearly showing that the Possum was still in the vicinity. Not to be outsmarted, Gerry placed his ear against the wall and punched a second hole in the wall and re-deployed his bloodied arm into the abyss. Still no success so another hole, and another and another until the wall was a mass of holes and resembled a slice of Swiss cheese. Gerry had not captured the Rascal but the sheer amount of activity had seemed to have caused the Possum to exit the area. Now facing a wall full of holes Gerry did what Gerry does and slid the freestanding wardrobe back to its original position which concealed 90% of the damage that he had created and back to bed he went.

Now that is not where the story ends as a number of months later (and the wall not being repaired), Gerry's wife opened the bottom draw of the Freestanding Wardrobe to find two baby Possums nestled into the jumpers that her mother had given her many years ago. She rarely opened the draw so they had a private room since their birth, not so long ago. The Possum, who we now know was a girl, had created a hole in the back of the Freestanding Wardrobe and had Gerry to thank for the idea. In addition the Possum had

Gerry to thank for the ease of access that he had provided in the numerous holes in the Wall. Gerry's wife told Gerry of the baby Possums while he was at work and Gerry said he would dispose of them when he got home. But Gerry's wife would have none of that talk and said that they were gorgeous and should be left alone. Her love of animals was well documented and the next story would add to the list.

Cats in the Cradle and Mums Silver Spoons

LITTLE LEGS WAS NOW in full flight and with the attention of ten or so of us he continued his stories almost seamlessly. The next tale was that of Gerry's wife and children's love of Cats. As Little Legs explained this love went well beyond the level of sensibility as we were about to find out:

Now Gerry was a very easy going fellow and prided himself on being calm in any situation, and even under pressure would hold his emotions all in. If someone would have a go at him or upset him, he would just brush it off or if he was upset with someone else he would use the phrase "Hey Booody". The more upset he was, or the more he was upsetting someone else could be judged on the length of the word Booody and how many 'oooooo's he slipped in.

The story started when one of Gerry's children brought home an adult cat that had followed him from the Bus Stop after school. Turned out that Tom was a Tina and an overweight one at that. Well not actually overweight – Yes you guessed it, and within a couple of weeks the Cat turned from Tom to Tina to Ten! Proud mum Tina was given the royal treatment along with her nine kittens and quickly took over Gerry's Garage leaving him to park his beloved car in the elements. Under protest, Gerry followed his wife's orders and left them alone but in the months that followed the same could not be said for the neighbourhood strays, and soon there were cats everywhere. Not only adult cats but litters all over the garage and beyond – it had gotten totally out of control. There was also issues with some of the kittens, as they appeared to be the product of interbreeding. All the while Gerry was paying the vet bills and again under protest!

But the day before Christmas Gerry had had enough and said to his wife that he was bundling up all the cats and taking them to the animal refuge. Because the issue was now impacting their budget and their ability to pay many overdue Bills, Gerry's wife relented and agreed to their disposal. As the Children were all at a relative's home for Christmas Eve, Gerry and his wife gathered all the cats into cardboard boxes and loaded them into the back of Gerry's Panel Van for their final journey. They arrived at the Animal refuge to find it closed, but determined to rid himself of the problem Gerry (under the shadow of darkness) unloaded the 50 or so cats onto the front steps of the institution. On the way home at around midnight they swung by their relatives place to pick up the children as they had a big day planned tomorrow. It was Christmas and they were going to Grandma and Grandpa's home for a big Christmas lunch. Grandma and Grandpa were Gerry's in-laws and they lived in the inner-city suburb of Kew, which in those days was quite a well-to-do suburb (not sure if it still is). Not only that but they had been very successful in life and were quite wealthy. This didn't mean a hell of a lot to Gerry and his wife but to their children at Christmas it added up to "receiving great presents!"

Fortunately as it was so late and with a big day tomorrow, when they arrived home the Kids did not even worry about seeing the kittens and went straight to bed. In the morning they awoke to presents under the tree, which ensured they would be distracted and not ask to see their pets (all 50 odd of them). In the rush of the morning and with all the pending excitement of Grandma and Grandpa's presents, Gerry was able to bundle them into the car around 10-00am without any awkward questions. Off to Kew for a lovely Christmas Dinner with the in-laws and it was not long before they arrived and were greeted by a gathering of family members all sipping Eggnog and chatting in the lounge. The children could not contain themselves and ran immediately to the proudly decorated Christmas Tree that was just short of touching the ceiling and loaded with presents. As they did Grandma announced: "now that all the children and guests were here, they could begin the present sharing!" As she was announcing this Grandpa slipped out to his bedroom where he donned his freshly ironed Santa suit and with a loud "Ho Ho Ho" re-entered the lounge room and directly to his favourite chair that had been strategically placed next to the tree. With Grandma taking up her position between the Tree and Santa, Grandpa asked all the children to form a Good and Naughty line with Good to the Right and Naughty to the Left. Then as ALL the children rushed to the Right he said the same as he did every year; "Well that's easy as you have all been Naughty so we can keep the presents for next year!" With a load roar of Noooooo!!!!! From the Children Santa said, then you should line up on "My Right" with a cheesy grin on his face. All the children rushed to the other side and the presents began to flow.

After all the presents were opened and the Eggnog devoured, it was now 1-00pm and Gerry's in-laws had set the huge dining table with their finest silver and fine China in preparation for lunch. The Formal Dining room was huge, as it needed to be, to accommodate the thirty-two family members who slowly found their places and were seated in anticipation of the pending feast. All the three daughters of Grandma, including Gerry's wife assisted in either the preparation or serving of the meal, as was the tradition. They all feasted for hours, and with the huge amount of food, wine and spirits the adults remained at the table while the children retreated to the Lounge to enjoy their newly acquired presents.

Just after 5-00pm Grandpa put the TV on in view of the Dining area as he liked to watch the Christmas Cheer from around the world. As they were all watching a live report came on about the ugly side of Christmas. This story was on something that would quickly disgust the room and send Gerry and his wife into a state of shock.

At this point of Little Legs telling the story there was a simultaneous roar of "No" as his audience clicked onto what the story was about.

Yes, you guessed it - it was a live report from the Animal Shelter and how some disgraceful person had dumped a huge number of helpless kittens on their doorstep. Everyone in the Dining room was disgusted except Gerry and his wife, as they were both trying to act as bewildered and disgusted as all the other family members. But with their red faces on full view they were in danger of having their dirty secret revealed. Fortunately Gerry's wife was able to leave the room with some token dirty dishes to disguise her timely exit, while Gerry sat there red faced.

Gerry's brother-in-law then asked Gerry if he was OK and Gerry let out one of his trademark "Boooooooooooody! I got a bit of fruitcake stuck in my windpipe". But before his in-law could administer the Heimlich manoeuvre Gerry ran to the kitchen and asked for a glass of water, while putting on a near death experience. Fortunately the children were oblivious to the TV story as they were at play with their cousins and newly acquired gifts. The mood also changed in the dining area as the shocking story gave way to lovely tale of generosity that had unfolded at a Melbourne homeless shelter.

Just as Little Legs had finished the story the Leading Hand came over to the hut and started allocating us jobs around the Mill, with the Machine crew and a few more experienced fellows working on the Machine in preparation of its re-start.

Back to the Job

With any re-start or shut down the use of high pressure water hoses is required to clean up the wet end of the Machine. In most settings this starts out as a work process but outside Monday – Friday dayshift it soon turns into a Star Wars type adventure for those lucky enough to have hold of the hoses. But to others not so lucky it is more like Dodgeball, with the traversing of the Paper Machines a task fraught with danger. Fortunately on this occasion we were on dayshift hours so travelling was 95% safe. I say 95% as being saturated still occurred to some but it was far less likely with the Bosses walking around, especially when a Start-up was in progress.

I was given the task of assisting in the Broke Room and with Stanley Knife in hand spent the last hour of my overtime cutting down Reel after Reel of rejected paper. As described earlier the Broke Room was for the recycling of reject and scrap paper from production and conversion. There was never a shortage of this stuff and it was a never ending job to cut it up for processing.

Typical skylarking with the Machine Hose - This was a poor fellow having his Birthday Party - could not have been too bad as he is all smiles!

Stuck in the Grind.....

WITH THE OVERTIME NOW finished I went to relieve my work colleague on No 1 Paper machine who was glad as always to see me. On this particular job, as nice as the guys are to work with, the job is tedious and for the most part uninteresting. It gave me very little mental stimulation, but hey it paid the bills and paid them well. Bruce and Ralph were great guys but they were much older than I was so the conversations were, over time, thinning out. At first it was great as they told me stories of the old days but as time went by the stories dried up and we didn't have a lot in common so it got a little boring and mundane. This pushed me even further into wanting to not pursue this line of promotion and I was forever on the hunt for a change. But the wheels of promotion turned slowly in the Mill and I would have to make the most of it for some time.

Fortunately though I did have a lot of friends on shift and with our days off falling on weekdays more than weekends we would often get together and go on trips away.

Flatulance ...

ONE OF THESE TRIPS was with Bobby (my Vietnamese friend) and Lance who was quite a character. Lance was a bit of a stoner but he was not your typical stoner who only hung out with stoners, and we got on well. The trip we had planned was to go fishing at Port Welshpool, as in those days I had a block of land with a shed on it at Venus Bay. We could stay in it and travel back and forth to the Port Welshpool Jetty. Bobby had heard that the night fishing was good there and was very keen. Lance was keen so "it was on!"

We finished Night shift on the Wednesday morning and decided to all go home and have a sleep, then after 2-00pm Bobby would swing by to my place and pick me up and head to Lance's. Then we would head off on the 2-3 hour drive and stop off along the way for dinner at some pub, I can't remember what it was called but it was in Korumburra.

Bobby swung by at just before 2-00pm so I know he is super keen to get some fishing in tonight or perhaps he just couldn't sleep. I on the other hand had slept like a baby and had only been awake for 20 minutes or so before he arrived. Fortunately I was prepared and my then wife had got the last of my clothes together for my trip. A kiss goodbye and it was off to pick up Lance. But when we got there Lance had his griller on and was cooking something. I said to Lance; 'what you cooking fella' and with a smile on his dial said he was toasting Mary Jane. I said mate I think that will not be too nice doing it that way, but Lance said he had forgotten to dry it and could not go three days with us crazy Bastards without it. I could see Bobby was not too happy as this was cutting into his fishing time and he was giving Lance some dirty looks. Must have worked though as Lance got ready within 5 minutes and we were off.

On the way by 3-30pm was still good and we arrived early in Korumburra, in fact it was just after 5-00pm when we got there and a bit early for a pub feed. So Bobby decided we should get our bait and any supplies that we needed at the Supermarket. Now with all the boring stuff done it was time to get a feed and a beer, or two, into us. The food at this pub was amazing (or it seemed that way as I hadn't eaten all day) and the beer was even better. So good in fact that it was flowing fast and so was time. In fact Lance and I were getting tipsy and Bobby was not impressed as he wanted to fish. But upon talking to the publican we were advised that the ocean was rough and it was extremely windy so the fishing would be ordinary. Bobby was disappointed, but we soon changed that by ordering shots and a double for Bobby who we decided was not driving anywhere tonight. As soon as Bobby spotted the double shot and we told him it was our shout he gave up the fishing plans and we got set in for a decent session. With the Beer flowing freely we asked the publican about accommodation and he offered us a room upstairs that had four single beds. He also gave it to us at a great rate as it was late now and it would be empty otherwise. I think on reflection though it was a business decision as we were spending shitloads on Beer and Shots.

By 2-00am we had had enough and we all crawled upstairs to our room for a sleep. As the publican had mentioned it was quite windy on the coast and even inland at Korumburra it was the same, and bitterly cold also. So when we got into our room it was also quite cold and I stumbled about trying to work out how to get the heater going. With that all done the room heated quite quickly, not because it was a great heater but more because the room was small. We all crashed into bed, and as it was a boy's weekend the shower was optional. About a minute or so later Lance got up and fully opened the window, to which Bobby yelled out "what the F**k are you doing Lance!" Lance said in a calm voice "trust me you will want this open," as the wind whistled in carrying the freezing cold into our freshly warmed room. Then Lance let go with a series of Farts that not only shattered the silence as we huddled under our blankets, but filled the room with a fog that not even the stiff breeze now flowing in could penetrate. Bobby and I were amazed at the intensity of the stench as even the blankets that covered our faces could not tame the Beast that Lance had given birth to. Not only that but they continued on and on for hours. Lance's response to our screams of protest was simply "I told you guys you would need the window open!" After about an hour of trying to hide from the Stench the alcohol and my lack of sleep won over, and I finally fell asleep.

The next morning we awoke to beaming sunshine and we quickly realized that we had slept in and it was a little after 10-00am. Lance looked as fresh as a daisy but Bobby and I looked as though we had been exposed to high levels of Radiation, and in fact we probably had been.

SPAGHETTI ON THE JETTY...

NOW THAT WE HAD awoken late we had better pull our fingers out and get to our fishing spot. As we travelled towards Port Welshpool Bobby stated that he did not want to stay at my shed at Venus Bay as it would be too confined and he would probably die with Lance sleeping in the same space! We all laughed and agreed, so we decided to stay at a cheap motel in "3" rooms. Although more expensive I agreed that it would be well worth it as last night was pretty horrendous.

We soon reached the Jetty and started fishing next to some locals. These fellows told us that they were here last night and caught dozens of Taylor and Salmon. Bobby was furious and said that the Publican in Korumburra had tricked us just to keep us drinking. I didn't think that was true but it did work out well for him as we spent a shitload last evening. I think it was the direction of the wind and maybe this place was sheltered from that wind.

Bobby started fishing and we got some nibbles early on but then it went a bit quiet. Lance said he was going for a walk and headed off the jetty and along the foreshore. Bobby said that he was off for a chuff, but I was more interested in something to eat so I asked Bobby if he wanted to share some chips with me from the Fish and Chip shop. He said he was keen but asked if I could get them as he wanted to keep fishing. There was no doubt that Bobby was the keenest of us three when it came to fishing. When I returned with the chips Lance was back, and from behind Bobby smiled and winked in Lance's direction, indicating that he was right about the Lance going for a Chuff.

Lance spotted the chips and asked if he could share, to which I responded "I bought them for you also!" He got stuck into them and then started to look a bit pale and the next thing we knew he was throwing up on the Jetty in front of us. Bobby was discussed and asked Lance "what the hell is wrong with you, do you have any normal bodily functions?" referring to both the vomiting and the Farting last night. Then Bobby looked at the offending pile that Lance had just dropped on the Jetty and said, "And you didn't chew your dinner last night, look at the spaghetti, it is all still long!" I couldn't help but burst out laughing and soon my friends joined me, we had a pleasant afternoon.

NO DEAL – JUST A SEAL...

WITH NO LUCK ON the fishing front we decided we better go and book a few rooms at the local motel and maybe get a few hour sleep before night fishing tonight. We found a nice cheap Motel and asked for three single rooms. The lady said that she only had two side by side and the other was in the far back corner near the carpark. As quick as she said that Bobby said "that's your room Lance!" and started paying the lady for the room. It was around 4-30pm and we were all tired so we went to our respective rooms to get a few hours shuteye.

I awoke about 7-00pm to deafening silence as this place was a bit isolated and the boys had not emerged yet from their respective rooms. I went to Bobby's door and knocked heavily. Bobby emerged and looking like shit said, - I am starving let's get some dinner. So we both got ready and went over to Lance's room to wake him and head off for a feed. Much to our surprise Lance was awake and when we entered his room the smell was overpowering. But this time it was not a pure fart smell but a mixed odour with a sweetish smell, which Bobby immediately recognized, giving me a wry smile. We packed the car with all our fishing gear before heading off to the Welshpool Hotel for a feed.

At the Hotel Bobby reminded us EVERYTIME we went to the Bar for a round of beers that we were here to go fishing. I am sure he was paranoid that we were in for a big session and that he would miss out on his beloved fishing again. Yes we were on a fishing trip but every Aussie knows this is code for a piss-up! But Bobby was persistent and by 9-30pm he had us rounded up in the car and on the way to the Port Welshpool Jetty.

We arrived at the Jetty and with only a few punters having a fish, we chose a spot and started fishing. Night fishing was a bit different in that we used a torch, which was directed into the water. We used coloured beads with small hooks on them and would jig the line around to attract the fish. We started getting attention straight away and we were soon catching fish, but alas they were small and we were throwing them back in. A lot of people keep them and put them through a mincer to make fish patties but we were not interested in doing that and I reckon it would be illegal anyway. Bobby did hook one big one and he was so impressed with himself that he was yelling for us to get the camera and photograph his achievement. He became so fixated on our lack of co-operation that he didn't notice that the fish was flipping himself on the jetty and heading for freedom. Then splash he was gone! Bobby was so angry with us and was silent for the next hour as we brought in one after the other undersized fish. It was farcical really, as we were just feeding them in a way. Although I am sure they didn't enjoy the process.

Then out of the dark waters we were visited by a seal who quickly rounded up the school of fish that we were feeding and started to feast on them. It was a beautiful thing to watch as the Seal was so graceful and quick in the water, herding the school into a group and then darting through the middle to gouge on his efforts. But as much as Lance and I were enjoying the spectacle Bobby was get increasingly angry as he knew more than we did. In fact it was only a few minutes into the show that the Seal took his smorgasbord out to sea, well away from us and our hopes of a good catch.

What do we do with the Drunken Sailor...

BOBBY WAS RIGHT AND for the next couple of hours we did not get a single bite and we contemplated giving it up as all the other fishermen had done (and I use the term Fisherman very lightly!) Then from the dark and onto the Jetty appeared a highly intoxicated youngish fellow who had a bushy beard and definitely looked like a local. He staggered towards us and asked how we were doing on the fishing front. Lance told him of the Seal and the events that had unfolded during the evening. He said never mind as he would be happy to take us out on his trawler and we would have no problems getting a good catch on the high seas.

Now I was not too keen as this guy was very drunk, but Lance who is super chilled most of the time said "come on we won't be getting any fish here tonight!" Bobby was also dubious but the lure of catching fish clouded his decision and it came down to majority rules, and I was out voted. I relented and he led us to his vessel a bit back from where we were fishing at the time. He staggered onto the boat and down into the hull where he started filling the tank up with diesel from the multiple Gerry cans below deck. When I say filling the tank this is really a half-truth as only half the diesel made it into the tank with a lot spilling all over the deck. "This was already starting to look like a very bad decision".

Fortunately though we got sailing without blowing up and he did really seem to be handling the trawler well, even though intoxicated. We travelled for about a half hour or so when he told us we would catch fish here and pulled up. With the engine still running we took our positions around the trawler and started to fish.

With the engine running and the lights on in the cabin our woolly young Captain decided to take a nap while we were having a fish. Problem was that with the engine running and the direction of the breeze we were sucking in more Diesel fumes than oxygen and this was making me feel quite sick. The anticipation of catching big fish kept me focussed, at least for a while it did, but I decided to move to the other side of the Trawler where the fumes were not as bad. Then about a half hour or so into the fishing I could hear the sound of water crashing onto the rocks in the distance. I went over to Bobby and told him what I was hearing on the other side of the boat. He thought I was joking until he got to where I had been fishing and then he got a very serious look on his face. We told Lance who had been taking advantage of the open air by creating his own type of smoke, but he was so chilled he wasn't interested. Bobby decided to fish on the same side of the boat as I was on as the crashing waves got louder and louder. I said to Bobby that this must be the rocks of Wilsons Promontory and we should do something. Being so dark outside the Trawler we had no way of judging how far we actually were from danger but we were seriously concerned now as in the still of night they sounded very close.

Bobby went to wake our Woolly Captain but he had locked the cabin and was not responding to our knocking on the windows. We told Lance again who decided to come listen for himself and when he got to my side of the Trawler he shit himself and went into a panic. Bobby increased the banging on the windows of the Captain's Cabin but with no response. Lance then grabbed some metal claw thing off the deck and started banging harder and harder until he smashed the side window. "Well that worked!" with our Woolley friend jumping to attention immediately as we all barged in and explained we could hear the waves crashing against the rocks. With no anger at us breaking the glass our Woolley Captain just clicked the Trawler into gear and said he would head back to the Jetty now. This made us wonder if it was his Trawler as he was not the slightest bit worried about the broken window and was more sleepy than concerned. Well that was a shitty waste of time said Bobby as we spotted the Jetty in the distance. Lance turned to Bobby and said, well at least we did something different and had some excitement. Little did he know what was coming up next!

As we approached the Jetty we could see all the coloured marine lights but the Blue flashing lights just beyond the Jetty were nothing that we remembered. We started to get a hint that things were not quite right quickly as we approached the Jetty. Captain Woolly was now wide awake and his eyes looked like dish plates as the Jetty lights started to take effect on the Trawler. We seemed to be travelling way too quick to dock but his skills sailing so far (while awake) had been great and we were all OK with it. But that soon turned to shit as we ploughed into the Jetty at speed. We were all thrown forward and the whole Jetty seemed to wobble and creak under the impact. He yelled at us to jump off and onto the Jetty, at which we were happy to oblige as it would end our nightmare trip.

As Captain Woolley tried to reverse the Trawler two police officers jumped onto the deck and wrestled him to the ground. Alas Captain Woolley was actually Deck Hand Woolley and further

Ex Deck Hand Woolley at that. All three of us were now shitting ourselves as we thought we would also be in trouble. Lance asked me if I could hold his tackle box for him as his hands were sore, but I clued on to him immediately as I knew he had Weed in there. I told him to F**k off and hold his own shit as I thought we were in trouble for sure and I was quite angry with everyone as I knew this whole thing was a bad idea.

But the police told us to go on our way and did not even get a statement from us. Poor Woolley was taken in handcuffs to the police car at the end of the Jetty and we soon followed them off the Jetty and into our own car. What a night "No Fish" but a shit load of action!

TO EACH THEIR OWN...

AS WAS THE NATURE of the hours required to work in the Paper Industry we all had our ways of coping. As a relatively young bloke mine was going away with the boys as well as having a relatively normal home life. Funny word that – Normal – as I have never been able to work out what Normal is.

Anyway....

My "Normal" was a family life and the occasional trip away with the boys which many would refer to as a "Traditional" way of life. But for many in the Industry, life had been harder to them and they turned to other ways of coping, with the number one being Alcohol. This book would not be complete without looking at the effects of Shift Work as stories of Alcohol can be Sad / Funny / Entertaining and sometimes all three.

Dodgy Flow Valve...

MY FIRST TALE IS that of Rex who was well known for his addiction and Grumpy façade. It occurred back in the days when I was stacking Scotties on the back of No 3 Rewinder a few years back. Poor old Rex had come in to work looking paler than normal and from the start of the shift he seemed to be relying heavily on Kev to keep the Rewinder going. Fortunately we were making napkin Reels which were much larger and took quite a while to run up, giving us all breathing space between jobs. Fred, Kev and I were all seated in the Rewinder Hut as was Rex, when he stood up and pale as a sheet of bleached paper, asked Kev to watch the Rewinder as he needed to go to the Shitter. He stumbled out of the hut and within five steps had placed his hand over his arse clenching his cheeks together, and within two more steps had inserted a finger to stem the pending flow. What a sight as he struggled across the walkway and we were all in fits of laughter. But really how sad it was, as Rex had a real problem, with this process occurring a further five or so times during the evening. As I stated earlier it was lucky we were running an easy product as if we were on Scotties we physically could not have covered for him.

FIT FOR WORK...

ON THIS PARTICULAR AFTERNOON shift I was working as 2nd Boy on Number 1 paper machine along with Bruce and Ralph, as usual. But on this occasion the Rewinders on Number 1 and Number 2 machines were running simultaneously. This was a rare event as Number 3 Rewinder was running the most of all the Rewinders and the 2nd Rewinder crew usually ran either No 1 or No 2 Rewinder. This meant normally that Gerry and Spider would have worked No 1 Rewinder with Rex and Kev running Number 2 Rewinder. But Gerry and Rex decided to swap and keep their respective crews with them. They did this as Rex preferred Number 1 Rewinder and Gerry was mates with Little Legs the No 2 Paper Machineman. Bruce was not too happy though as Rex did smoke and Bruce hated smoking in the hut. But that was the way it was so Bruce had to suck it up (so to speak).

My job was easy when the Rewinder was running and with Rex at the wheel we were not in for a Gerry Gee type of catastrophe that he was famous for. In addition we were running wax based paper that took an hour and a half to run up on the Machine and 45 mins approximately on the Rewinder, giving us all plenty of free time. The shift started well and was quite uneventful until around 6-30pm when Rex told his crew to have a half hour meal break. Rex said he was off to the Canteen for a meal with Bruce requesting if Rex could get him a plate of Spag Bol (Spaghetti Bolognese) on his way back.

At the end of the half hour meal break (that the Rewinder crew were on) Rex had still not returned. Now this was unusual for Rex as he had a military background and was a stickler for perfect time-keeping. Bruce said he was a bit concerned as it was now 35 minutes so he requested that I look after his job for a few minutes as he wanted to check on Rex. Not sure of Bruce's real motivation but I suspect he was more concerned about his dinner than Rex, so off he went. Ralph said he would throw the next reel out for Bruce and told Bruce to take his time. Truth was Bruce never let me do his job and Ralph knew this and wanted me to have a go. As the reel got close to full size I called out to Ralph who came down and told me to get into it. Extremely nervous I executed the Reel change and nailed it – (up to the end that was until I raised the slitter). But Ralph picked this up and dropped it quite quickly, so no major harm done. We loaded the Rewinder and I helped Kev get it going before I did my next task which was to load the new Corebar ready for the next Reel change.

No 1 Paper Machine – 1st Boy Reel eject Control Panel to the right – Wet End of Machine straight ahead.

This is what I loved about working at this place as the guys all helped when someone was out of action for a while. Sure some shifts were not as co-operative but I know Gold Shift guys had each other's back. About twenty or so minutes later we were all starting to get a bit worried. Then when informed by the Forkie that an Ambulance had arrived outside Conversion our concerns escalated and we immediately started wondering if something had happened to Rex. The next minute Larry (shift Leading Hand) came flying around the corner and said that Rex had had a fit in the canteen. By the time Larry had reached the Canteen though Rex was already on the Ambulance stretcher and being wheeled through Conversion to the awaiting vehicle.

A short time later Bruce came back to the Number 1 Mill hut and we all asked what was going on.

Bruce took centre stage and began - the Story went like this;

I went over to the canteen to find Rex and I could not see him anywhere in the Canteen – (At this point it would be best if I describe the Canteen as it is hard to picture the events without this). The Canteen that we used after day shift was actually the Conversions Sections Lunchroom with a number of chairs and tables laid out in a standard formation with approximately 20 tables and at least 6 chairs to each table, so a fair sized room. Now in this room was also a set of dispensing machines that were loaded with meals and snacks by the day shift canteen staff. Apparently the main Canteen used to be open all the time but costs meant that it was put back to day shift only. (Cost cutting without affecting the Suits!) This was not a popular choice for meals as it was accompanied by a bank of microwave ovens that ensured that all who partook, ate to a standard well below what they were accustomed to (judging by the general physique on show). This disappointment gave rise to the 'Jagenberger' which I will outline in a future chapter.

Unable to sight Rex, Bruce noticed, (above the half wall) that some of the table and chairs were displaced and then he saw a chair which appeared to fly over by itself. Upon closer inspection he spotted Rex in a kind of foetal position with his arms and legs thrashing about. Bruce immediately ran into the Lunchroom to assist Rex who was in grave danger of seriously hurting himself.

Now at this point I will add the account of an eye witness (an ethnic fellow) who saw Bruce in the Lunchroom. It goes like this;

I walked into the Lunchroom and saw a large man on top of a small weak man. The large man had the small man pinned to the floor and was gouging at his face. I told him to get off him and leave him alone – you are bigger than him – what did he do to you!

Now to explain the serious side of this Bruce was trying to keep all of Rex's arms and legs still so he didn't break anything on the surrounding tables and chairs. The Gouging was actually Bruce trying to extract Rex's tongue from his throat.

Bruce went on to say that Rex then started to calm a little and with Mick (Gold shift Conversion Leading Hand) arriving on the scene they were able to call an Ambulance that arrived in less than 10 minutes. Then all tucked up on the Ambulance Stretcher Larry arrived and accompanied Rex to the Box Hill Hospital.

Now even though not directly linked to having a problem with Alcohol this event did mean that Rex was placed on light duties for a long period of time. Eventually he did get back on the Rewinders though and our paths would cross again.

QUICK NIPS...

OTHER SHORT TALES OF Alcohol related incidents went like this;

- Mick (the fellow just mentioned in the Rex story) admitted he slept with a bottle of Scotch under his bed and had to take a nip every hour to keep sleeping.
- Allan Billing (shift fitter) who drank Ouzo during his time away from work so when he was at work he could drink water to re-ignite the Alcohol in his system (not sure if this works or not but I have studied reports that say it has an effect).
- Another fellow who worked in the Pulp Yard and Conversion prior to that – told me a story of how he had to constantly drink beer, and he would bring a six pack of frozen cans into work every day. He told me that he would keep them in his locker and periodically sneak out to the locker room to have one. He also told me of a time when he was on night shift and the weather was bitterly cold. He described going to the locker where he found the Beer still frozen, then out of desperation he cut open the can with his Stanley knife and ate the can of beer.

GILLIGAN...

ONE CHAP I REMEMBER who stood out as having an outstanding ability to consume Beer was Simon Bend (a First Boy on No 2 Paper Machine).

His appearance was quite normal with the exception of his very long hair and Gilligan style hat, and boy did he have a talent for drinking beer, amazing. When drinking he appeared to just pour the contents without swallowing – just like a wide mouthed funnel into a Gerry Can.

His vehicle was a Panel Van that doubled as a recycling bin and the process went like this. Slab on passenger seat – grab beer – pour down gullet – toss over seat to rear. The vehicle would ting around corners as the number of empties in the rear generally numbered in the hundreds. Only emptied when they started coming back into the front cabin upon harsh breaking!

When asked about distance travelled he would reply in stubbies ie; how far is your home from work? – Answer – "two stubbies!"

I remember going to a 21st Birthday party once that he was attending. It was on the Western side of Melbourne and a fair distance, (possibly five stubbies) and when I arrived Simon's Panel Van was parked in their front yard on the lawn. Obviously he was there for the duration (as long as the Beer lasted). I watched in awe as over the afternoon and evening he consumed two slabs of VB – I would be dead with this amount. The host had bought a keg for the party and with most guests driving home it still had contents at the end of the evening.

I was told that Simon awoke from his van early the next morning and proceeded to drink until after Lunch, only leaving when the Keg was dry!

That's Not Cricket...

ANOTHER SOCIAL EVENT THAT was popular with the boys was Cricket and all the shifts had teams with some taking it more seriously than others. It was a logistically well planned event as the teams playing would have to be on Night, Afternoon shift or RDO's (rostered days off). This then allowed for the game to begin at 8-00am with the Night shift crew going directly from work to the ground while the Afternoon shift crew could play until after lunch. This was plenty of time to get a game in and it was popular amongst the lads. Another bonus was that we could play any day of the week ensuring that we had the ground to ourselves. The warm up to the game was always a Beer or three which not only hydrated us but made the cricket far more entertaining.

I remember one game as it was about 8-30am and we were fielding. The batting side, and a few of the outfielders were enjoying a brew or two. Then this old bag come out of her home complaining of the noise we were making and getting quite agitated. She started ranting about how we were all a bunch of Alcoholics and she was calling the police to have us arrested. We all actually laughed at her as we were not that loud and it was not the middle of the night or anything. One fella asked her why she chose a home near a park if she didn't like sport, to which the old bag retorted; Sport, is that what you call it, you are just a bunch of pissheads. A touch of truth, and we were all in fits of laughter as the old bag retreated. Expecting a visit from the Ponies we played on, but alas we must have looked like true cricketers as we saw a divvy-van cruise past without intervention.

A New Direction...

AS I HAD MENTIONED earlier I was not happy doing the second boys job as it was either full on or boring and I wanted something a little more interesting. By this stage Larry had the shits with me complaining about it and told me he would train someone to do second boy on Number one machine and I could go back to the Rewinders. This was great news to me and within a couple of weeks I was back on the Rewinders and working with more people in my general age group.

My first step back into it was on number two Rewinder with Gerry and Spider, where they were running Scotties. Now Scotties on Number two Rewinder was more difficult as it was not designed well and the layout was cramped and antiquated. But at least it was interesting with Gerry Gee running the Rewinder and Little Legs telling the stories. I will come back to the stories in a moment but first I would like to describe the working conditions so you can get the gist.

The Papermachine area although not as sophisticated as Number three was similar with only the Reel extraction being majorly different. On Number three Machine the Corebar was pulled near the back of the machine with the Rewinder being at the very back of the plant. But on Number two the full Reels had to be craned over the Rewinder to the Corebar extractor. Add to that the Rewinder and Machine shared the same weighing scales, the Rewinder Corebars were removed manually about three feet from the Machine Reel extractor, and it all adds up to a tight fit. Also remember that these Reels are over three metres wide, about 1.6 metres high and weigh in excess of two tonnes. As cramped and as treacherous as this may seem boy I loved the vibe of working here as it was a laugh a minute.

Now with all that you have heard about Gerry Gee so far you would think that it would be pandemonium, but the truth was Gerry was very busy and this kept him on the straight and narrow. Perhaps add to this that he was on his second written warning and you get the picture that Gerry was a little more focused. I was also to learn from Little Leg's stories that Gerry was having other issues at home. As a footnote I will go over the Warning system and Union representation in a future chapter.

Fish and Chips...

EVEN THOUGH I EXPECTED heaps of drama and action, my first week on the Rewinder was quite uneventful. As we had now just finished Afternoon shift the next would be day shift which normally meant bosses around and a more serious vibe. But we started dayshift on a Weekend so it was going to be less formal and when I arrived I saw that Number two Rewinder was not running. This meant I would be doing odd jobs and getting to chat to different blokes around the place. I loved this as most were older guys with tonnes of interesting life stories.

My job for today though would be a different one as not only was it a Weekend but Spider was having a sickie and I would be doing his job. Fortunately there was no Rewinder running so this did not mean working in 'close' with Gerry Gee, but with no Spider and No Rewinder it was the Fish and Chip run for me. Spider loved this job and he made it last the entire shift so I knew that if I dawdled I would not be hassled by Larry (my Leading Hand). Not only that but Spider had told me that he went to the Fish and Chip shop on Whitehorse Road – I think it was called Boccy Burgers, and Jim would give him his order free as there was usually over 20 orders from our shift.

Jim outside his Famous Boccy Burgers in Box Hill.

The Red Sigma Wagon that we all used for errands – including the Fish and Chip Run. It is pictured left of the onsite Fire Truck.

What a great day this was going to be. The hardest part would be making sure I found everyone to take their order as I had to ensure that I had the order into the shop by 10-30am. This meant I could take my time but if I wanted to spend time with some particular people then I would need to see the others first and keep an eye on my watch.

I started with Larry and Pat (My Leading Hand and Supervisor) as once they knew I was doing the Chip Run they would leave me alone. I then did the CR Lab and phoned the TC lab that was above them. Then I headed to Number 3 Paper Machine and took their orders. I spotted Rex hiding in No 3 Rewinder hut so I dropped in to see him on the way to the Stores area. I Asked the Sparky and the Fitters if they wanted anything, then off to see Grumpy Tony in the Stores. Typical smartass comment from him along with a huge chip order and I was off to see John in the Broke Room. Had a cuppa with John and we had a chat – top bloke John and didn't mind a chat as he was on his own most of the time. Then off to No 1 Mill were I spotted Gerry Gee chatting with Bruce and William in the Hut – Three big orders here and I was off to find Ralph (number 1 Machineman). Couldn't find Ralph so I thought I would catch him on the way back when I went to see Little Legs on Number 2.

Up to stock prep to see the Kraut Hans and Rob who I knew would have a huge order. Now Hans was a grumpy old bugger and didn't mind being called a Kraut, as he said he loved the dish and knew of nothing about the term used in a derogatory sense. I called him Hans though as I didn't want any fuss and I thought the word Kraut was disrespectful. He was tight also, and never bought anything but chips. Whereas Rob who was a large lump of a man bought Chips, Potato Cakes, Pickled Onions, Fried Cabana, Fish, Hamburger and 2 cans of coke. This was his standard order and if my memory is correct it was almost $20-00 worth way back then. He was a nice bloke though and every time he spotted Larry or Pat coming up the stock prep stairs he would splash water on his face and complain about how hard his job was on that particular day. Truth was Stock Prep on Number 1 machine was one of the easiest jobs – or so I was told. I think he was just doing it so Larry would not get him cutting reels down in the Pulp Yard, which they were supposed to do when quiet.

Then I was off to the Pulp Yard for my second last stop. But the fellows up here were quite self-contained and rarely bought anything. I was lucky to catch Roberto (Stock Prep 3) here though, as I had missed him when I dropped into Number 3 Machine earlier. I hadn't seen Kev either and thought I would find him in the Pulp Yard. When I asked Rex, all I got was "how the F**k would I F**king know. I then made my way down the Back of Number 3 machine, along the rear alleyway, and then headed back towards the Broke Room so I could loop back to Number 2 mill without going past the office. But as I looked through the motionless Number 2 Rewinder I spotted Kev chatting to Larry in his office. Didn't want to go back in there but never mind and I went and got Kev's order. As I was heading back to the Number 2 Machine I spotted the 2 Forklift drivers Rick and Enzo, so I called out to them. Even though not technically part of the Mill they were always picking up product from the Mill and Enzo lived around the corner from me in Seville. They both put in an order and said that they will be in the Conversion Canteen around 11-30am. Just had Ralph to find and then I could go to my last location and that was to see Little Legs.

Now I had left Little Legs until last as I wanted to catch up with the Gossip on Gerry Gee. Little Legs had hinted at something the other day but we were all too busy to have him elaborate. Finally found Ralph, who was always fiddling around the back of Number 1 Machine, took his order then I was off to see Little Legs for a catch up. Being now only 9-25am I still had an hour or so until I needed to have the order in, "Fantastic!" now I could get all the gossip on Gerry Gee.

BILLY, BILLY DON'T YOU LOSE MY NUMBER...

LITTLE LEGS WAS HAVING an easy day, and with the Machine running well, he "let sleeping dogs lie" as did most of the Machineman. I asked him for his order and he had a pot of tea on hand so we sat back and had a yarn.

Little Legs made the Gerry Gee stories sound fantastic as he conveyed them with Vigour and enthusiasm. I told him that I loved the horse story that Spider told us in the canteen some time back and with that Little Legs was into it.

He started with 'did Spider tell you about the Goat?' I said 'no' and off he went. As you know Craig, Gerry was in on this farm trend and not only was he going to make a small fortune out of the Horse Agistment, be he wanted a whole menagerie of animals for his kids. Turns out though that his first purchase 'a goat named Billy' was fonder of his missus than any of the kids. This disgusting stinky beast would stand by the trees outside the main house and dry hump the air and soil itself for all to see, apparently a common thing for male goats. Billy was also very stinky as he always urinated on himself or anyone else he took a fancy too. Gerry would quite often get a call at work from his missus who complained that she couldn't get out to hang the washing or any of the other outdoor chores required. She would ring to check that Gerry would be coming straight home and on time so she could attend to these choirs in safety.

One day before afternoon shift Gerry, who had been for a counter meal with Spider at the Glenburn Hotel came home around 1-30pm to find his missus bailed up on the front patio holding a fence picket and swinging at Billy to try and keep him from having his way with her. She had forgotten about Billy, as when Gerry was home Billy was always well behaved. It was unusual for Gerry to be out before afternoon shift so his missus forgot about the crazed animal. Spider was laughing his head off when they turned into Gerry's driveway but Gerry could see the fear in his wife's eyes and knew that he would pay the price for not being home when needed. May (I forgot her name until just now) was screaming and soaking wet when Spider and Gerry started herding the goat away. On returning and entering the home Spider turned to May and said 'You stink' as he realized that May was urine soaked not just wet from the washing. May, shattered and unimpressed, started to get depressed with her new life as her dream of living the fantastic farm life was being shattered by the reality of 'life with Gerry' wherever that may be.

The Man from Dixon Creek...

NOW THE GLENBURN HOTEL was to become Gerry's new obsession, and as he perused the patrons he envisaged a look that would bring him in line with his newfound status. Spurred on by his new self-inflicted farm owner title, Gerry went out and bought the finest of the gear that would help him blend in with his mates at the Pub. The Akubra hat, full length Driza-bone drover's coat, cowboy style high boots and spurs, Gerry was now a true farmer. And with the addition of a stockwhip he was sure to impress, regardless of all the bills mounting in the background mainly from the gammy agisted horses dumped upon him.

Fresh from the tag removals Gerry strode into the Glenburn Hotel to the applause of the awaiting regular patrons and a slap on the back from each as he strode clumsily in his new boots to the bar. The fact that Gerry had never ridden a horse in his life mattered little to him as he now felt accepted in his new establishment. Of course Gerry was so pumped and focused that he did not see the smiles and laughter that was occurring after he passed each of the patrons. These guys continued to pump-up Gerry's tyres as they knew that the more they did the deeper Gerry would go with his new image. He was continually complimented on his look as all the while becoming a bigger and bigger laughing stock to the locals as the word spread of his antics. The Publican was not going to say anything either as Gerry was now beginning to draw a crowd with many locals coming just to see Gerry and his clobber.

Not only was Gerry blissfully unaware that people were taking the piss out of him, he also came to work and bragged of his antics, while Spider told us all of how he was really being perceived. Poor Gerry he was really spiralling out of control and I think the dressing up was a distraction from how his life was really going to shit. "Never underestimate the power of denial!"

Erectile dysfunction...

WITH HIS LIFE IN turmoil, and his ability to bury his head in the sand, Gerry did not pay enough attention to his family and was about to pay for it. The offer which came from one of his farming neighbours was a Godsent, in Gerry's eyes, and was in the form of an offer to Gerry and his family to move into the old farmhouse on his property. Gerry saw this as an opportunity to clear his debt and not having to be responsible for the abandoned lame horses on his rented property. All he had to do was move his family out in the still of night and his problems would be over forever.

So with this Gerry took up the offer and they all moved into the old farmhouse which was located within close proximity of the generous farmer's new home. Somehow Gerry and his family had foiled the Rental Agents attempt to locate them. Although they lost their Bond, they came out of it well in front of what it would have cost the owners of the property to right all the problems left behind.

Settled into their new home, the reasons for the kind Farmers offer became painfully obvious, to everyone, except Gerry that is! He was lavishing attention on Gerry's wife in Gerry's absence and a relationship began to bloom. When Gerry started night shift, May would put the children to bed, get herself all dolled up and slip off to the Friendly Farmers home. This went on for a considerable amount of time before Gerry was alerted to "the goings on." The sad fact is that it was Gerry's eldest son who ended up telling Gerry what was going on after being awoken one evening by Gerry calling home. Gerry was on Night Shift and May had completed her routine and was over at the Friendly farmer's home when he called to see how his daughter was as she had a cold. When his son answered the phone Gerry asked him to wake up May. His son paused and then explained to his dad where his mother was and that she was there almost every day. Gerry was floored and decided to stay calm until he saw May the next morning.

As per usual May had returned to her own bed in the early hours of the morning and was asleep when Gerry arrived home as it was a Saturday. Gerry woke May and challenged her with the news; that he knew about her and the Friendly Farmer. May denied that anything was going on and said that she just needed someone to talk to. Gerry "still in his constant state of denial" believed her and so it went on.

A week later and having a beer at his watering hole, the Glenburn Hotel, he confided the news to his good friends at the bar (another example of his level of denial). They told him not to be concerned as the Friendly Farmer had served his country where he received a wound that denied him the primal function of manhood. This put Gerry at ease and even the stories from their sons who had witnessed May in the Friendly Farmers bed did not concern Gerry. Or if it did he was showing no signs that it did. At this point I told Little Legs that Gerry had told me of his marriage issues but not in any detail. He had confided in me that May had struck up a friendship with a neighbouring farmer and explained that she was depressed and lonely and needed someone to talk to. "WOW! – Never underestimate the power of denial. This continued on for months. I saw May and Gerry at one of the Shift shindigs and May confided to my then wife that Gerry just didn't get the hint that their marriage was over and asked if we would tell him. My ex-wife told me when I got home but I didn't know how to tell Gerry this so I kept out of it. Upon reflection I maybe should have said something but I was still young myself and felt overwhelmed by the responsibility of it.

Inevitability and the Shift...

I continued telling Little Legs the story that I knew of, it went like this;

WITH GERRY FINALLY ACCEPTING that his marriage was over he switched from the naïve doting husband to a husband scorned. He proceeded to pry his children away from his wife with some degree of success. The boys had witnessed mums sneaking around and supported their father. They were also teenagers now and were excited to move closer to the city as the farm life was boring to them. The daughter though was only nine and her place was with her mother so she remained on the farm. May and the Friendly Farmer played the happy family with their daughter while Gerry made the shift to rent a home in Blackburn, close to work.

Gerry moved into a weatherboard three bedroom home that was quite basic but tidy, positioned on a main road. The backyard was nice though, as it had a garage plus a separate brick shed. It also backed onto a wholesale plant nursery, making it quite pretty and private. Happy with his lot Gerry continued working and even settled down slightly as he had just received advise that he would start training as a Machineman with the retirement of a couple of older crew members. Although not getting a Machinemans job it was policy to have staff trained up as Machineman for when required in the future. This gave Gerry a pay increase and on a more positive note something else to focus on. Not that the company wanted Gerry there, as he was not highly regarded in management circles due to his antics and poor record. But Seniority ensured that Gerry was chosen and "that was that". Gerry did stay on the straight and narrow for some months and even Larry and Pat (Leading Hand and Supervisor) noted the improvement and conveyed it to the Chief Paper Maker and Management.

Truth was Gerry did improve and if not for his sense of necessity to be liked and popular may have done OK. But alas not the same could be said for his two boys who had turned into little hooligans with new freedoms and a distinct lack of supervision. Even though not the best mum in the world May was there, and without that the boys ran amuck. Now Gerry didn't know this as his basic personality of denial shone through all that had happened both marriage wise and in the workplace. Again the first hint that his boys were up to no good came from someone else's comments. This is how it all unfolded after almost a year in his new rental home.

Gerry had invited a group of us from work around to his home to give him a hand moving a motor out of his backyard. As per Gerry the Motor was a project for another vehicle that he was putting together as he needed a vehicle for travelling to work. His last vehicle died in the Northern Car Park of Bowater and stayed there for some months as Gerry was not too good at following things up. Gerry had removed the plates so it could not be traced back to him (even though most of us knew it was his car). Management had put out a memo on the vehicle as it had been reported as abandoned and could not be identified. The memo was distributed while we were on Night shift which worked out well for Gerry. He simply borrowed a Forklift, opened the four windows of the vehicle, picked it up by placing the Tynes through the opened windows and dumped the whole thing into the onsite industrial waste bin (job done).

Back to Gerry's Place...

AS I WAS SAYING, we were all around at Gerry's place one afternoon after day shift to give him a hand to move this motor of his. Turned out the motor was a dud and was not worth repairing, so Gerry's plan was to get it out the front and a scrap guy would pick it up the following day. Now I mentioned before that Gerry's home had a shed and a garage in the backyard, and the layout meant that no vehicle could access the rear yard as the garage was only a metre or so from the back corner of the home. With this in mind Gerry's plan was for us to push the motor along the concrete and out onto the front verge. We started to do this, and in fact could have moved the weight, but because of the motor's size we could not all get a grip on it. With this Gerry came up with the idea to tow it out with a cable that had in the garage and two of us could guide it from behind. With Gerry's mate Bill's 1968 Chrysler Valiant VE Safari Wagon all hooked up and the motor on the other end of the cable, we started the move. It was all running smoothly while the motor was on the flat concrete surface, but as we progressed to the straight part of the driveway the engine slid into the turf that separated the two concrete driveway strips and dug in. Undeterred Gerry retrieved a shovel from his back yard and dug a bit of the offending dirt from the front base of the motor. He then flipped the shovel and placed it under the front of the motor so it could lift, under tow, away from where it had dug in. Mike said to Gerry that he should move back from the front of the motor but Gerry smiled and said "all good Booooody!" As he just finished saying that, with Bill at hard throttle (yes you guessed it) the cable snapped spearing within inches of Gerry and straight through the back window of Bills pride and joy!

Bill was furious, flying out of his car and confronting Gerry who was pale as a sheet from the incident. Bill was ranting in Gerry's face with Gerry spluttering and stuttering Boooooooooooooody I I I will buy you a n n new one! Of course we all knew this would never happen, but the truth is, it was as much Bill's fault as it was Gerry's, and deep down Bill knew that.

With the engine now propped half way down Gerry's driveway, we all decided that that was enough excitement for one day and we still had some Beer to drink and a BBQ to enjoy. The engine would be fine where it was and although the Scrap guy had told Gerry to have it out on the Verge it would be easy for him to back up to it and collect it from where it was. In fact being on a main road that was probably a safer option. Now as the chore for the day was complete, and with Bill's blood pressure dropping we all retreated to the backyard for a cold beer and a warm fire.

Gerry lit the BBQ fire as we raided his fridge to locate the Beer, but in typical Gerry fashion he had forgotten to buy any, and we had to do a Bottle-O run to fulfil our needs. All sorted and we sat back and traded yarns while enjoying the beer and the food that Gerry "had got right", thanks to his mate who worked in the abattoirs. Bobby, who had just made use of the rear of the shed, asked Gerry what was in the shed as he noticed it had a padlock on the door. Gerry told him that all his late grandfathers' tools were in there and he wanted them kept safe. Bobby asked for a look, but Gerry made up some excuse about losing the key when he moved in almost a year ago. At this point Little Legs interjected that in fact Gerry didn't have a key at all, and the Grandfathers tool story was a crock of shit. The truth was that his two boys, now fourteen and fifteen had the key and not even Gerry was allowed in there. His boys were not only Hooligans but thieves and had the shed full of stolen Motor Bikes and other items.

I never heard what happened to these boys long term, but they were nice boys and I hope they straitened themselves out. The behaviour and dynamics of their relationship to their father was typical of Gerry as he liked to live in fantasy land and seemed able to completely block out reality. I left around 7-00pm as it was starting to get dark and I still had to drive to Seville (home) and grab a few supplies on the way that my then wife asked me to collect.

Little Legs then carried on from where I left off and explained that after I had left some more shenanigans had gone on. Intrigued I said – do tell, and Little Legs broke into the next episode. Well after you left Bobby and Mike were pressing Gerry about the property over the back and if Gerry had been over there. Gerry explained that an elderly couple owned the Nursery and they lived onsite. Bobby and Mike then started chatting and decided to lighten the load for the old couple by giving them less to water. Soon after, they disappeared from the group and a while later when Gerry went to see where they were Bobby and Mike had amassed at least a trailer load of mixed plants. Gerry was in a panic and said Ohhh Booooooooody ya ya ca can't do oo that! But alas his want of being liked outweighed his sense of justice and he even helped them load up both vehicles. Apparently this went on night after night and only stopped when the old couple let off a shotgun round over their heads while in the act. Fortunately they did not know where the thieves had come from or that their neighbour was in on it, as if the police had visited Gerry then a lot more would have been discovered.

I'm Hungry...

FORTUNATELY MY STOMACH INTERVENED, as I checked my watch to see that it was now 10-20am and I had to phone in the Fish and Chip order. I said to Little Legs "to be continued" and with that I was over to the Supervisors office to phone in the, all important, Fish and Chip order. Wow what a big job that was with 23 orders plus my freebie, it took almost 10 minutes to convey to them. Jim asked me 'what I would like', and I replied; one of your famous burgers and chips would be great.

Just before 11-00am I jumped into the Red Mitsubishi Wagon that Bowater provided and went to collect the order from Boccy Burgers. True to the form that Spider had advised me, the order was ready and waiting. After sorting all the money and ensuring I had enough change for everyone back at work I was off.

Now this job would become a big rush, as cold chips are not popular with the guys, so I was under pressure to get them all delivered promptly. I do recall Spider not being so efficient and everyone would complain of cold to mildly warm food. In saying that the orders never got smaller as it was still a heap better than microwaved machine food. The lack of quality fresh food onsite was a big issue, and one that would soon give rise to the "Jagenberger!"

To streamline the process, and remembering the advice of Spider, I delivered the orders first and then did the same round again to give them all their change. Truth was Spider didn't do this for the sake of hotter chips, he did it to drag the job out and not have Larry allocating him jobs towards the end of the shift. Fortunately Larry was busy today with issues on Number 3 Mill and didn't have time to find me and allocate me shitty jobs. After doing the first round I tucked into my Boccy Burger and chips and immediately recognized why this place was so popular, "it was sensational!"

Noseberg and the Shitty Twins...

AFTER FINISHING MY FEED and doing the change run I was keen to get back to Little Legs and see what other stories he had for me. But unfortunately he was busy with a blade change and required adjustments on the Machine, so I went over and had a chat to Ralph on Number 1 Machine. Lucky to catch him as he was normally fiddling with the Machine, must have been the big feed of Fish and Chips that he devoured. In fact he was perched in his hut staring at the dry end of the Machine. I popped into his hut and on doing so spotted that Bruce was not there and Shane Iceberg from Blue Shift was in early. I said to Ralph what is the go there, where's Bruce, too many chips for lunch? Ralph laughed and said that they had a working arrangement and Shane was paying Bruce back two hours that he owed him. I said; he must have been stressed that I wouldn't get back from the shop in time for him to eat his chippies. Ralph laughed and said; you got that right he was looking everywhere for you at eleven o'clock.

I asked Ralph what Shane was like to work with and he said that he was OK on the job but most of the 2nd boys didn't like working with him. When I asked why Ralph told me he had a habit of emptying the contents of his nose with his finger and swallowing the evidence. Not only that but he was not shy about it and would do it in front of anyone. Now I twigged as to why they called him Noseberg and obviously why he was not popular with the 2nd boys – "Grose!" Fortunately even though I worked for a number of months as 2nd boy on this machine I hardly ever saw Shane and had never worked with him. Ralph then went on to say that if I had a few minutes he would tell me another story about Shane.

Ralph started by telling of it being back on the four shift roster days when Shane was on Green Shift and Derek Sorters was his Machineman. This was before my time and I was keen to hear the story and any others that Ralph had time to tell me. Apparently well known for his appetite Shane was regarded as someone who would eat anything (and thus the Noseberg nickname was born). But not only would he pick fruit from his own tree but was also accused of removing other members lunches from the communal fridges that were dotted around the Mill. This drew the wrath of many in the Mill who suspected Shane but had no proof. As the venting was directed towards Derek on more than one occasion he decided to play a trick on Shane that would become a legend in the annuals of the Mill shindigs.

Completing a microwaved meal from the Conversion Canteen machine, Derek placed the thick cardboard plate onto his hut bench and reached for his stomach. The meal had given him a belly ache and there was only one way to relieve the pressure that this food had thrust upon him. As he rose to exit for the shithouse, a beam of light hit him from the skylight windows above and he grabbed the cardboard plate and rushed to the locker room toilets. Upon exiting the toilet he was holding twins on the plate that were destined for greatness and he carefully concealed them on his return to the paper machine. No good in their current state for the plans Derek had for his newborn twins, he decided to bake them in the machine's after dryers all while staying out of Shane's view. A few hours later Derek's freshly baked goods were carefully cleaned with a light air hosing and placed in a container inside the communal fridge for chilling.

To complete the sting Derek told Shane that he was off to conversion for an hour or so to chat with the Fitters over there and asked him to keep an eye on the machine while he was gone. Being lunchtime Derek knew that if Shane was in fact the culprit that the now sausage like twins in the fridge would be too much for Shane to pass up. And with the opportunity of an empty Machine hut to hide his crime, Derek and that of many others in the Mill's suspicions were realized. Within twenty five minutes of Derek leaving Shane had gone to the fridge to get his own lunch when he spotted the twins and could not help himself. On this particular day Shane's wife had prepared him a plate of left over Chinese food from the prior evening. Fortuitously this included a fork and knife which could be used in the devouring of the home made sausages. I say fortuitously as for without this fork and knife Shane would have probably just picked up the sausage and hooked into it. But as he sliced the first of the twins, the texture and odour wafted into his freshly cleaned nostrils and his head flew backwards, immediately identifying the origin of the twins. During this process Shane had dropped the fork and part of the offending twin rolled onto the hut floor. In his panic Shane stood on the beast, making it impossible for him to hide the fact that the incident had occurred. He tried to mould it back into shape with his knife but on returning it to the communal fridge it was obvious that it had been tampered with. As Shane moved back towards the Machine hut to eat his own lunch, William Citiham (Green shift 2nd Boy) came up to tell him that the reel was up to size. This meant that Shane had a bit of work to do and that his lunch would have to wait. He quickly got through his chores, but not quick enough, as Derek had now returned and was heading for his hut. Shane caught up with him and explained that his lunch was in the hut as he was keeping an eye on the Machine while he started eating. In the panic Shane did get his lunch and his eating utensils but clean forgot about the sausage stub that had been trodden into Derek's hut floor.

Derek sat in his hut after Shane had retreated to his own space and a minute or so later noticed a foul smell. The smell in fact was his own, and after locating the offending patch on the floor he went to investigate the communal fridge. His suspicions and that of his colleague were correct as the twins, or at least one of them, showed signs of being tampered with.

Funnily enough no more needed to be said as the Communal fridge stayed sacred for many years after, with no further incidents of lunches going missing.

Ralph then looked at his watch and said; shit I still have to do my checks around the Machine its 2-30pm, and with that he was off.

Cash was King!!!

TO DESCRIBE THE 80S as the last of the true Cash era was an apt description, as this was the beginning of the end of the dominance of cash in the general population. I say general population as in "Wog society" it still rules today. Being 50% wog I feel comfortable saying this as I embrace my ethnic side and am extremely proud of my heritage. The reason I am mentioning this is to give an insight into the culture and a description of how things were performed. A lot of older people will be ho-hum about this, but for the newer generations it will be an insight into how things were.

The Pay Office (or pay dispensing office) was located on the Southern side of Conversion A and on the Eastern side of the Conversion Canteen. It was a ghost town for most of the week, but on Thursday afternoons it was the most popular area in the entire Factory. You got it "Payday!" From memory it started at 2-30pm to allow for the afternoon shift to get their pay before their shift started and went until 3-30pm or 4-00pm to allow for day shift. I think also there was a 7-00am one to cover for the night shift crew, with only the Armaguard guys doing the pay dispensing. My memory of the times is sketchy as it was a long time ago, but my memory of the process is quite clear. It went like this;

The ladies from the Pay Office (who worked in the admin building) would come down shortly before time and prepare the rooms for the dispensing. This usually included dusting in general and cleaning of the bank teller like glass windows. Then the Armaguard boys would arrive, with two carrying the box full of pay packets and one riding shotgun with a mean glint in his eye. With the queue stretching for a large portion of the Southern wall of Conversion 'A' it was all systems go. We got good money in those days so the amount of cash would have been substantial. So it made sense that the Armaguard boys stayed for the entire proceedings.

When negotiations started between the Company and Union for the implementation of the Direct Credit system many conspiracy theories were circulating through the "Red Brick Walls" of the Factory. In fact it was argued that some employee's did not even have a Bank Account for this type of transaction to occur. But this arguments roots were more in line that many of the fellows in the Factory didn't tell their wives how much they earnt and thinned it out prior to handover. The Company overcame this obstacle by allowing up to three accounts for their wages to be deposited into, so negotiations continued. It was also revealed that up to three percent would be charged by banks for the Direct Credit, so this also became a stumbling block. The Company must have done a Deal with a local Credit Union as they stepped in and offered the service free of charge (no fees). The Credit Union, in return, got their foot in the door as by offering this gained a pile of new clients. Bowater also allowed them to set up an on-site office.

My own Credit Union Card from the era.

Later we learnt the true reason for the company wanting to change to the new system of Direct Credit into our Bank accounts. "Cost cutting" - and this came in the form of removing the pay office on-site and reducing staffing by two in the process.

I am not sure exactly when this stopped but it was not a popular decision on the Factory floor.

Some of the shenanigans that went on were directly related to the fact that Cash was immediate, and there were plenty of creative characters who could help relieve you of your recently acquired load. One amazingly creative fellow decided to have a raffle, with the prize being his pay packet. He sold tickets to the workers standing in line for their pay and rumour has it he made a lot more money from the raffle proceedings than was in his pay packet.

"Wanna Bet!"

AS CREATIVE AS THE Raffle Ticket salesman was, by far the most effective way to remove a man from his money was by gambling. The weapon of choice at Bowater was the Game of Cards, it was rampant and with cash being the main currency it wasn't long before the amount escalated. The location for the card game was always the same - the Eastern side of the Conversion Canteen tucked in a bit of a corner that was created by the Pay Office Dispensary room. This location was also chosen as it was beside an exit door, very handy to nip out for a quick Ciggie between hands.

Now the Supervisors of Conversion turned a blind eye to this for two reasons. One; it appeared to be just for fun, when in fact they ran the numbers on paper that was not displayed. Two; the main ringleader was related to the Supervisor on his particular shift. This shift was also the one that had, by far, the highest stakes. Good old Nepotism raising its ugly head again. Well this practice continued for a long period of time, not sure how long exactly, but came to a head in a fiery fashion.

It wasn't long before novice players were lured into the game, resulting in large losses to the entrepreneurial ring leader who, it seemed, had the blessing of his titled brother. But one rainy afternoon a fired up and rather large ethnic lady arrived at the Gatehouse demanding to speak to management. Not sure if Schultz was on the gate but it was his style not to be confrontational and the lady entered without much resistance. Storming into the admin building and causing a ruckus she was given immediate attention in the interview room by a number of senior managers. Her complaint was that her husband had brought home a savaged pay packet each week for over two months now and last week none at all. Assured that the issue would be rectified the poor lady returned to her car and off home.

As upper management was involved this could not be swept under the carpet like many things were, and the next day a memo went out to all Supervisors and managers that the gambling must cease immediately.

A large sign was also placed on the Conversion Canteen door stating – "There will be no Gambling on this Site" by order of management. It was placed there on the Friday afternoon so that new shifts starting over the weekend would be informed along with their Supervisors who had memo's in their inboxes. By Monday morning large red stickers had been created and plastered over all signs with the words "WANNA BET!"

Social Outlet!

MANY WOULD SAY THAT a lot of these guys were just looking for a social outlet in their lives as rotating shift work can be a socially isolating form of occupation. This precise thing gave rise to many different forms of Clubs that were formed by different shifts within Bowater and the Bowater Social Club was one of these. My memories of these events are sketchy but I do remember that to be a member it was set up as a deduction on your weekly pay. The gatherings were good though and my two young boys enjoyed the Christmas events with Santa and presents immensely. But rewind 20 years earlier to the 60's and I remember as a child that these events were paid for by the companies. Sad really how socially we have deteriorated, as it seemed that when it came to Company Cost Cutting these type of things were the first to go. Go back even further to the 50's and my Grandfather told me of the Melbourne Show. Apparently Show Bags were free samples given out by companies to show their products to the public. We speak of advancement in society but I think we are using the wrong tools to measure these advancements with social awareness being the biggest casualty.

You Don't Talk About Fight Club!

(But I Will Write About It!!!!)

WHILE WE ARE GOING further back in time and talking about clubs then I must write (not talk) about "Fight Club!" I am guessing by the freshness of the stories, and the age of the gentlemen telling me, that these stories being told to me back in the 80's about Fight Club must have occurred mainly in the late 70's.

It all started as a way for the boys on the floor to resolve disputes in a civilised manner and was conducted and overseen by two masters of manipulation Seth Azure and Little Legs. Both also known for their ability to stir a pot without a spoon and spin a yarn without a Spindle. They took their role very seriously and Fight Club was conducted in the Basement of the Paper Mill and the rules were those of "The Marquis of Queensberry Rules." Not knowing WTF this was and only remembering the name "Queensberry Rules", I looked it up and here is an outline of what they are:

1. To be a fair stand-up boxing match in a 24-foot ring, or as near that size as practicable.
2. No wrestling allowed.
3. The rounds to be of three minutes' duration, and one minute's time between rounds.
4. If either man falls through weakness or otherwise, he must get up unassisted, the boxer has 10 seconds to allow him to do so, the other man meanwhile to return to his corner, and when the fallen man is on his legs the round is to be resumed and continued until the three minutes have expired. If one man fails to come to the scratch in the 10 count allowed, it shall be in the power of the referee to give his award in favour of the other man.
5. A man hanging on the ropes in a helpless state, with his toes off the ground, shall be considered down.
6. No seconds or any other person to be allowed in the ring during the rounds.
7. Should the contest be stopped by any unavoidable interference, the referee to name the time and place as soon as possible for finishing the contest; so that the match must be won and lost, unless the backers of both men agree to draw the stakes.
8. The gloves to be fair-sized boxing gloves of the best quality and new.
9. Should a glove burst, or come off, it must be replaced to the referee's satisfaction.
10. A man on one knee is considered down and if struck is entitled to the stakes.
11. That no shoes or boots with spikes or sprigs (wire nails) be allowed.
12. The contest in all other respects to be governed by revised London Prize Ring Rules.

Now I don't know how strict Little Legs and Seth were on this, but I do know by one contest that they described that some adaptation had occurred. In fact it was the only contest that I remember as I worked with one of the contenders and know that by any means this individual wanted to be popular. Yes, you may have guessed it – Gerry Gee, and my memories of him was not the stature of a prize-fighter but more a carnival attendant. I will describe him again as I knew him but in the 70's the pot belly and grey hair may have been absent, in fact I am sure they were. But his basic frame was not big and certainly no match for his opponent at the time, a fellow known only as "Pud!" But a name can tell a thousand words and he sounded like he would easily crush Gerry to a pulp. (Pardon the paper pun!)

The tale was told to me like this;

With the ring set up with large cardboard sheets on the ground and exactly two 24 feet lengths of rope and four bollards wrapped in wads of paper (cut down Scotties) the arena was set. In one corner was a lively Gerry Gee (not how I remembered him – but OK he was younger) and in the other a very large fellow with an apparently very mild temperament and an acquired dislike for Gerry.

Seth was the referee and before proceedings began he professionally checked both contestant's gloves and made sure that their footwear was appropriate before bringing them together and making them shake hands (or touch gloves). Then sent them both back to their corners.

The Fire Bell was rung and the contestants approached each other in what they believed was a boxers stance. Gerry came at Pud with a flurry of lefts and rights that seemed to be more annoying to Pud than do any damage and he just brushed his face as if to shoo a fly. But the annoyance of Gerry's 'love taps' (as they were described to me) meant that Pud had to bury his good nature and smack Gerry a bit. So by the second minute of the first three minute round Pud let go with a right hook that slapped Gerry out of the ring and into the arms of an unsuspecting spectator. But to Gerry's credit he was still on his feet and by the time he was back in the ring the bell for the end of the first round rang.

Seeing the unfair balance between the two contestants Little Legs approached Seth at the bell and suggested that some levelling of the playing field was in order. So with the agreeance of Pud, and I dare say the joy of Gerry, a piece of rope was tied to Pud's right hand and strapped to his waist to "balance the contest". But as round 2 started it was clear that Gerry's punches were doing nothing to Pud and within the first minute of the round Pud had knocked Gerry out of the ring "again", but this time with his non-preferred hand. Again the two adjudicators stepped in, this time with a rule change – now Pud could only hit Gerry when he was given the OK by the referee Seth. Unbelievably Pud agreed and called a two minute break before Round Three. The break was ordered as with now only two punches actually laid on Gerry he had blood running from his nose and required some light attention.

Round 3

Gerry, fresh from a two minute rest, came out full of beans and laid what seemed like dozens of punches to Pud in a very short time. But again with little to no effect on his much larger opponent. In fact by the second minute of Round three Gerry seemed to be tiring from all the effort. At approximately that point Seth said "OK Pud you can hit him now!" and with that single punch, with his left hand, and only his third hit Pud put Gerry to the Cardboard. Shaken but not hurt Gerry got himself up and Seth gave the contest to Pud – by knockout!

Battered Around the Ring...

ANOTHER CLUB THAT I was told about in the 70's was a club of a more sharing and loving nature but ultimately more destructive by all accounts. The Key Club was a rage in the Swinging 70's and Bowater had their own version with a fruit bowl and car keys being the only required props. How it all came about is a secret, but the process was that a party was organized for the boys and their wives from a certain shift. (As Gold shift had not been developed until the 80's there were only four shifts who could have organized such an event.) Couples would arrive at the start of the party with the driver dropping his keys in the Fruit Bowl located just inside the front door. Then towards the end of the evening the host would take the said Fruit Bowl around the room and the ladies would take a set of keys out and go home with that particular owner.

Famously made into a movie called Swinging Safari in 2018 staring Guy Pearce, Kylie Minogue and even a cameo by Jack Thomson, the 70's was a time for "Sharing" apparently. I have since requested feedback from some of the boys who were around in that time and one said that there were quite a few broken marriages because of those debaucherous parties. Another told me that upon arriving at one of these parties his wife was horrified and demanded to be taken home (I suspect by her own husband!) One chap who was not there, but became that Shifts Supervisor not long after said; I heard many stories about the "Car Key Parties" but also said that none of the performances that he was told of were Book Worthy!

Obscene Outcomes...

WHILE ON THE TOPIC of parties I would like to tell you of a few parties that I did attend in the 80's and although not as sharing they are a good yarn. The first was a Bucks Night for a particular fellow who was on my shift and just a year or two older than myself, Mark.

We had planned an evening in the City of Melbourne which would include Strip Clubs and Pubs, as is of right to all young gentlemen on the verge of a forever commitment. It was a great evening and we were all quite smashed by the time we arrived back at Lance's place. We chose Lance's place to crash as he was the only one of us that was unhitched and no matter what happened we could not make it messier than it already was – perfect! We all kept drinking, all except Lance that is, who much preferred the Maryjane, and the night continued to flow without incident.

Then at about three AM Fred came out from the bathroom with a small bottle in his hand. We all said; what's that you got Freddy? To which Lance replied; you can't drink that shit Fred! WTF is it was our thought. Lance piped up again saying it was Mercurochrome, to which we responded; WTF do you need or want that for Freddy? With a cheeky glint is his eye and a wry smile he pointed in the direction of Mark, who was now passed out on the sofa.

Within seconds of asking, Freddy had whipped Mark's pants off and emptied the entire bottle of Mercurochrome onto his Pecker. His plums were now more true to colour and the whole area got a good soaking. Amazingly Mark stayed passed out and it was not until some three hours later at 6-00am that we got a response from him. Wow and what a response, as he screamed the house down while doing circles in the lounge room with his pants around his ankles. He later told us that he thought it was blood and was in a state of shock. Glad that it was not blood and seeing the funny side of it he wondered off the bathroom laughing.

Now Mark's joviality lasted less than a minute as he realized in the bathroom that he could not get it off. With a handful of his pants holding them up at the front, he turned to as and asked; what is this shit? To which Lance responded; Mercurochrome - and you have to wear that shit off! By this stage Mark was enraged and with his Wedding on late this afternoon he was already panicking. Fred then piped up and said; you can either save it for later or try and wear it off solo! We all roared with laughter - all except Mark that is, who stormed out and caught a cab home.

Big mistake having your Bucks Night on the night before your Wedding, and it was at least three months before Mark spoke to us again. We asked; what happened when Rachael spotted it. Mark said he had been successful in getting most of it off his Pecker and he used mood lighting to hide the remaining evidence. He added that in the morning light though his plums were aglow and Rachel spotted them immediately. She cottoned on to what had happened and if not for her wicked sense of humour Mark may never have spoken to us again!

TOTALLY PLASTERED ...

ANOTHER MEMORABLE GET TOGETHER was that of the party we had for Spider leaving Bowater. As I mentioned earlier Spider was always in trouble because he never gave a shit about being late for work. His work colleagues from other shifts, who had to wait for him to take over, were always complaining about him. This meant that Spider was always being reprimanded and given Warnings. Still he didn't care, and as I knew his wife 'Slippery Sam' earnt a shitload of money stripping I knew why.

But believe it or not he actually left of his own accord, which surprised me, as I knew he had not long been in his new home and he had just purchased a brand new Ford Bronco for $23,000. Now $23,000 does not sound like much these days but some five years earlier I had purchased my first home for the same amount.

Off track and not so relevant we had a party to plan and we owed it to Spider to add some spice for all the practical jokes and cold chips that he had served us over the years. Turns out Slippery Sam had a film offer in Sydney and with a big cheque in the waiting Spider wanted to make sure he got his slice. Never heard what sort of movie it was but you didn't have to Albert Einstein to work it out. They would be leasing their property for six to twelve months and as it had lots of land and was set up for horses they already had a tenant lined up – "No not Gerry Gee!"

To have a party that size we could have it at Lance's place and we all chipped in for a Marquee and a BBQ spit to cater for the bigger numbers. Nearly all the guys from our shift came as well as guys from Conversion and other shifts who were not working.

With over 50 at the do we were having a great evening with Spider doing shots with anyone who would join him and the 'Slippery Nipple' was his favourite. Poor bastard got so sick on that Sambuca that by 11-00pm he was driving the Porcelain Bus and the sounds were horrendous. By midnight he had passed out not far from where Mark did some six or so months earlier. I said to Lance as a joke, hey fella you got any Mercurochrome? Lance replied; No Mate Daniel has got a payback all lined up for Spider and she should be here by 1-00pm. When I heard "she", I immediately thought they were getting him a stripper or a Fat O Gram. Then I thought well neither would be of any use to Spider in his state and doubly so with a stripper, as he went to bed with one every night.

Apparently Daniel had lined up one of his wives friends who was a nurse practitioner to come and set Spiders leg in a cast. Now that will be very funny in the morning when he comes to. Running a bit late the Nurse rocked up to the party, drank the shot she was offered and started her craft. The minute she touched Spiders leg he stirred and we all thought the gig was up, but alas he collapsed back in the chair and the Nurse was able to complete the full leg cast.

We were still partying at 7-00am when Spider awoke with a squeal and we all tried to contain our laughter as he tried to focus and see what was on his leg. As he tried to get up Lance ran over to him and said; take it easy fella you have had a bad fall and the doctor said you should only walk with crouches for the next six weeks. Looking totally confused and looking over his body for other signs of injury

Spider had nothing to say (a rare moment). He looked devastated and asked Lance to help him over to the phone so he could call Slippery Sam to come pick him up. More than devastated he looked genuinely scared and with Slipper Sam on her way we all knew why.

Slippery Sam was furious with Spider and had a go at us for letting him get so drunk and injure himself. She was yelling at him all the way to the car and I remember distinctly her saying that "he better not have Fucked Up her new career opportunity" and that she would "leave him behind" if he was a roadblock to her.

We continued partying until around 10-00am when most of the boys got picked up and went home, or the likes of myself and a number of others who found a soft quiet place to get some sleep.

We never heard from Spider again as he would not return any of our calls. But Gerry Gee, who he spent the most time with at work, did get hold of him some three or four months later. In typical Gerry Gee style he could not keep the secret that Spider had told him to keep and blabbed to us as to what happened. Apparently they had to re-book their flight to Sydney as Spider couldn't travel in a normal seat and all the exit seats were booked. So they spent five hours at Melbourne airport and then when in Sydney he had all sorts of drama due to the height that the plaster was taken to. The delayed flight meant that Slippery Sam was late for her first meeting with the "Movie Producers!"

Furious with Spider she took him to their motel room where she continued her verbal abuse. Apparently it was ugly and loud everywhere they went, and she was creating quite a spectacle. No longer able to deal with the height of the plaster cast he asked Slippery Sam to take him to a doctors. She did this and that is when things changed. Now you see Spider told the Doctor that he was passed out when the plaster cast was put on so he didn't know to what extent or where the break was. He explained to the Doctor that he would not ask us what happened or what hospital he attended as he was angry with us. This is when the Doctor had a lightbulb moment and smelt a rat.

When he ordered an x-ray and it came back with no break his suspicions were confirmed. He removed the plaster cast and Spider walked out into the waiting room where Slippery Sam was waiting, and her jaw nearly hit the floor. One last outburst in the Doctor's waiting room, but Spider didn't mind as it was no longer directed at him!

"Can you believe that Spider never spoke to us again!!!!?" Some people have no sense of humour!

This particular party was a Birthday Party held on-site. The Birthday boy was tied up in the Basement and the guests only attended to wet him down again when he started to dry!

MOVIN ON UP...

AFTER WORKING IN THE Paper Mill now for about 5 years it seemed like it would be many more years until I achieved the position of Winderman. I had chosen this line of promotion as I enjoyed the crews I had worked with on the Rewinders, and if later on I decided to become a Machineman I could. With the departure of Spider I got an Assistant Winderman's job and I resolved myself to the fact that it would probably be another 5 years, at least, until I achieved the status of Winderman. The good thing was that I was able to remain on Gold Shift, as guys who were in front of me (in Seniority) did not want to swap shifts to take up the new position that had been advertised. I could understand this, as it was comfortable to remain on the same shift and I felt lucky that it had worked out well for me.

But my idea of remaining as an Assistant Winderman for at least five years was about to be blown apart with some amazing turn of events.

The first was;

The Sacking of a Dummy!

WITH ALL THE TRAUMATIC events that had occurred in the life of Gerry Gee it was near impossible for him to maintain his good behaviour and the recently acquired skill of "Giving a Shit!" Alas it was not long until he started to slip into his old habits of not turning up for work and if he did being late. This infuriated management and especially Mr Cogers, who seemed to have shielded Gerry from dismissal while he made genuine efforts as a Trainee Machineman. But now Gerry Gee was back as Winderman with Spider gone and Rex now permanently put on light duties after his fit/seizure in the Conversion canteen. With this he could now not be shielded from the complaints that were rolling in from his fellow Winderman, who had to cover his shift when he did not turn up, and worse still wait for him when he was constantly late. But alas this did not push him out the door, and with a lenient Warning System in place along with a strong Union it would take more than this to dislodge the infamous Gerry Gee!

With the second Rewinder crew not running on our night shift it was a fabulous time for Gerry Gee to sneak off and get some sleep under the guise of Training as a Machineman. I, on the other hand was hounded by my Leading Hand (Larry) who had me doing every shitty little job that he could find. The main Rewinder crew were running No 1 Rewinder as No 3 Machine was also down for maintenance. This also meant that Gerry was training as Machineman while other shift Winderman were covering for Rex who was now off the Rewinders completely. This seemed very silly as Gerry Gee could have done the job, but as per the Union agreement with Bowater it was Rex who was off so his colleagues were entitled to the overtime.

I was doing my basement hosing at about 1-00am when Larry came down to me and asked if I could run number 1 Rewinder. I thought the prick was going to give me my next shitty job as I was already saturated and covered in the smelly stale pulp that I was cleaning up. But it turns out that the Green Shift Winderman had left instructions that he did not want the overtime and that at 3-00am they would need coverage. This to me seemed strange as Gerry Gee should have been brought over. But it turns out that he was not to be disturbed in his Training as Machineman as it would breach Union guidelines on its agreement with the company. More to the point I don't think that they could actually find him and Little Legs the Machineman pulled that line to cover for Gerry being off asleep somewhere. I said to Larry that I would like to go 'now' as the Winderman that was there until 3-00am (Don Finder) could give me a refresher on a few things as I felt a bit rusty. Reluctantly Larry agreed and I was stoked to be getting out of this wet clobber and away from this shitty job! I headed to the change rooms, had a hot shower, got into some fresh clothes and was at the No 1 Rewinder within twenty minutes.

Don was pleased to see me rock up before 1-30am as he knew I would be competent to take over with a bit of a chat and refreshment. But more to the point he now knew he could go at 3-00am and not be stuck for a double shift. We were running Wax Based paper so it would be a doddle and we could have a good chat. As we started talking about Gerry Gee, Don stated that Gerry was not the only dummy that was nearly out the door. Intrigued at his comment I asked him to elaborate, and the story went like this;

With No 3 Paper Mill down for maintenance, the day shift Supervisors along with the Chief Papermaker were checking over the whole machine, from Gas Hoods to Basement bearings. Mr Cogers, while inspecting drive shafts in the Basement had spotted in the corner of his eye an employee who appeared to be hiding behind a series of motors and in a blind spot, (if you were not crawling all over the place inspecting for faults). Unfazed by the presents of the Chief Papermaker the employee did not move and Mr Cogers kept going with his inspecting. On his way up the stairwell of the Basement he glanced back to see if he could catch a glimpse of the lazy employee. To his horror he could just see the fellow's leg and that made his blood boil as the fellow had not moved in almost 15 mins. Fuming, Mr Cogers powered up the Stairwell and flew across the floor to the Shift Supervisors Office. He burst into the door and yelled at the Red Shift Supervisor (who had not long got into work) that he wanted that "Lazy Prick" in the Basement of Number 3 Paper Mill sacked on the spot and marched off site! Cogers was seething and he made that Gesture that he made of pulling his pants up with the inside of his wrists, while crinkling his neck to one side in a twitching motion.

Panicked by the severity of his rage the leading hand ran over to Number 3 Basement and located the offending employee. On approach Eddie realized that the said employee was in fact a pair of overalls stuffed with paper, with rubber gloves, gumboots and a rubber face mask that he believed Derek Sorters had made some weeks earlier and used in the "Cherry Bomb Incident"(I will tell you that story in the next chapter).

Unable to control his laughter and in the true spirit of the Papermaker, Eddie picked up the Dummy and marched it up the

Stairwell of the Basement, across the Mill Floor and straight up to the Clock cards. Watching in bewilderment from the Mill Supervisors Office Mr Cogers and Geoff (Red Shift Supervisor) looked on as Eddie raised the dummies right glove, clutched at his timecard and clocked the offending employee off. Eddie then proceeded to march the Dummy off site, but was halted by Mr Cogers, who by this time had replaced his furrowed brow with a huge grin.

By this stage all of us in the No 1 Rewinder hut were in hysterics of laughter, and if not for the paper reel being ready to unload I am sure that Bruce (the first boy with the Hyena laugh) would have wet himself. "I loved working on the Rewinders!"

Cherry Bomb!

AS PROMISED I WILL go back to the incident that was nicknamed "Mission Cherry Bomb," which occurred some two or so weeks prior. I call it a Mission as a degree of planning went into it and a lot of effort also. The Dummy that was produced would have taken some time to create also, as it looked quite realistic (just ask Mr Cogers). Now Charles Blueberry was the main man when it came to introducing new staff and Visitors to the Bowater facility. He was the gentleman that took me on a tour of the site when I first started with the company, as you may recall, early in this book.

On this particular day he was to take a group of New Zealand Papermakers and Managers on a guided tour as part of an upcoming possible merger. Now I will need to describe the scene of the crime as it will be foreign to most who have never seen an industrial Paper Mill facility. I dare say this would be at least 98% of the population. The area in question was near the Scotties stacking area at the rear and to the South of the No 3 Rewinder and almost directly opposite the Stores where supplies for the Factory were located. Now these facts are not as important as the height and set up, but may help those who have seen the site. The roof of the Paper Mill in this area would be about 40 – 50 feet or around 14 metres, and in this particular corner was an access point to the roof along with access to the overhead crane (the crane that is used to take reels of paper from Machine to Rewinder etc). The Access is for Maintenance Crews and Electricians to mount the overhead crane when breakdowns occur or as the name suggests, maintenance is required.

With the Number 3 Mill in full swing and the Rewinder running Scotties the area was busy with workers going about their business. The only difference to the guys on the floor was that the walkway that normally only had yellow lines marked on the concrete also had bollards and tape today so that the tour group did not encroach into the work space. This was for their own safety as Forklifts operated in the area and steel bars were swung by the workers at times when the paper plied together and they needed some persuading to separate. Now this safety barrier had been in all weekend so the perpetrator of this planned event (Mission Cherry Bomb) knew that it was an ideal opportunity to do it on this tour as the barrier would keep all visitors safe from the pending prank. Hard to believe that no-one on the Mill floor noticed the Dummy that was located at the entry to the overhead access point, but apparently they did not.

The planned tour started at the Admin Building at 9-00am and with the rear section of number 3 Mill being planned for early in the tour it was about 9-45am when the group of around six to eight guests were gathered near the Scotties area, led by Charles.

Then as Charles was pointing to the boys stacking the Scotties biscuits a loud AHHHHHHHHHH!!! cried out from overhead as the Dummy crashed onto the floor some three metres in front of the group. Charles was shaking like a leaf but some in the group realized it was a prank immediately, as from where they were standing a gumboot had fallen off and they could see paper where a leg should be. The shock gave the perpetrator a few seconds to get out of sight and he must have made his escape over the roof towards Conversion as he was never caught. It took Charles a good minute to find his feet after he realized it was a prank and after an apology he continued the tour.

Management was fuming over the incident but with nobody talking and nobody caught it all died down and was soon forgotten about.

Must not have upset the Kiwi's too much either as they ended up buying the place a few years later.

Fiery Finish!

GOING BACK TO THE night shift where I was running No 1 Rewinder, a chapter or so ago ***(The Sacking of a Dummy!....)*** Gerry Gee was indeed sleeping when he was supposed to be training. I was enjoying being back on the Rewinder as it was far more entertaining than standing around with a high pressure hose with no-one to interact with. Don had left at a few minutes before 3-00am and I was finding my groove running the Rewinder, and taking the speed easy. Which pleased Bruce (the first Boy) as he did not want a repeat of the Gerry Gee fiasco that occurred many years earlier. Bruce never trusted my skills as he never let me throw out reels on the machine when I was second boy here either.

Now ironically Gerry Gee would create a fiasco that would involve us all without even being on the Rewinder.

It starts like this;

Gerry normally hid in the Broke Room to have a sleep, but as many machines were down, the Broke Room attendant (John) was in his hut a fair bit and Gerry could not use it to have a peaceful rest. So Gerry found a dark quiet spot in the form of the Number 3 Rewinder hut, that was not being used and was perfect as the Paper Machine was also down. All the overhead lighting was off and there was almost no-one in the area so Gerry felt well pleased with his choice. But trying to nod off on such a cold night was not easy so Gerry trotted over to the Broke Room and cut himself a wad of paper off a reject reel which he took back to the hut and made into a cosy blanket.

At about 4-30am the Fire alarms went off, and being a member of the Gold Shift Fire Crew I was required to respond. In most cases these were false alarms but in all cases we were required to respond and investigate. There were Alarm Station boards located around the Factory, both Mill and Conversion, and these housed displays of locations around the whole site. They displayed a number of lights which when lit up indicated the location of the alarm / detector that had gone off. On inspection it was indicating the rear of Number 3 Paper Mill. Myself and my Assistant Greg, who was also on the Gold Shift Fire Crew, took off towards No 3 Rewinder at a reasonable pace until we got passed the Mill Supervisors Office and spotted the smoke. "Now" it was obvious that it wasn't a false alarm and with the Fire Brigade also alerted automatically by the alarm we bolted towards the source of the smoke.

Upon arrival we spotted that Larry (Leading Hand) was already dousing the flames and Gerry Gee was assisting with a second fire hose that was much smaller than the Machine hoses we had in the Mill. Gerry Gee helping seemed very strange to both Greg and I, as we knew he would have been off sleeping somewhere under the guise of Training on No 2 Paper Mill. Immediately we noticed that No 3 Rewinder Hut was the source of ignition and had been completely destroyed in the blaze. The Perspex windows were melted (the cause of the Black Smoke) and the entire hut had caved in on itself. Fortunately the Paper Mill was down, as if not the area would have been thick with dust on the walls, ceilings and overhead crane. The shutdown allowed for clean ups and these areas had been washed thoroughly over the past few days. If not for this the fire would have almost certainly spread.

Soon after the Box Hill Fire Brigade arrived and took charge of the scene, which by now was totally under control, as the flames had been extinguished mainly by Larry. But the Fire Brigade kept dousing the area and moving items to ensure no re-ignition could occur. The Brigade then taped off the area and instructed Pat (Gold Shift Supervisor) that the Investigation squad would return in the morning, only a couple of hours away by now. This comment brought a pink glow to the face of Gerry Gee and it appeared that Larry already had the answers to the pending investigation.

Turns out that the following occurred;

With Gerry Gee all snug and asleep inside the No 3 Rewinder hut another fellow worker had snuck up to the hut, opened the door quietly and lit the wad of paper that Gerry had wrapped around him. Gerry had sprung up immediately and thrown the wad of paper off into the hut while barging out the door. He then ran to the fire hose and started trying to extinguish the flames. But as the door was on a spring close he struggled to hold the door and use the hose, allowing the fire to take hold. Larry, who was just heading from his office to No 3 Paper Mill spotted this and grabbed a machine hose to assist. Now this was very serious as Gerry could have been severely injured in this, so called Prank.

A full investigation by the Box Hill Fire Brigade could not find an ignition point in any electrical fittings so no further action was taken by themselves or any other outside Bodies. But internally Gerry Gee was in a shitload of trouble as Larry placed him at the scene and no-one believed Gerry's story that he had spotted the smoke on his way to retrieving something from his car in the adjoining Carpark. Management, who already wanted Gerry Gee out called for his sacking stating gross misconduct as a reason for dismissal. But in true Bowater fashion the Union successfully argued that even if Gerry was asleep in the hut he was not the arsonist, and that Gerry Gee's only offence was sleeping on the job. They further went on to say that they would fully support the sacking of the arsonist once Management had located that individual. That never happened!

Unrelenting in their desire to get Gerry Gee out of Bowater, Management met with Des Onion and other Union Officials to propose a payout for Gerry. The Union said that they would put it to their member and if Gerry agreed they would support Management. The sum of $6,000.00 plus all accrued entitlements was offered to Gerry in a meeting of the three parties and Gerry Gee jumped at it. A reasonable sum of money at the time but not really a lot. In fact most Workers would not have accepted it but Gerry Gee was not your average guy. In fact $6,000 all in his wallet at one time would have made Gerry Gee feel very special indeed. Rumour has it that he took the money and immediately bought a Removal Truck. Uninsured he crashed the vehicle on his second or third job and in addition to not being able to afford the repairs he was successfully sued by the client of the removal job and put on a payment plan by the courts. Never heard any more about the life and times of Gerry Gee, but it would be hard to see a "Silver Lining "to his disastrous life's story.

Chicko Rolled!

NOW WITH GERRY GEE gone more opportunity was opening up for promotion on the Rewinders, and my prediction of being stuck for five or more years as an Assistant Winderman was looking shaky – In a good way! But the next series of events meant that more and more time would be shaved from my wait. The first was by natural attrition and the second by investment, this chapter covers the first.

Without doubt there were some characters in this place and Chicko was absolutely one of them. An unusual chap who was also an Assistant Winderman and was one of my "Reliefs" (*fellow worker who did your job on another shift – who took over when your shift ended or you took over from*). Now we only crossed paths on limited occasions, as with five shifts you were rostered on a rotating basis. I was also just new to the main Rewinder crew and Chicko was already turning into a pain in the ass. He was forever late and unapologetically so. He would have no consideration for his fellow Relief's and with his Supervisor being very aloof, not much was ever done about it. I complained to both him and his Supervisor a few times but it seemed to fall on deaf ears.

One story I remember about Chicko was a tale that could have ended up very nasty it went like this;

With the Rewinder down and Red Shift on Night shift it would not be long into the shift before Chicko was off somewhere having a sleep. On this particular night he chose a quiet corner of the Broke Room where he was assigned to assist. He nestled into a paper waste skip bin that was loaded nicely with soft white paper. (*Like sleeping on a cloud if you get one like this*). At this point there appeared to be nothing wrong with his choice, but as the shift went on all of the bins that were between him and the conveyor (that ran into a Hydro-Pulper) started to dwindle. Again should not have been a problem as the Broke Room Attendant knew he was there. But along came Tex Bogan, the Forklift driver from Conversion, and he was chasing a bin as they had a big pile of Broke (reject paper) that needed cleaning up. Now this is where the problems began as Tex spotted Chicko's bin (not knowing what was inside) and with the Broke Room Attendant not around decided to retrieve the bin and empty it onto the conveyor himself. This happened by a rotation attachment on the front of the forklifts that would lock, load and turn the bin upside down, emptying its content. Problem was that this bin also contained Chicko who had slept through the pick-up stage of Tex's process.

As the Paper from the now upside down bin hit the conveyor belt a startled Chicko emerged looking like a lamington, as the bin also contained a large amount of paper dust in the bottom (now the top). Tex shit himself when he saw Chicko and was relieved that Chicko appeared uninjured. In fact Chicko was extremely lucky as if Tex had of emptied the Bin in the opposite circular direction then Chicko would have landed on his head rather than on his legs. In saying that, many fellow workers would disagree as they believed Chicko was very thick skinned, especially around the Head!!

Ringmaster (Little Legs)!

I WOULD AGREE WITH the thick skinned bit, as no matter how often I would ask him to try and get to work on time when relieving me he didn't listen. Even when I started relieving him late that did not work as he would just get one of his co-workers to wait for me on the hope that they may get overtime out of it. Alas it turned out that I was getting through to Chicko, but his response was not that of a reasonable person as I was soon to find out.

Arriving at work one morning and in the process of clocking on I saw that No 2 Rewinder was running Scotties and we were now working over here. Turns out that yesterday afternoon No 3 Machine had some issues and had to be shut down. But Tissue supply was required by Conversion and No 2 had come to the rescue. Truth is that this Rewinder was very impractical at running Scotties, as the area was cramped and the Rewinder itself was quite antiquated. I headed towards the Hut to relieve Chicko and noticed Little Legs in the hut, and that the place went a bit quiet as I entered. I was my jovial self until I noticed that Chicko was agitated and staring at me. Then I spotted him clenching his fist and I knew he was going to take a swipe at me. I moved back out of the hut deciding that putting my bag in there at this point in time was not worth a smack in the chops for. I moved strategically in view of the Supervisors office in case Chicko took it outside. But he didn't and soon realized that I was aware of his intentions and he headed off to his clock card and off home.

Fucken Little Legs, the troublemaker was trying to stir the pot again. I did not realize how dangerous his antics were until I was the target. They say "Empathy is easier acquired by involvement than observation" and I could now vouch for that. Turns out that he had been employing his tactics on Chicko since the early hours of the morning as he had been called in at 3-00am. The Ringmaster of the 70's Fight Club appeared to be wanting its return in the late 80's – for his viewing pleasure! Truth was that with Gerry Gee now gone he had to focus on others to stimulate his twisted sense of humour.

Falling Like a Dekka Cards!

Definition: An unstable or weak structure or plan

NOW THIS FELLA HAD no problems getting himself into trouble and his favourite catchcry was "I'll Fuckin Deck Ya!" From memory he was a transfer from Conversion and we soon learned why they were so keen to get rid of him. With a catchcry like that you would expect him to be a big fella, but alas he was like a string bean with a protruding jaw full of crooked teeth, and bad skin that was sickly pale.

In search of a Gerry Gee replacement Dekka was an easy target for Little Legs who was happy to promote Dekka's ability to take down larger opponents. It was like the 70's all over again but this time there was "no ring" and "no rules"! I believe other people were involved in stirring all this up but in general it became a bit of a game for many of the Mill boys who thought Dekka deserved whatever was coming to him. Now funny enough Chicko would be Dekka's first opponent in the unofficial title of "King of the Mill!" How I came to learn about the fight was by being called in on overtime to cover Chicko who was not in at work 'AGAIN!'

He had apparently injured his hand somehow on Dekka's face and the wound got infected. But that was the unofficial story as he was officially on light duties due to cutting the webbing between his knuckles on a Rewinder Slitter Blade. The second was the story I got when called in on overtime. The first story (what actually happened), I was told by Don soon after I arrived. He gave me a full description of the event and it went like this;

Apparently fired up by another worker, Dekka was told that Chicko wanted to punch his lights out as he was such a dickhead. Loaded up with this Dekka confronted Chicko and said "I'll Fuckin Deck Ya!"you Mexican Prick. With that Chicko took a swing at him and missed with the first punch but got him clean in the mouth with the second. Dekka immediately sprung a leak and grabbed a wad of paper to contain the stream of blood. It was all over in a few seconds.

Even though Dekka had lost the fight he was not badly injured, and as he could keep working, the two were separated and the whole incident was covered up by the Shift Supervisor and Leading Hand. In fact Dekka's wound healed quickly and Chicko ended up with worst injury, albeit to his hand. It caused him grief for months and was still a problem when it eventually healed as he had movement issues, possibly permanently. With all this happening not long after Gerry Gee was paid out it appeared that management must have had more knowledge of the incident than we thought, as Chicko was also offered a payout and left shortly after. Truth is both Gerry Gee and Chicko had terrible work records and even the Union knew they were on borrowed time. I didn't hate Chicko but I was certainly glad he was gone as I would now get home on time more often.

Even with Management seeming to be cracking down, Little Legs and his buddies did not stop pumping up Dekka's tyres and it was not long before he was at it again. The next incident happened on a night shift and this time it would be serious enough to put an end to the "Unofficial Fight Club." The story goes like this;

With Dekka coming off second best against his first opponent Chicko, it appeared at first that he had chosen his next opponent more wisely. Ewan was a small Scottish Fellow with a mild disposition and kept to himself, as he had not long started with the company. But he was very popular as he worked well with those around him and was always there when needed. Again though, he did have a dislike for Dekka and had told him to shut up on more than one occasion. He was not one for a lot of talk and Dekka never shut up, strutting around like a peacock. Probably validated by Little Legs and all the shit he was feeding him. It all came to a head when Dekka pushed Ewan as Ewan was exiting the Hut to do his next task after a cuppa.

Ewan pushed him back and said to him "pull your head in!" Dekka sprung into his line "Ill Fucken Deck Ya!" and at the same time hit Ewan with a right to the side of the head. Well what came next shocked everyone working in the area as Ewan sprang into action with a series of lefts and rights that you would expect to see in a professional bout. Dekka did not stand a chance, and the first punch that he got in was the only one as Ewan continued the onslaught. With Dekka reeling backwards Ewan moved forward with blow after blow until Dekka "hit the deck" on the concrete floor beside the machine blade rack.

Knocked out cold and not too healthy this incident could not be covered up as an ambulance had to be called.

When the next shift started the news of the big fight had already spread like wildfire and this was a perfect opportunity for Derek Sorters to apply his artistic talent. Derek went to work at 7-10am on creating a chalk outline where Dekka had landed. It looked amazing and covered up by loose broke, none of the managers would see it during day shift (or so he thought).

Word came down later that day that Dekka's mum was at the Admin office letting rip on Cogers and other managers on how she was going to sue the company and have those responsible arrested. Banging on about how her poor son was being picked on. This guaranteed an investigation would ensue and soon the Union, Supervisors and Management would be in discussions about what would happen.

With that Cogers had called the night shift Supervisor and Leading Hand back to work for a meeting at 11-30am and instructed that Ewan would be suspended with pay until the results of the investigation were concluded. The meeting would be held at the Mill Supervisors office as they wanted to have an inspection of where the incident had occurred. Now this was not conveyed to the boys on the floor and the Broke covering the Chalk Line body shape was still in place, as was the Chalk Line. Cogers walked past the pile of broke on his way to the Mill Supervisors office and looked very stressed and focused by all accounts. During the course of the meeting they all walked over to the No 2 Mill Hut and Cogers requested the Broke be removed to inspect the scene. Hesitant to do this the 2nd Boy tried to make up some feeble excuse but Cogers was now seething and said "NOW!" When removed Cogers roared out "For Fucks Sake!" and did his little jig of raising his pants with the inside of both wrists. Ordered to remove the tape immediately all the boys got stuck in and had the place shining within minutes. Not one of them stopped working for one second for the rest of the day.

Many of the Boys from that night were interviewed and their stories all matched, saying that Dekka was the instigator and that Ewan acted in self-defence. We were all impressed with Cogers as he stuck by Ewan only giving him a warning and stating that if he was involved in fighting ever again it would be an instant dismissal. The Union also saw this as fair and didn't challenge. Dekka on the other hand was dismissed immediately for instigating the altercation. Dekka's mum returned to the Admin Office and was told that an investigation was held and all workers stated that her son was the instigator. Management stated if she wanted to pursue it further that the company would vigorously defend its findings. Alas no more was ever heard of Dekka and his mummy, with Fight Club being shut down permanently.

Misplaced Investment!

TISSUES SEEMED TO BE one of the two strongest parts of Bowater's business, second to toilet rolls, but still as strong in the marketplace. As such modernization of Conversion was required mainly for auto packing of toilet rolls but also to house the new Jagenberg that was on order from Germany. Nicknamed No 4 Rewinder it needed to be housed in Conversion but would be part of the Mill. This is the Investment I was speaking of in earlier chapters that would assist me in climbing the slow tree of progress that was the "Bowater Seniority System."

But before all this was to occur a re-design of Conversion would need to be drafted in order to accommodate it and the modernization of the antiquated manual packing systems still in place. The Jagenberg would be a multi-function Rewinder that would run many different types of paper and even light cardboard for core-making.

The supposed "best" Blueprint Architects were commissioned to do a factory overlay of Conversion incorporating the new machines as well as re-position existing machines that were to be retained. All this with efficiency input from Papermaking professionals and productivity engineers. Sounds complex hey, (sorry been living in Queensland for 30 years now, that slipped in) and it was, with the planning process taking seven months and at a cost in the tens of thousands of dollars.

Problem was that no-one had calculated in or reported the positioning of the structural beams that held the roof up, with 30% of them ending up through the middle of the new or re-positioned machinery.

Option one; No Roof

Option two; Re-draw

I hope you are with me on which one they choose. Yes totally amazing, and shows that money spent doesn't equate to quality outputted.

Well a further three months on and with the Jagenberg due to arrive very soon the Architects fixed all the issues and work commenced on getting the area cleared firstly for the new Jagenberg. As mentioned this new machine was commissioned to run all types of paper and Bowater specifically wanted it to make more Scotties Tissues for the hungry (or snotty) market. No 3 Paper Machine had now been upgraded to increase its speed and No 3 Rewinder would be left as is. This meant that as Scotties were being produced on No 3 Paper Machine the Rewinder would get behind. So every third or fourth Reel being made by the Paper Machine would be slit on the machine and manually transported to the Jagenberg or No 4 Rewinder as it was nicknamed by the boys. The Jagenberg was a half width Rewinder and would produce 8 Scotties biscuits per set compared to the 16 on No 3 or 2 Rewinder. It could also run stored reels which meant that when Paper Machines were down Scotties could still be produced.

In theory this sounded like an extremely practical and efficient process, but in time to come we would all realize that in practical terms there were many flaws and efficiency issues.

Here Come the Germans!

KNOWN FOR THEIR ENGINEERING excellence the Germans arrived for the installation and commissioning of the Jagenberg (No 4 Rewinder) with great pride and an air of excited optimism from Bowater Management. The assembly of the Jagenberg seemed to happen quite quickly but this was probably because most of the construction happened before it arrived. The whole concrete floor had been removed, deep footings dug and poured in specific areas where major support would be required, and Trim Chute channels were set in preparation for installation. When completed and the Jagenberg erected, a specialist crew from Germany was sent over to commission it and train staff in its use. Of course during its build another team from Germany were onsite to supervise the build and train the maintenance staff.

Ready to produce and Mr Cogers was assigned to oversee its maiden run. But alas the anticipation of a high speed producer was soon dismissed as a number of issues prevented it from being run at anything over 25% of capacity speed. At first these issues were thought to be alignments and adjustments, but no amount of adjustment could stop the Barrel Wrapping and Reel Thumping that were the major issues. Mr Cogers and his German friends worked tirelessly trying to get it right but alas it appeared that a miscommunication in expectations had occurred and the Germans blamed the conditions rather than the equipment.

Stuck with what they had purchased Bowater now had to man it's new machine and the Union was pushing for as many new members as it could get. They argued that for Health and Safety reasons three workers should be allocated per shift to the machine. But due to its lack of ability to hit speed Bowater successfully kept the numbers to two, a Rewinderman and an Assistant Rewinderman. This new machine was to be my pathway to a Rewindermans position and not only that but I was able to do it on my own shift (Gold Shift). My Assistant was Aaron Softing who, after almost 20 years of working in Conversion, had transferred to the Mill only a few years earlier. Weird thing was that he worked on the edge of Conversion for a fair amount of that time, on the printer in fact, and now with this promotion was physically also on the edge of Conversion again. Anyway he was a good fellow and we got along quite well so that was the main thing.

THUMP 'N' WRAP!

WHEN I FIRST STARTED on the Jagenberg I was keen to make a good impression and worked really hard to get this machine to a better speed.

Aaron was also great to work with and he was on the same page as I was, he also had a good work ethic. But alas not all the shifts shared our enthusiasm and it was not long before I was criticised by other Rewindermen for producing too much per shift and making them look bad. Truth was it was extremely difficult to lift the bar as the Barrel Wrap was ridiculous and could create many rejects if not kept in check.

Me Running the Jagenberg – Around 1991 I would think.

NOW TO EXPLAIN BARREL WRAP:

The paper runs over a series of rolls and these rolls help keep creasing out of the paper as it is unrolled from the main reels. Then at the point of cutting there is a Barrel that has the Slitters (set to size) set into it. This is where the paper of specific sizes are first created and wrapped onto a biscuit. The Barrel Wrap starts at the point of the Slitter cut and there were numerous reasons why this occurred. The problem was that it was near impossible to stop it occurring on the Jagenberg when at speed. To explain Barrel Wrap – it is where the paper breaks free from the main sheet, at the Barrel, and wraps to it rather than where it should be on the new Biscuit. Hope this makes sense!

The Thump was caused by the shape of the new reels that were supplied. The problem here was that the paper had been transported by the grab Forklift, usually from storage where it had been squashed in transit. This grab would squeeze the Reels out of shape. Being belt driven and with hydraulic pressure arms the out of shape reels would create a bounce, that at speed would cause the belt to bounce free from the Reel and the paper would break or go loose. This sometimes caused Barrel Wrap due to the creasing or would cause the cut Biscuits to interweave and be hard to separate. The faster you went the worse it got. We did find that if you went very fast you could get past the bounce, but at that speed if you got Barrel Wrap it would be so bad and thick, that by the time you stopped the machine the Slitters were damaged. The softer the paper, the worse the shape of the Reels became, and because one of the main objectives of the Jagenberg was for Tissues production, well you can see the quandary.

Keen to prove this Aaron and I, on a night shift, organized for two fresh Reels to be transported directly from No 3 Paper Machine to us on pallets. The Reels had to be smaller to fit but we were able to get them to the Jagenberg in almost perfect shape. We ran these reels at 75% speed without incident. Problem was that transporting this way was impossible to achieve on a regular basis.

I always maintained that if we had a floating bar like they had on many of the Conversion Machines and that the angle that the paper hit the Barrel at was flattened we would have got better speed out of the Jagenberg. Of course the Thumping would still be a problem. Never mind, it didn't work like that at Bowater and it was best to go with the flow. Both Aaron and I soon settled into a groove and kept production sensible so we didn't upset our colleagues.

It was a good job and we had our own hut to be able to relax in away from the noise, so life was pretty good. I say that as the

Conversion boys, who were now just across the walkway from us did not have huts and had to be in the dust and noise all shift. We at least got to take off our ear muffs and still oversee the operation of the Rewinder.

Site Layout (forgotten)
Bring on the Nasty Nurses!

This chapter was going to go in a few chapters ago **Misplaced Investment!...... (Site Layout)** *but as you will soon see I have the concentration span of a man and well...... read on!*

IN AN EARLIER CHAPTER ("Roll Change") I spoke a bit about the layout of the Factory and more specifically the area where I went to catch up with Des Onion about my career path question. Now to talk slightly about this I will touch on my theory on the layout of the overall site. My theory is that in the early days, prior to the erection of the Administration Building, it was like this: I believe that the area where the TC and CR testing labs were in the 80's and 90's was originally an office block for Paper Mill Staff, as it always seemed like an overkill building for a testing department. Further to that theory, that the offices of Des Onion's and the Medical Centre / Nurses Station, located between Conversion A and Conversion B, were also an office block but for Conversion Staff. (There were a string of offices in this block – not just the two mentioned).

Now I added the 'heading' to this section prior to writing it and it read "site layout". Which means with the above title I am committed to digressing as I am in a memory flow and cannot stop. But truthfully the main reason for my digression is far more primal, as when I mentioned the word Nurses my mind wondered. Not to the first Nurse I met onsite but to the second, or the third if you include Annie (but I will get to her later)!

The First Nurse was more a Matron than a Nurse, in my eyes anyway. Uma from Upwey was a nugget of a lady, not very tall and almost as wide as she was tall, with her uniform always looking stressed and under pressure. She was Nasty, but in a mean way, and was not as popular with the 99% male contingency that formed the Factory Floor as the second Nurse Anita. (Or third Nurse if you include Annie). Fortunately I never had much to do with Uma as I was still a young fella and quite healthy (not so young now – but touch wood – still healthy).

Now to Annie;

To be honest I never knew that Annie had a name until a conversation just recently with a colleague from back then. I was chatting to him about some of the crazy stories from the past and one of his stories was the same as I had heard in my time at the Mill. The unusual thing about this was that we were both from different Shifts and also from different locations in the Factory, as he was from Conversion. I had also heard the story from many others of that era and as it affected a number of people then you may start to understand why.

See Annie was a Resuscitation dummy and an integral part of the First Aid training program. Training was huge in the Hawke/Keating era and Bowater spent heaps on it in many different areas. The guys loved training as it was usually one hour's overtime before afternoon shift and a pretty good boost to the pay packet. (We actually got Pay Packets in those Days).

After a quiet weekend Uma arrived at her Medical Centre all primed for the week ahead, but as she opened her office door, she was greeted with a grotesque sight. Letting out a loud squeal she was joined by Des Onion who had also just arrived at work. The sight they were confronted with was that of Annie alone on the examination table facing the doorway and showing obvious signs of interference. I will not go into great detail, other to say that there were scrape marks up the walls and the room was a mess. Someone had had a great time with Annie "and had left proof"! To my knowledge though, no-one was ever disciplined over the incident even though it was only First Aid attendants who had keys and only 3 shifts who worked over that particular weekend.

The story of Annie was broadcast all over the Factory, both Mill and Conversion, even though staff tried to keep the incident quiet while they were looking for the culprit. But alas nothing was a secret in this place and when the next First Aid training session was held and Resuscitation was on the menu no-one was going near Annie. In fact they had to purchase a new dummy with a completely new design before they could resume classes.

Not long after that Uma resigned from the Nurses job and we got a lovely new Nurse named Anita. This proved to be a hit in the Factory with attendance at the Medical Centre tripling overnight. Anita was quite an attractive lady but more so she had a happy and confident demeanour that made her extremely popular. Very professional though and would take no nonsense, which she had to extend on many occasions especially in the early days.

Whereas in the past with Uma the guys would see their own First Aid attendant for a band aid or bandage, when Anita arrived they went to her instead. It got ridiculous and the Shift Supervisors had to intervene and put a lid on the practice as it was affecting productivity. On one occasion there was an ethnic fellow who went to

Anita with a muscle issue to his calf that was causing him great pain. Anita examined him and as she did the fellow complained that the pain was coming from higher up. 'Well onto this', Anita advised the fellow that it could be serious and that she would call the Doctor in for a more thorough examination. All of a sudden the pain stopped and he quickly exited the Medical Centre minus the limp he entered with. Thus was the "Miracles" that Anita could perform.

My first meeting with Anita was when the Doctor was in, as I was suffering from an infected ingrown toenail and it had gotten so bad that I had made an appointment to see him. I was running the Jagenberg (Number 4) Rewinder at the time and as I was on dayshift and midway through my shift rotation I had not been to my local doctor and I was trying to work with it until my day off. To do this I was wearing a gumboot on my right foot, as it was so infected that I could not put my work boot on that foot. I choose an oversized gumboot for this task as it was the only thing I could wear with a steel cap that both complied with 'Health and Safety' and was comfortable enough to work in. Although I was quite a sight with one Gumboot, one shoe and a wicked limp. But I didn't care as it enabled me to work and I had 'bills to pay'!

I made my way down to the Medical Centre as I had taken an early Lunchbreak and was greeted by the lovely smile of Anita who asked me to take a seat. The Doctor emerged from his office a few minutes later and upon examination asked me to sit up on the examination table as he would operate on it. He told me that he would firstly drain the affected area and then cut a slither of toenail from the top to the hyponychium (quick). Sounded good, and when he drained the affected area it was such a relief as the throbbing stopped. But it also made the area more sensitive and when he started cutting I nearly hit the roof with pain. Anita stepped in and said "are you going to give him a local anaesthetic?" To which the Doctor replied "he is tough, he will be right", but Anita insisted as the pain was obvious. That made Anita number one in my books and after the anaesthetic the procedure was a breeze. Not sure why the Doctor didn't do it first up, but boy was I happy Anita stepped in. After the procedure I got back into my mismatched footwear and hobbled back to the Jagenberg.

Exposing the Underbelly!

LOCATED TO THE WESTERN end of the Jagenberg, near where we prepared the Reels for loading into the Rewinder to run, was the Conversion Shredder. This created bundles (cube shaped) of recycled paper that came from Conversion waste and could be stored for future use in the Broke Room. Nifty was the operator of the machine on our shift and we would quite often have a chat as he was quite a nice fellow. A bit of a hippy type and always good for a chat as he had one of the better jobs in Conversion, if you liked to be away from the action that is.

Aaron was always chatting to Nifty as he did most of the new Reel preparation while I was watching the Rewinder. Aaron and I had only just started on the Jagenberg but we did feel a bit isolated as we were away from all our mates in the Mill and we didn't know a lot of the Conversion fellows. Aaron would have if he was still on the same shift but he swapped shifts to go into the Mill and was also at the opposite end of Conversion from where he used to work. So chatting to Nifty was nice and we got on real well.

Then one day on our first day back from a three day break Aaron asked me who the bloke on the Shredder was as he didn't speak English and didn't know where Nifty was. I thought Nifty must have had an extra day off by pulling a sickie, but when the ethnic bloke was still there after 7-00pm I guessed he was Nifty's replacement for some reason. Around 7-30pm I spotted Mick (Conversion Leading Hand) and asked him who the new bloke on the Shredder was and where Nifty was now working. Mick was a bit coy and just said that Nifty was no longer employed by Bowater. Aaron and I were puzzled by this as Nifty was a pretty good worker, who everyone liked and hardly ever had a Sickie by all accounts.

Bewildered by this Aaron and I kept probing to see what was going on and were gobsmacked when we found out some four or so weeks later. Apparently Nifty lived in a share house with the Minogue Brothers (Craig and Rodney) and he had been put into the Witness Protection Program, never to be seen again. If you don't already recognize their names they were involved in the Russell Street bombing in Melbourne in 1986.

Flaming Legends!

LOCATED NEXT TO THE Shredder was a portable office that was the home of the Fire Officer – Roy Bayonet, along with Barry Virgo who looked after all the Cleaning Staff and Reel Storage. Roy was an older fellow who had been there a while and when he left Bowater one of the boys from Red Shift, who was keen to get onto day shift, Stan Rollen stepped into his position. Timing would be good for Stan as the Kiwi's had just purchased Bowater and with his extract 'could only be a good thing!' I have a good yarn about their incestuous relationship that I will share later.

The Shift Fire Crews were an integral part of the Fire protection of Bowater as they manned the facility after hours. So with a 24 hour operation they were more than integral, they were essential. The reward for the guys who joined the crew was one hour per month training which was paid at double time and occurred when each shift was on afternoon shift. We would come in at 2-00pm instead of 3-00pm on Fire Training Day so it was very convenient and did not eat much into your day. It was good for us as members, but was also good for Bowater as it gave them a crew on-site after normal business hours and on Weekends, at a cheap price. In fact training was big at Bowater and a Safety Meeting was also held once a month for all shift workers and was well attended. Bowater would like to think for the right reasons, but really it was a few bucks for little effort that drew the crowd. Conversion I believe also had a Safety meeting but the Mill had theirs separate to them.

BACK TO THE FIRE CREW

Now having a Fire Crew was one thing but being co-ordinated in a response and well trained was equally as important. This is where Stan Rollen shone. Now Roy Bayonet was a good bloke and had all the skills but Stan was a better communicator and had most of the crew's respect. He appeared to really enjoy what he did but more importantly was able to empathise with us shift workers, as he was one of us a short time ago. His only problem was though was that he was a F***en Kiwi and us Aussies (broad interpretation if you looked at us) were (and are) not enriched with a love for our neighbours "over the ditch!"

The Gold Shift Fire Crew minus the person taking the photo and Me (Craig) as this was sent to me a few years later.

STAN TO ATTENTION!!

Here is the story I spoke of earlier, all in Stan's words;

> We all have interesting stories of Box Hill, and stories that have never seen the light of day - and this is one of mine... Hope I don't offend anyone.
>
> So Carter Holt Harvey - the Kiwis - buy the site, and for some reason, as usual, I was asked to take photos to send to CHH Auckland Headquarters as the Kiwis wanted to see what the place looked like. Off I go from the red fire hut, click, click, click, 'Vic Admin', 'overview of the pulp yard', shot of 'Mill 4 Building', and I wandered into the No 4 Mill to let the Machineman know what I was up to - where I met up with Green Shift, Derek & Crew on day shift. "Gidday Stan what are you doing...?" says Derek. "Just getting some photos of the best of Box Hill to send to the new owners Deks, how are you...?" Bit of small talk - and I off I went to the toilet - leaving the camera on the Mill 4 control panel. Came out, - picked up the camera, - and off I went again, click, click, click, around the site. (Some of you can see what's coming right...?). Well I put the photos into the 1 hour developer and picked them up, I was putting them into the envelope to send them to New Zealand, and thought, "better check that they are all in focus...." So I'm flicking through them, - Vic Admin check, - pulp yard check, - Mill 4 building check, - erect male penis..........!!!!!! Don't know who the guilty party was, but thank the lord above I didn't send that off. And SHAME on me for leaving a loaded camera around a Mill Control Room. - - - So what happened you ask....? Next time Green Shift were

on days I wandered into Mill 4 Control Room, "Gidday Stan how you going..?" Says Derek. Says I - "I'm going really well thanks Derek, - one of the Kiwi girls from Headquarters has rung me up three times now asking for a date.....!!!!

BACK TO FLAMING LEGENDS!

Bowater on Fire in 1972

Back to a more serious note, Fire was a big concern for the plant as back in September 1972 the whole Factory was nearly destroyed in a huge fire. The nature of the product made the place susceptible to fire as it produced a volatile mixture of dust that filled the air in some sections. Couple this with the Gas fired drying systems on the Machines and you had a lethal combination. Other sources were; Fires starting when paper built up around rollers running at high speed and friction causing ignition. Bearings overheating or seizing up and igniting paper dust build up. Then of course there was man made causes, like cigarette butts.

Bowater was very pro-active with fire safety for these very reasons and another benefit of being on the Fire Crew was that when maintenance staff and outside contractors were doing grinding or cutting, a member was given overtime on Fire Watch. This was a large expense for the company, but a fire would be far more expensive and devastating for all the workers if they had no place to work in. We also received outside training on Fire Fighting which included live action and simulated rescue. It was great training and something I will never forget. Stan Rollen did a great job at organizing this for the crews and we even had our own onsite Firetruck.

1995 Fire - some of the damage after the Fire was extinguished. Also above the Box Hill Fire Brigade in action on-site at Bowater. The Bowater on-site Fire Truck can be seen a few pages back and in a Photo of the Sigma (Fish and Chip) Wagon earlier in this book as well.

I spoke earlier about the Fire ignition points and to go into a bit more detail the preventative measures that ensured the least possibility for fire, was cleanliness. With most of the issues being created on the Paper Machines themselves, the crew of Machineman - 1st and 2nd boy were trained to be vigilant on cleaning at every possible opportunity. These opportunities were in some cases only when the paper sheet broke and the machine Yankee blade was being replaced. A technical event for those who have never worked in a Paper Mill and one that I have described in an earlier chapter *"Back to the Roll Change"*. But general cleanliness was highly stressed to all workers, with all areas doing complete clean downs at the end of every eight hour shift.

I have chopped around a bit here but I will be a bit more specific now about what I believe was the biggest creator of the issue of fire;

The main drying area on a Paper Machine is called the Yankee Roll, and on many Paper Machines it is topped by hoods that are gas fired. Now if paper worked its way into this area, from whatever source, then it could ignite and create sparks that then can make their way into the new paper reels being created (run up). Now this process rarely causes a fire immediately but rather is trapped and starved of oxygen (required for flame/fire) to possibly raise its head another day. Working on the Rewinder there were some occasions when we were plying paper and making biscuits (cut to size reels) that the sparks trapped in the Reels would ignite the sheet and even the dusty air around it. These mini fire balls would scare the heck out of you, especially if the Machine Crew had not warned you of the possibility of sparks in the reel. It did not happen often, but it did happen. It was standard practice to then mark up all paper reels made on the Rewinder around these incidents "Warning Sparks!" All Machine made reels, and Rewinder created product that were marked "Sparks" were then stored in an isolated storage area in case of combustion. Conversion had the same issues as the Rewinders as they also ran the product and had fire ignitions often. From memory they also had an equipped Fire Warden on duty when running "Sparks Reels!"

PROMETHEUS!

ANOTHER CAUSE OF FIRE was one that seems to not fit in with the general causes and apparently made it all the way from Bowater to an employee's home,

It went like this;

"NEWS TODAY!"

Crews from the Lilydale Fire Brigade were called to scene of a house fire at ****** Street Lilydale. Officers on the scene were amazed at the ferocity and intensity of the blaze, especially in the roof space which a spokesman for the Brigade said; 'was extremely difficult to extinguish!'

"TWO MONTHS LATER!"

Chief Officer ******* from Lilydale Fire Brigade reported that the recent fire in a Lilydale home was traced to an industrial electrical motor that was incorrectly installed. He added that the ceiling was lined/Insulated six inches thick with paper sheets similar to facial tissue which significantly added to the intensity of the blaze. He further added that investigations quickly determined the source of the paper and that the owner was assisting police with their enquiries.

Robin Hood... because... Robin Could!!!

To pilfer is to steal something, typically of small value. Minor thefts, like taking a roll of toilet paper out of a public bathroom or napkins from the Early Bird Buffet are what your grandfather, for example, might pilfer.

The verb pilfer comes from the Old French noun pelfre, meaning "booty," or "spoils." Now pilfer is used when talking about the act of stealing loot: you may find that you have to really restrain yourself from the desire to pilfer your friend's new fur-lined gloves, even though you're pretty sure she pilfered your headphones. Robin Hood was able to pilfer from the rich to give to the poor.

IN THE EARLY DAYS of the Factory the company allowed employee's to take home reject toilet rolls and other paper product that had made their way to the Broke Room (reject paper area). This was a nice gesture but one that over the years was abused. Stories of this abuse were extensive and wide reaching, they extended far beyond the simple Toilet Roll as you will soon hear.

A good time now to add that these are only stories that may or may not have some basis of truth. At the very least they are embellished and at worst reprehensible.

A story emerged that an employee of Conversion had been stopped at the Gatehouse by a vigilant Security Guard that had spotted full cartons of Toilet Rolls on his back seat, under a blanket. Now at this stage it was still classified as a minor incident, (unbelievable in today's world) but the stupid fellow started complaining that he was being picked on and that everyone in the place did it. He then went on to name another employee who was subsequently investigated. Being on a day off, Police were sent to his home to investigate the nabbed employee's claims. Upon entering the said offender's home they spotted a room off to the left with its door ajar and loaded with Bowater product. They then went into the rear yard to find a six by six metre shed loaded floor to ceiling with the product. It was so full that they had to remove the metal sheeting to retrieve the goods. Another tale was of many employee's selling product at their local markets on a Sunday. The abuse was rampant and went way beyond the meaning of the word Pilfer.

In one reported incident, two fellows pulled up at the gatehouse requesting entry to fill up their car with free toilet paper, just like their mate who works there does.

Now various paper product pilfering was one thing, but the theft (and really that is what this must be called) went way way beyond that. In fact the theft became almost a sport within the red brick walls. The items it included were as broad as one could imagine and were best summed up by Spider's (Gerry Gee's Assistant Winderman) comment in an earlier chapter "If it ain't bolted down – its mine!" Here are some tales of the adventures that this Culture created;

JUMPIN JACK!!!

THIS STORY IS OF Spider, back when he travelled to work with me from my first home in Flowerdale. As you may remember he moved to Yea with his wife Slippery Sam to buy a small horse ranch, which we nicknamed Footrot Flats, due to its consistent flooding issue from the Yea River (Muddy Creek). It went like this;

Night shift was the same as usually for me, busily stacking Scotties on the back of number 3 Rewinder. Far from the most pleasant of jobs on night shift due to the dust and physicality. As per what regularly occurred, we were the only Rewinder running, with Gerry and Spider playing their normal game of hiding from Larry and Pat (Gold Shift Leading Hand and Supervisor) and avoiding the cleaning jobs they were meant to be doing. Gerry spent most of these times sleeping but Spider would split his time into sleeping and finding things to "Pilfer!"

Trouble was that it was my vehicle that he travelled home in, so quite often my Ute would have Pilfered goods under the tarp without my knowledge. This would infuriate me as he took advantage of the situation and put me at risk. But this particular morning pissed me off to a point where I lost it and flew off the handle at him. The morning went like this;

Nice and refreshed from his four hours of sleep Spider quickly sneaked from the locker room and clocked off himself and Gerry before Larry or Pat could catch him, and he was out the door. He would then wait for me at my Ute as I had to wait for my relief before heading home. On this particular morning I was quite tired as my work mate had a sore back and I had to do most of the heavy lifting. I did not mind this as Fred was a top bloke and would do the same for me. What pissed me off is that Spider was all take and never offered to help. All that aside that was part of the way it was so I could accept it. But what came next was 'out of line' and I had no problem letting him know so.

As we pulled out of the Northern Carpark and towards the Gatehouse all was normal but as I took a sharp left to exit past the Gatehouse and onto Ailsa Street I heard a ***"boom - boom - boom - crash"*** as the whole back of the Ute shifted in the Gatehouse direction. "F**k" I said "what the F**k was that!" I thought I had broken an axle or the tail shaft had snapped or something until Spider said Go Go, just keep going. As we continued down Ailsa Street he explained that he had acquired a Trewhella Jack and then started to describe to me what that was. I immediately cut him off and said I F**ken know what a F**ken Trewhella Jack is. (We used them in the Tyre game to lift Forklifts as they were both heavy and very close to the ground). Turning onto Middleborough Road I proceeded slowly to ensure no more damage occurred and then a kilometre up that road I pulled over to survey the damage. The Jack was a monster and had scratched the back of the tray and smashed an interior side panel which would need to be replaced and painted. Not a hugely expensive job in those days but one that would involve a considerable amount of my time to repair.

I was seething and let rip on Spider. Fortunately he was not aggressive as otherwise I am sure we would have been in a punch-up.

He offered me the Trewhella Jack as a peace offering but I refused telling him; what the hell am I going to do with that big piece of crap! The rest of the journey home was quiet, and when we reached my home in Flowerdale he asked me for a hand to lift it into his car.

I just walked off into my front door thinking "is this bloke for real!"

He had a sickie the next night, which happened to be the last night of nightshift. Not sure whether it was because of my reaction or not, but by that point I didn't really care.

NICE DROP!!!

LOCATED IN FRONT OF the Factory was the Admin Building that was idle on night shift and weekends as it was the home of the shirts and skirts we fondly named "Them". This area was where we did some training and had safety meeting, but apart from that, never went near. True 99.5% of the time but on this particular occasion the temptation was too good for Robin Hood who had caught wind that the Boardroom had just been restocked with some fine top end beverages.

Senior Management were having some guests or something so the stock was for some sort of Shindig.

But in the shadow of the night some of the lads got in through the roof of the building, dropped into the Boardroom and absconded with the lot.

International Sex Line!!!

PILFERING OCCURRED IN MANY unusual forms, but none more so than this one. As mentioned in earlier chapters in the middle of conversion (between Conversion A and B) there was a series of small offices that now housed the Nurses Station and Des Onions office. I think there were other Staff members using some other offices there for other purposes, can't remember who or what for, but there were still some that were spare / not used.

One of these offices contained an unattended phone on the wall. The only type of phones we had in those days, ones with wires attached. Now some clever cocky worked out that Telecom had a way of opening up any line to make International calls. I believe that a series of numbers were entered before the actual phone number to access this service and that each company had its own special numbers. It may have been through Telecom that this number was obtained or by an insider in the Administration Building, but either way the news got out to members on the floor.

It was very popular on night shift, and with a huge number of migrants working in conversion, you can understand why.

Now apparently this number, when used for International calls, was not registering on the Company phone bill. So from that I am gathering that it was specifically a Telecom code, and the practice went on for many months undetected. This was until some freak started dialling a London Sex Line (probably the same perpetrator of the Nurse 'Oral' Annie incident). Apparently as a "Service" this was charged separately and Bowater got the Bill. The phone and line were promptly removed and to my knowledge, as was the case with most Pilfering, the perpetrator was never apprehended.

MANY OTHERS!!!

As mentioned Pilfering came in many forms, some that are weird and some very expensive. One was of a Bobcat that was stolen from a locked wire cage when No 4 Machine was being built. Bolt cutters were used to cut through the fencing and God only knows how they got it past the Gatehouse.

Another was that a worker bought in an axel and two wheels on a drawbar to begin Night Shift. Then in the morning drove out with an entire caged trailer. All for the price of 2 slabs of beer!

The list goes on and on but this next story, I believe, put the writing on the wall for this engrained behaviour.

Unauthorized Planting (The Mini Golf Course)!!!

A RUMOUR SPREAD THROUGH the "Rumour (Paper) Mill" that a mini golf course had been established in the Admin building, just outside the Managing Directors office windows. The comment was also made that the Managing Director was furious and after blood. I only heard bits and pieces of this story and was inquisitive as to its context.

We were on Night Shift so most of the action happened during the day, as far as Admin went. I pressed Little Legs further and he told me we would hear more this evening from Pat the Shift Supervisor. At around 12-30am that evening Pat did the rounds of the Mill discussing the issue with each work group in their particular area and Smoko Hut. No 2 Rewinder was running so a large group of us were in the Smoko Hut when Pat came to speak with us. He started with what had occurred and it went like this:

A week ago or so a number of plants were put in around the Admin building to help freshen it up. This was done as the owners from England were on route to do an inspection prior to selling to the Kiwi's. Apparently the most attractive of these were planted in the area in front of the Managing Directors office window, as that was where a lot of the meetings of Upper Upper management would take place. Last evening (our first night of night shift) these plants were stolen, about 18 in total. Snoozy piped up and said (to huge laughter) "they could have turned the holes into a mini Golf Course!" Pat even had a slight smirk on his face until he realized what his role here was, and that it was taken very personally by his big boss. He continued by saying that, as we are on Night Shift, that Upper Management believed it was someone from our shift. Further they have extended an offer that if the perpetrator returned the plants that only a Warning would be given, but if not and the perpetrator was caught they would be instantly dismissed.

All in the Hut thought – Des Onion would like to hear about this, as the Union leader (in our belief) would not stand for that talk.

We later learned through a phone call Des had made to Larry (the Leading Hand) that Des had argued that the Plants were installed by non-union members, therefore not recognized as existing in the first place.

A few weeks later the plants had still not been returned and no further action was taken. "BUT" soon after that incident more security was employed and the Gatehouse Staff were now required to do Security Rounds of the whole facility. This was the beginning of the end of the Pilfering free-for-all that had gone on for many years.

A MESSAGE FROM A PAST EMPLOYEE!!!

With any company there comes a time when some pencil pusher wants to make a name for himself by strengthening the bottom line. By making the Security Staff at Bowater start bag searches was a way to cut this Pilfering down at the very least and improve the Company yield / profits.

Back to the Jagenberg!!

While describing the surrounds of the new Jagenberg I have digressed into other events that happened over all of my ten years at Bowater. I cannot promise that this will not happen again, but I can promise that any digression will be entertaining!

Due to our geographic location in the Factory, Aaron and I tended to associate more with the Conversion guys than the Mill guys. Even though we were Mill employees. One story that I will share now was born of this association and in line with the Theft theme that I have been running.

G-PACK!!

MY LOVE OF TORANA'S re-emerged when my pockets refilled. This occurred due to the great wages we were paid and me now settling in to our second home. I also worked for 'Foster Parents Plan' in Kew on my days off so my pockets were happy. This led me to rush out and impulse buy a Yellow Torana again. This one though was a four door version, a G-Pack which were nicknamed the Greek Pack due to the ethnicity of the majority of their owners.

It was not all that good though with a fair bit of rust in it that magically appeared after the fourth or fifth time that I gave it a bath. But when I spotted it in a tiny caryard on Middleborough road on my way to work I couldn't resist it and bought it the next day. Thinking back I didn't buy the car itself but the memories that it invoked. Did I mention how much I loved my 77 LX SS Torana Hatchback!

Anyway I soon grew tired of the car as it was no match for my original Torana and the novelty soon wore off. I decided to resell it and put a sign on the back window as was the way most of us did things back then. The other way was in the Trading Post 'Paper', but at this stage I was in no rush so I stuck with just the sign in the back window. Turned out that worked out OK as Dimi, the Conversion

Supervisor and brother to the two shift Forklift drivers spotted the sign and came over to the Jagenberg to ask me about it.

He too was just after the look so the rust did not over concern him, he just wanted a run about for too and from work. He handed over the cash, and I handed over the papers along with the Roadworthy Certificate and that was that – Or so I thought!

About two weeks later I received a phone call that awoke me at 2-00am from the Dandenong Police. They asked if my name was Craig Nelson, to which I sleepily and dubiously answered 'Yes' to. Then when they asked me if I owned a Yellow G-Pack registration number 123-ABC the penny dropped. Bloody Dimi had not yet lodged the paperwork to transfer the car into his name. Fortunately this was the days before Fixed Speed Camera's, Toll Roads etc, so it wasn't for traffic infringements. Turned out that they had found the car still running in a local park with no-one to be seen. They concluded that it must have been stolen from my home and taken on a joy ride or something of that nature. Made sense as the car was a magnet as far as looks go and was very easy to break into and steal.

I then had to explain that I was now not the owner and that Dimi was meant to change the name over last week. They then asked for his number, which I did not have as we were at work together all the time and I didn't really need it. Remembering again this was the pre-technology era, so no mobile phones. I asked for their number and said I would ring work and get the Conversion Supervisor that was on at the time to ring Dimi and get him to call the Police Station direct. They agreed and said they would lock up the car and do a run past at the end of their shift to check it again.

Again at 7-15am I was awoken by the Dandenong Police and was told that Dimi had not called and the car was still there. Being on Afternoon Shift it was too early to get up so after again ringing the

Conversion Supervisor that was on I asked for Dimi's number – rang him direct, told him to ring the Dandenong Cop Shop and went back to sleep. At that point I did not think to ask him why he didn't call but thought I will ask him at work later today.

What a shocking sleep I had, as after the first call I tossed and turned and it seemed as though I had not been asleep when the phone rang at 7-15am. But alas I must have been as the time seemed to pass too quickly for me not to have.

When I arrived at work that day I spotted Dimi and asked why he hadn't called the Cop Shop at 2-00am. He told me the Supervisor on Blue shift rang him with the info and he wrote the number down and fell asleep. I could not believe my ears, how in heck could you fall asleep with your car missing from the driveway and knowing that the Cops had it. I said nothing, turned around and walked away. I was so tired and grumpy I thought it best, as I might say something I would regret. With his two brothers on the forklift's that supplied my machine I let it be as they could make my life difficult.

I did ring and check with the Dandenong Cop Shop though and they told me that they made Dimi change over the name there and then. They told him that if he didn't the car would be returned to my address. I lived in Healesville around 60 kilometres away which would have given Dimi a big Tow bill.

Back to the Jagenberg!!

RUNNING THE JAGENBERG WAS a great advancement for me as I had started at Bowater at a time when it had started expanding. For 15 or so years prior to this not much had happened in the way of advancement with many Paper Mill workers holding the same position for over 10 years, waiting for advancement.

The biggest movement for promotion occurred when the 38 hour week came in, as this required the inclusion of a fifth shift (Gold Shift). So as you can imagine a 20% increase in staff opened the gates to a fair amount of promotion. An example of this was Larry (my Leading Hand) who had been a Machineman on Number 1 Machine for 20 years. Another issue that had kept the lid on the bottle for all those years prior to the inception of Gold Shift was that very few of the Leading Hands would take a promotion to Shift Supervisor. The reason for this was due to the increased responsibility and that the Supervisors role was a Staff position with no Union Representation. They also received no overtime payments for covering their absent colleague from other shifts when required to cover. Management said; "it is in your salary package!" The poor buggers also only got paid monthly, where we were paid weekly. I remember when one of the Supervisors retired and the other Supervisors had to cover his shift for months as no-one would take the job. They complained consistently until finally management put one of the Leading Hands into the position as a temporary fix.

This lead to create a situation where the job was then opened up to all staff, with or without Machine experience. This position was filled by an external Staff member, but I cannot remember where he was from. The next occurrence of this situation allowed my then Uncle "Uncle Fozzie" to apply for, and get the job. He was from the CR Lab (paper testing area). Neither of these two had ever run a Paper Machine and it must have been a huge challenge for them, especially with the characters we had in the place, who just loved to stir the pot. To their credit though these guys handled it well and eventually blended in.

Going back to the inception of the new shift, this required the creation of a new roster, and it was a masterpiece. Its duty required it to now include a fifth shift while evenly distributing weekend work and Christmas breaks. The story goes that Management worked on it for ages with many working on the project full time, but it took a guy from the floor to put it together. This gentleman created this masterpiece largely on his own and it ran over a five year period (the printed Roster that is). I was fortunate enough to reach out and contact this gentleman and in his words this is what he wrote back to me when I asked if he was the author of this complex puzzle:

> Yes Craig I designed the thing - worked it all out. There were a few problems, the shifts didn't get the same number of weekends, and then some worked less days than others. After much fiddling around managed to get all the shifts to Work same number of days per year and the same number of Saturdays and Sundays, it all had to do with the "stuff up"

> period. It was a pain but got everyone the same conditions each year. Couldn't get everyone Christmas hols every year though. Spent a lot of time working the sucker out.

A humble answer from who I remember as a soft spoken gentleman.

I on the other hand am neither humble nor soft spoken, or too bright for that matter. But what I do do well is always look for an opportunity and when I spot it grab it with two hands. I think this is partly in my DNA but also from the life experiences that attuned me to be like this. I did the same working in the Tyre Game, but there I was passed over with no help from others, and no experience behind me.

My drive to achieve also came from the fact that I had a wife and two boys to provide for, along with a hefty mortgage that reached the dizzy heights of 17.5% right when my boys were young and my mortgage was at its highest, in my third home. But unlike today we just worked harder and longer to stay afloat. It was a difficult time in my life on the one wage and there was no support in those times, you just worked harder or lost your home. So with no option in my mind, I just worked harder.

This work included my 38 hours a week at Bowater, my 20 odd hours a week at Foster Parents Plan Australia as a handyman and my small landscaping business on my days off. This kept us above water but I was always looking for more ways to get us ahead.

This desire, and the fact that we could not run the Jagenberg at speed (due to **Thump 'n' wrap!........** see past chapter of this name), gave me time to do a bit extra while the Jagenberg was running. This free time (or time at idle) gave rise to;

The Jagenbergers!!

AS MENTIONED IN THE Chapter "**Fit for Work....**" the Canteen was only open on day shift Monday to Friday. At great expense automatic vending machines were installed in Conversion 'A' canteen, which were stocked by canteen staff from the main canteen before going home for the day. As for weekends there was hardly ever any meals left and if you saw one there on Sunday,

1. You knew it was 2 days old
2. It must be bad if nobody wanted it

Now sometimes on Weekends the Mill would send someone out for Fish and Chips (in the Red Sigma Wagon) but this depended if there was any spare staff. And as for Conversion they almost never got any Fish and Chips. Apart from those facts on Night Shift people wanted fresh – not crap from a machine.

At first I started selling soft drink cans and at 70 cents each cold, which made them better priced than the vending machines at $1.00. I was able to do this as we had a fridge in our hut to keep them cold and the boys loved it because I ran a tab. To ensure a healthy profit I would buy the soft drinks in bulk at a local supermarket when they came on special. From memory I would purchase them at 33 cents per can (for Coke Fanta etc), and sometimes would get other brands for even less, which added to the variety "and The Profits!" Now I cannot take credit for thinking of this idea as it was first started by Phil Yockers, Winderman on another shift. But things in the Entrepreneurial world were about to grow and soon we had the birth of the Jagenberger!

With a distinct lack of quality food onsite on Weekends and Night Shift I was trying to work out what food could be served that was reasonably simple and yet inviting. "No concerns about what to serve the food in, as we had an endless supply of napkins and paper towel!" But what would be the best to get people in? Simple answer "Bacon!" Once you put this stuff into a pan you could smell it a mile away. The two meals that I thought would work best would be 'Egg and Bacon Rolls' and Hamburger's, which soon received the nickname "Jagenberger!" Named obviously because of the Machine Brand that Aaron and I were running while I cooked this feed for the boys.

I carefully planned the menu as I needed to create the best food I could in the easiest possible manner. Fortunately my drive to and from work (Healesville to Box Hill) took me past Lilydale and the fresh food market there. Fresh lettuce, onions (for added aroma), and tomato was available here along with fresh minced beef, bacon and eggs and bakery bread rolls. I would purchase these items fresh in most cases, but when unable to get to the markets due to work commitments I would always have hamburgers and bacon in my freezer at home.

It did take a bit of preparation as I would have to slice the tomatoes and onions, shred the lettuce and put them all into Tupperware containers for ease of serving at work. I bought one new frypan and now I was ready to go.

Any reservations about my ROI (return on investment) were put to bed on the first Saturday where I prepared and sold 30 Bacon Rolls in 30 minutes. (Could have sold more but I ran out of Bread

Rolls). 28 of these were retail sales but the other 2 went to Aaron and I for free as I sometimes needed a bit of help. Aaron was cool though as he was happy with a free Bacon Roll and a Coke for a bit of extra work.

I didn't do Hamburgers as well that day as I wanted to see how I would go. With this response though I wouldn't have any problems selling them. Turned out that doing 2 cooks per shift was a bit much and I only did that for a short amount of time. There were also bad sales days when the Fish and Chip run was done and I sold half the amount. Fortunately though with two growing boys at home the food never went to waste as they loved the Bacon Rolls especially.

Earlier I mentioned making egg and bacon rolls, but this became too finicky so I went to just Bacon to make life easier. The profits were good, and on average paid our entire home grocery bill while I was on shift. My only concern though was that my Supervisor or Leading hand would put a stop to it, as a conflict to my work. But my productivity was very good, and the cooking showed no signs of interfering with my output. A lot of this was due to Aaron being supportive (Free Feed and Coke) and the fact that the Jagenberg was a Lemon, and unable to live up to the expectations of why it was purchased.

The isolation of the Jagenberg was also a factor as we would often never see Larry or Pat for days on end, neither were interested in the Jagenberg as both were from a Machineman background. This was also the time that Number 4 Paper Machine was being constructed and a lot of interest was focussed on it. The only time I thought I would get in strife over the cooking was one Saturday morning when Mr Cogers popped his head around the corner of our hut while I was frying away. But he said nothing!

For days though I was shitting myself thinking I would get a Warning or something, but it never happened. I spoke of this fear with my Union guy (Des Onion) who told me he had not had anyone say anything about it to him. He went on further to say that the only thing he had heard about my cooking was from the boys who said they loved the food and would be pissed off if Bowater shut me down. I am not trying to say I was doing a service for everyone on shift, as my main objective was to make a quid for my family and I, but I was not hurting anyone either. That was probably why management left me alone.

Incoming!!!

AS I STATED EARLIER we were a bit isolated on the Jagenberg, as we were located in the back corner of Conversion 'A' while being classified as part of the Paper Mill. This seems ridiculous now as I am writing this, but back then there was so much of an "Us and Them" culture that we were isolated by Geography from the Paper Mill and almost culturally by Conversion.

One group that breached these boundaries were the Forklift drivers. The Drivers on our shift were Dimi's (Conversion Supervisor) younger brothers Rick and Enzo. Enzo, as I mentioned in an earlier chapter, lived around the corner from me in Seville and was always up for a chat. One day between flipping Jagenburgers he sat himself down in our hut and told me he had a great story to tell me that he had just heard from Little Legs on Number 2 Machine. Always up for a good yarn I passed him a complimentary Coke and said; I am all ears.

Enzo broke into his story, and it went like this:

With the construction of Number 4 Mill under way there was a lot of interest as to what Bowater was doing at its Box Hill plant from our major competitor Kimberly Clark. (Which I made reference to in my first book "One Simple Journey!" as on day 135 of our travels we drove past their Millicent Factory in South Australia). An unidentified helicopter had been seen circling the Box Hill Plant on numerous occasions. This helicopter was rumoured to be a spy craft from Kimberly Clark taking photos in an attempt to see what its competitor was up to. As I mentioned earlier Bowater seemed to be on an expansion mission and it appeared that Kimberly Clark was concerned about losing its market share.

So far I was Ho-hum about Enzo's story and thought it not even worthy of the free Coke that I had parted with. But alas I should not have been so hasty as the next line that came from the mouth of Enzo was that the Police were called. Not by Bowater for the intrusion but by a local neighbour. This still was not too exciting as the Neighbours were always complaining about the Paper Mill, even though they were separated from it by an 18 hole Golf Course and more importantly moved in after the Paper Mill was fully operational. No noise complaints this time but a report of the sighting of an anti-aircraft gun on the roof of Number 3 Paper Mill. Not sure how or why, but the Police launched their own helicopter to investigate the sighting and immediately called for a ground crew to be dispatched to the site as they confirmed the neighbours sighting. The ground crew immediately entered the site fully loaded with rifles and body armour. It was rumoured that Sargent Schultz (not his real name) was on the gatehouse at the time, but this is unconfirmed as the Gatehouse Attendant at the time of entry was nowhere to be seen. In fact rumoured to be hiding under his counter. The ground crew made its way to the reported site area and were shocked with what they found. In fact they did find a twin barrelled anti-aircraft gun, carefully constructed from pallet wood, cardboard and two Rewinder Cores for barrels. All painted black and strategically positioned to point over the under construction No 4 Paper Mill.

Oh Who...

Hot Summer Nights!!

AS MENTIONED IN THE last chapter the local neighbours seemed to be always complaining about the goings on at Bowater. Believed to be driven by a desire to have the facility closed down, a steady stream of complaints were always talked about by the 'Shirts and Skirts' and generally generated by the actions of the boys on the floor. This story is no exception;

Located on the roof of the Boiler House was a giant freshwater tank. Now one would have thought that the primary function of this tank was for the use of its content to be used in the creation of steam. But the boys on the floor had other ideas. They believed that its primary use was to 'keep their Beer cold!' To do this fellows would lower a six pack of beer into the chilly water on a piece of Pulp Yard wire and hook the top end of the piece of wire to the side of the tank. Now as I am writing this I realize that some would not know why a six pack and how this is possible, as today six packs come in light cardboard packs. But back then a six pack came in a plastic extrusion that kept them together. Totally environmentally unfriendly for waterways and birdlife but very effective as a way to hold and carry your Beers!

This process proved to be very effective to chill your Beers, but it also allowed others to prank their mates by removing the wire. The result meant that their owners would have to dive into the chilly exposed tank to retrieve their beloved beverages. Can you see where this is going?

In order to do this though the Beer owners would have to strip down prior to their retrieval efforts and expose themselves to the world. Not too much of a problem though as the Beer was generally chilled over summer and generally after business hours. I am told that the dip was quite invigorating also on those Hot Summer Nights.

How the heck the neighbours saw this is the part that puzzles me, as even if they could see the figures in the distance, the chilly waters would ensure that nothing of any great interest could be viewed.

ENTREPRENEURS!!

NOW I WAS NOT alone in my entrepreneurial endeavours, as it seemed as though there were many others who used their concentration of days off to pursue additional business activities. A lot had small scale business which allowed them to take on jobs as time permitted. A good occupation for this was landscape gardening which proved to be a popular choice.

One fellow was Mike Fonzerelli who started at Bowater before I did but was in Conversion until a year or so after I started. He then transferred into the Paper Mill. This was about the time my Jagenberg assistant Aaron transferred also. There were many who came over around this time, I am not sure where the gap came from, but there must have been a few retirements or something I guess. Another was Bobby Dan who I spent a fair bit of time with and we went fishing together (see chapter Spaghetti on the Jetty). Back to Mike who did a fair bit of Landscape Gardening and it must have been lucrative for him as he had a lovely home and a nice car. In this day and age you don't equate that to doing well as debt is so easy to obtain, but back then you had to be pretty solid to afford what he did. I think the ethnicity also helped as it did with many on the floor.

One such gentleman was an old ethnic fellow who lived on a main road in Blackburn, in a home which was quite run down and dilapidated. To look at him you would think that he slept under a bridge. He walked like he had Rickets and looked very ill most of the time. Upon speaking to other ethnics that worked with him they said he was super tight with his money and never spent a cent at the canteen or vending machines. ("No chance of him buying a Jagenberger or a Bacon Roll from me then!") They went on further to say that he didn't have power connected to his home and wore Bowater issued clothing 24/7. I remember one day, late in my time at Bowater when I was told that he had passed away. Apparently his nephew worked in the Factory somewhere and he along with his wife were the sole beneficiaries, as the old man never had children of his own (too expensive I guess). Aaron was in on the conversation and as he had worked in Conversion and knew where he lived, piped up and said; 'not much to inherit there – his home was a dump!' But we were then told that he actually had a string of rental properties both here and in Canada, along with a small shopping Mall in Canada also.

Another fellow was one who was close to blind (Nicknamed Blind Jimmy), not a funny story really, more tragic actually. These facts did not stop the jokes that were played on this poor fellow and here is a bit of what went on;

- Other guys on the floor would put chairs in his path which he would bump into.
- They would dangle pieces of paper on a piece of string and touch him on the head. He would wave frantically thinking there was a fly or a bug on him.
- They would move his clock card to another spot so he could not find it, and not be able to clock on.

They were terribly mean to him which was not justified. Yes, he was a super tight ass but that was no reason to treat him so badly.

To keep working with his near blindness he had set a routine and a path that allowed him to get to work, clock on and get to his workstation with relative ease. He was able to do this as the blindness had come on over the many years that he had worked there.

Jimmy also sat in exactly the same spot each day in the Conversion canteen to eat his lunch (which he 'always' brought with him). On one occasion someone had stuck a five cent piece to the table with Araldite where Jimmy would sit. During the Lunch Break the whole canteen watched and laughed as Jimmy attempted to secretly pick up the five cent piece. Unaware that everyone was watching, and in fact laughing at him, he worked on that five cent piece for his entire lunch break.

When on his job, which was manually packing toilet rolls into a box, he was excellent at it. But his time was limited as the inception of Automatic Packing Machines would require him to learn more skills. Something that this fellow, with his condition, could never achieve. The company caught wind of his issues and the Union could only fight for a decent severance pay for him, which I believe they got. It was sad really as I heard that during his dismissal he sobbed. With his pride broken he protested repeatedly over and over how ashamed he would be to tell his family that he could no longer provide for them.

Again I have digressed slightly here and will get back on track.

A fellow who did a bit of Union work around the place and who worked on the Rewinders on Green Shift was a chap named Morris Stevens. Now Morris had a talent for fixing cars that was only surpassed by his talent for breeding. He told me he only had five children, but every time I took my car to his place in Woori Yallock, to get looked at, it appeared that he had twenty or so. They were everywhere, no shoes on and always looked like they had been swimming in the local creek. Don't get me wrong, they were not neglected, they were just super active. (No Ritalin in the cupboard I guess – If it existed back then!) Morris was always tinkering with Cars, and his hands, no matter what time of day or night were always cracked with ingrained black oil in them. He loved it. The problem with Morris was that he didn't make a lot of money out of fixing cars as he never charged enough. Back then, like today, there were always plenty of people around who were happy to take advantage of your good nature.

I bumped into his old Winderman work mate, Ron Rascal, a few years back who told me that Morris had Parkinson's and was not that good. He also said that he had borrowed his car and never returned it. 'Not sure what all that was about.'

Another entrepreneur was Dimi's younger brother Rick, who owned a small Fruit shop on the Maroondah Highway East of Lilydale. He had this for a while before selling it to another fellow at Bowater. (A story for another chapter)

After selling the Fruit Shop Rick decided he would go into the Car Rental business. He set up a yard in Bayswater and created his business model around the budget market. No that's not 'Budget Car Rentals', that's the dodgy cheap shit boxes to battler's budget market. From all accounts he did a roaring trade and this was reflected in the fact that he quite often didn't bother coming to work at Bowater. The other Shift Forklift drivers would whinge all the time about him. It must have been tough for Dimi as his Supervisor and brother. Sadly I found out recently that Rick passed away at a quite young age.

Sad, as he was quite a talented fellow just rough around the edges. He was also the Master Card Player in my earlier chapter.

Driven by Eight Day Week!!

THIS ENTREPRENEURIAL TREND WAS driven mostly by the Eight Day breaks that we received on a number of our shift rotations. This block of time was used by most for R and R, as it was intended, but some like myself could not help but to use it to get ahead in life. I chose Landscaping as a way to make some extra bucks as I enjoyed doing it on the new homes I purchased and others in the Paper Mill had made a go of it with good success.

I started with a neighbour's place who hired me to do some paving and it grew from there. Another reason for me doing Landscaping was the ease and abundance of natural resources that we had at hand and more to the point the price. I remember in the 90's buying used railway sleepers for $1.50 each. I also remember recently enquiring about the same product and being quoted $75-00 to $120-00 each depending on quality. I believe this to be a reflection of how we are selling off these resources to resource poor and highly populated countries.

NEEDS AND GREED'S!!

ALTHOUGH A POPULAR WAY to make an extra quid or two, not everyone was into giving up their Eight Day breaks to work hard. Most relied on overtime to achieve this and the place was full of people who would do anything to get a chunk of it. As we were all on a 24 hour rotating shift overtime was dished out in 4 hour slabs to cover for missing staff or extra work. This was paid at double time so you earned as much on the 4 hours of overtime as you did for an entire days work, or more if you got called in! The call in rate was a half hour at double time and you even got a free taxi to work if you asked for it. Even more lucrative were some of the Electrical staff and engineering staff who would receive 10 hours call in if on days off and got the phone call.

The title of OT King was one that was highly sort after and the most joked about, as some blokes went crazy trying to get the extra hours. The only place that they were not as keen was on Scotties stacking, as this was a lot harder than most of the jobs. But some of the older guys were so hungry for the OT that this shitty job didn't even stop them. One OT King was Seth Azure (Little Legs mate in the Boxing era) who would do just about anything for the extra hours. He also pushed his opinion around a bit when he thought others were getting OT when he thought he should have been asked first. It made no difference to him how legitimate someone's claim to OT was, he would bend the rules and manipulate the system to his advantage all the time. The greed for overtime was not limited to the Paper Mill, as Conversion also had its players who would do anything for the extra hours at the great rate. And with that, where there is someone blinded by greed, there is always someone who will take advantage. This leads to the story of;

The Generous Supervisor!!

IN THE POSITION TO allocate overtime as required Petro the Conversion 'A' supervisor was particularly generous to Jose, a machine operator with a hunger for overtime. Now Jose thought highly of Petro, his Supervisor, as he was consistently given overtime on afternoon shift by him. This meant that Jose would finish work at 3-00am. Little did Jose know that it was not because he was a nice fellow and a good Supervisor that this occurred. In fact what was happening was that Petro would dish out the overtime to Jose and then slip around to his home and dish out a bit to Jose's misses in the four hours. This apparently went on for years until eventually the cheating couple decided to be together and announced their intentions to poor Jose. All that overtime and hard work only to lose his wife and half his home in the process. I am sure the hourly rate did not cover that!

TAKING A BREAK!!

AS PART OF OUR role running the Jagenberg Rewinder we were occasionally required to run number 1 Rewinder, as we were still the second Rewinder Crew. The purchase and installation of the Jagenberg Rewinder was meant to put an end to the number 1 and 2 Rewinders as they were old and in the case of No 2 Rewinder quite unsafe. I say unsafe as it was very tight and required a lot of awkward manual handling.

Having to go and run No 1 Rewinder was a nuisance for me on weekends as it meant I could not cook for the boys. The first time it happened I was caught off guard and came into work with all my ingredients to cook "Jagenbergers", it was our first day back after an eight day break. From then on if I was to start a rotation on a Saturday or Sunday after a break I would ring before going in to check if we were on the Jagenberg or not. Fortunately it only happened once or twice and I did get to use the Jagenberg Hut fridge so nothing went to waste. With two young boys at home all the fresh produce including the Hamburger's, Bacon etc did not last long, and only a few bread rolls went stale. Even these went to the local wildlife and birds that made short work of them.

The job we were running on No 1 Rewinder on this particular Saturday was a wax based paper that I think was used as surgical sheets or the like. Not exactly sure of the end use but it was a slow running product that was quite strong. This ensured an easy workload and being the weekend we quite enjoyed the pace as it gave us heaps of time to tell stories and have a laugh. I must say it was good not to be trying to do two jobs at once on the weekend and I was having quite a relaxing day. In fact we even got Fish and Chips, as there was a spare guy in the Paper Mill who Larry instructed to do the honours. The day was pleasant and it was good to catch up again with Bruce (who was still First Boy on No 1 Paper Machine) along with his new assistant Bary who had transferred from Conversion 'A".

On the Sunday we were having a good time again with work running smoothly and the stories running freely. But this was all about to change as you will soon read;

Bruce was in a super jovial mood and decided that he would give his old mate Craig a bit of a rib tickle. Now, as I described earlier, Bruce was a brick of a man with forearms the size of most people's upper thighs, due to his previous occupation as a solid plasterer. So his rib tickles were more intense than his laugh (which I can only describe as the sound a Hyena being kicked in the guts). With this in mind as Bruce lunged at me with those sausage fingers I jumped up and headed towards the Hut door. But as I did this Bary thought it would be funny to retard my exit by blocking my pathway. With Bary sitting on the bench and his legs propped up on the front bench my only exit was now severely obscured. I now had two options;

- Push my way past Bary or,
- Take a savage Rib Tickling from 'the Beast' Bruce

So really I had no choice and Bary was going to have a struggle to keep me there. As I pushed against Bary's legs there was roars of laughter from all in the Hut as Bruce got hold of my ribs and went to work. I am not sure what was more painful, Bruce's grip or my uncontrollable laughter that was more a cry for help than a laugh. With all this noise, laughter and action going on no-one noticed that Bary's left leg was buckling under the strain of holding me back with Brutus Bruce ripping into me. It wasn't until Bruce backed off me a bit that we heard Bary's screams of pain and his pleas for us to stop as his leg was trapped. Turns out that it was pretty bad with Bary in tears as we untangled. As he tried to stand his left leg just gave way and it was obvious that he had done some damage.

The mood on Number 1 machine changed dramatically and it was decided that it would be best to make it into a workplace accident so Bary could be taken to a doctor. Technically it was a workplace accident but not one that the 'Shirts' would look too kindly on. So a story was quickly invented and with all in agreeance Larry (Shift Leading Hand) was called over to get Bary off to a doctor. With Bary carted off to the doctors the mood was sombre for the rest of the shift.

The next day (Monday) we all arrived at work to the news that Bary had broken his leg and would be on Compo for at least six weeks. No surprise that we were all concerned for him, and upon calling he was angry with us all as, although he would be paid, he would not receive weekend penalties. A little unfair really as he made the choice to stop my exit and thought it quite funny to do so "initially!"

YOU WON'T CON THE FRUITERER!!

WITH BARY BEING SO pissed off at being short a few bucks we all decided to have a whip around and chip in a bit to help him with the bills. But Bary was also working on a plan of his own and we soon learned that Rick the forklift driver had sold him his small fruit shop on the Maroondah Highway East of Lilydale. (This is now a residential estate – the fruit shop was roughly where Tudor Village Drive Lilydale is today)

Bary did not seem to be a 'Fruit and Veg shop' kind of guy, but as the Cash was 'said to be good' and Rick letting him have it free for a month to get a taste for it, Bary jumped at the chance. This meant that all the cash he made for the first month would get him through until he could work full time again.

Turned out to be a reasonably good earner and gave Bary a steady income even after he came back to work. He would employ someone to help his wife in the shop on a casual basis and work there himself on his days off. It also allowed Rick to free up his time to pursue his passion of the Budget Car Rental game which he had not long got into. This was a great relief to his colleagues on the other shifts as Rick would now turn up for work more regularly.

Dodgy Compo!!

IT WOULD NOT HAVE been the 80's without a solid scattering of Dodgy Compo Claims and at Bowater it was no different. Those not of the era may remember a scene in 'Wog Boy' Movie that captures the mood magnificently.

I have been reminded of a few tales by an ex-employee I worked with and I will start with his stories to get you in the mood;

The first was a Conversion 'A' fellow who had taken Compo after apparently badly hurting his back lifting 'broke' into a broke bin (Broke is the name given to paper of no further use that would go back into the mix via the Broke Room). He had visited his own doctor and was given two weeks off to then be re-assessed. This was normal practice, as the company would allow a maximum of two weeks prior to seeing the Company appointed Doctor. Difference in this case was that while on the two weeks Compo he headed to Lake Eildon with his Jet Boat. Then to add insult to the injury he tried to put in another claim after crashing his Jet Boat and breaking his leg. "Claim Denied!!!!!!!"

The second was a Paper Mill boy who, while on holidays, contracted a disease from a low cost St Kilda Hooker. On his return he lodged a Compo claim stating that he would not have been there if the Company had not made him take the holidays. "Claim Denied!!!!!!!"

The third was again a Paper Mill gentleman who claimed that he had 'Tunnel Vision' which was caused by the bad paper dust in the Paper Mill. He claimed that this had sent him close to blind. But one clever Day Shift Supervisor caught him out when he placed a $2-00 note to the side of the walkway on route to the Nurses Station. While escorting him to the Company Doctor the guy spotted it from 50 metres away! "Claim Denied!!!!!!!"

Oh Me Back!!

THE CATCHCRY OF THE No 3 Rewinder was that of "Oh Me Back!" As the stacking of Scotties was one of the most consistent physically demanding jobs in the Paper Mill. Personally I did not find it difficult and believed that doing Roll Towel as Second Boy on Number 1 machine was far more demanding (that was where I had my back injury). To my surprise after I hurt my back I was told that prior to the five shift roster they had two men doing this job, which, to me, confirmed my belief. Most of the other shifts would lend assistance in the form of a spare man to this job when available and No 1 Mill was running this product. I described the process in an earlier chapter **Back to the "Roll Change"** But not my Leading Hand Larry, as I was not popular with him and he always had his pets that he would look after.

I found stacking Scotties easier as you stayed warm because the work was at a consistent pace. Whereas the 2nd Boy was hot and cold work and you were always rushed when running Roll Towel, especially when inexperienced. The job required far more skill and when you got it wrong those seven feet high Roll Towel reels were very hard to manually turn.

All that aside the Stacking of Scotties was widely perceived as the hardest of work in the Paper Mill and in so was the target area for those wanting a few weeks off with a quick cry of **Oh Me Back!!....**

Lucky Escape!!

NOW NOT ALL ACCIDENTS that occurred in the Factory were from skylarking or Dodgy Claims, and the Paper Mill especially could be a very dangerous place to work. There were a number of serious accidents that occurred and the one of Dom Furr was one that sticks in my head as one of the worst.

The Plant was generally a 24/7 operation with the exception of Christmas where I believe the plant was closed down for two days. Now in Conversion this was not too difficult, but in the Paper Mill a lot of work went into cleaning for restart. It was also one of the only times that the whole place could get a thorough clean. I mean a real thorough clean. Conversions clean down was a dry clean down with dust being the biggest hazard. And what a Hazzard it was, the paper dust was absolutely all consuming and required a minimum of a dust mask and eye goggles, just to see and breath. In some confined areas mechanical breathing apparatus was required, similar to that used by the Fire Brigade. The Paper Mill had a combination of both Wet and Dry, with the Rewinder area following similar procedure's to Conversion while the Paper Machine was mainly Wet Cleaning with high pressure hoses. There were some dust areas on the Paper Machine, mainly in the drying areas and the top of the Yankee

Hoods (Big main Drying Cylinder and generally Gas fired hoods). On Christmas Shutdown these areas were intensely cleaned, as it was the only guaranteed time that this could be done. I cannot remember how long prior to the two day Christmas break we were shut down for but I tend to recall it being at least a day or two.

Now dust was not the only consistent thing that required cleaning, and wet pulp also provided it unique challenges. It built up in some areas worse than others and although the machine operators would keep cleaning these spots at every opportunity during normal running, there were some spots that only got a proper clean on Shutdowns.

Another area that was crucial to be cleaned was inside all the Hydro Pulping Machines. If this was not done thoroughly then the pulp would dry solid and potentially cause damage to the motors that drove them on restart.

The accident of Dom Furr happened in this area as he was the Stock Prep attendant on Black shift with Uncle Fozzie being his Shift Supervisor. From memory Uncle Fozzie had not been in the job for all that long prior to the Christmas Shutdown. So I would say it was either the very late 80's or very early 90's. Now Dom, who was a very fit fellow, worked alone in the area, unlike No 1 and 2 Stock Prep. The shift I believe was afternoon shift and as no-one had seen Dom at the meal break around 7-00pm and for an hour or so after the then Machineman on Number 3 brought his absence to the attention of Uncle Fozzie and his Leading Hand. The search began and all knew that it was not in Dom's DNA to sneak off and have a sleep, and definitely not without letting someone know. Then the First Boy on No 3 Machine did a check around the Hydro Pulper as he had found a High Pressure Hose shooting around in that area unattended a few hours prior. At the time he just thought someone had set it up to wet an area down by wedging it between pipes and then going off to other jobs. Not something that was either recommended or done often, but had been known to happen. But when he heard Dom was missing he just had a feeling that this may have something to do with it.

His suspicions were confirmed as he peered into the inspection window that was located on the side of the Hydro Pulper, as he thought he could see a work boot. His heart skipped a beat as he saw it and bellowed out to his 2nd Boy to quickly get Uncle Fozzie or the Leading Hand. Normally you could not just yell out from this distance, but with no machines running the 2nd Boy got the message and by the tone of his Work Mates voice he knew to hurry. Within a minute half the Paper Mill crew were on the spot and upon inspecting down into the Hydro Pulper through the opened top hatch they spotted blood on one of the cutting blades which lit up in the torchlight.

This sent a shudder down the spine of all in attendance as they feared that no-one could survive a fall onto such sharp and hard machinery that was designed to smash pulp to pieces. But the constant calling of Dom's name brought him to, and a faint cry for help could be heard. That was the simple part – now was the challenge of how to extract Dom for his twisted wedged position, in his injured state. The team, with the help of the Box Hill Fire Brigade and Shift Fitters, managed to pull enough of the panels away to reach Dom after almost three long hours. In fact Dom was only extracted around 10-30pm which was 30mins before the next shift (my shift) was to start the night shift. He had been in there, badly injured for over four hours. The 1st Boy though it was around 5-30pm – 6-00pm when he turned off the hose so it could have been six or more hours that Dom was there.

We found out the next day that Dom, although severely injured would make a full recovery. It was also said that it was his fitness level that had most probably saved his life.

The poor 1st Boy took it particularly hard as he felt he should have checked at the time of turning the hose off. But while visiting Dom in hospital he was reassured by Dom that he was the one responsible, as he was working alone and told no-one what he was doing.

Nightmare Ending!!

WHILE APPROACHING THE CLOCK card area to clock on for dayshift, on this particular day, I noticed that the boys in Number 2 Hut were all sitting soberly with their heads tilted downwards. Not unusual for night shift, but highly unusual for the end of night shift, as the boys would generally be upbeat about it being time to go home. It was also unusual in the fact that the area was still dusty and messy and appeared that no 'end of shift' cleaning had taken place. After clocking on I made my way back towards the Jagenberg and decided to pop my head in and say hi to the boys on Number 2 Machine. Snoozy, Simon and Little Legs were in there by this stage and were in the midst of being told of the tragic events of that evening.

For a while they had been having trouble on Number 2 machine with the paper not wrapping onto the Corebar after a blade change. This created a lot of work and mess requiring the second boy to get under the Corebar and Reel drum area and pull the unattached paper out as it quickly piled up. The problem was so bad that any spare members in the Paper Mill would be dragged over to help on the blade change in anticipation of the struggle ahead.

Now would be a good time to explain the process again as it will give a better understanding of the events that unfolded. Looking at enclosed pictures of the machines will also help to visualize what occurred on that dreaded night. I will try to explain in broad terms to keep the explanation of the process brief (as some may find it boring), but detailed enough so as those interested can follow.

It goes like this;

The paper starts its life as pulp, (in a large variety of forms) which is dropped into a pulping vat (Hydro Pulper) to be made into a liquid mash. This mash is pressure sprayed onto what is called a wire (some 3-4 metres wide). This wire (similar to flywire but far more tightly woven) is the start of where the water is extracted from the mix to eventually turn it to paper. Remembering that this sheet is over three metres wide, the paper (in its earliest form) is picked up by a felt (called a pickup felt – strangely enough) that is a continuous piece of material fitted over a set of rollers (some of which are called suction rollers – removing more water). All running at speed, the paper attaches to the felt and is taken through a series of rollers, secondary felts and onto the Yankee. All the while having more moisture drained from it.

The Yankee is a huge metal reel (I guess, from memory, to be about three metres in height or perhaps more) that is the main dryer of the paper. Encompassing the Yankee are its Gas Fired Hoods. The paper then hits a blade that strips it from the Yankee cylinder (similar to a giant paint scraper) and into the After Dryers (again a series of felts on high speed rollers). The paper then reaches the Corebar area where it is attached to the Corebar (like a toilet roll on Steroids).

Now the part where this story has its origins is created when the Blade is changed. The Blade is changed because being constantly in contact with the Yankee surface it wears, and this can allow the paper to penetrate the point of scrape on the Blade. Which in turn creates a bubble like lump in the finished paper product (called a blade mark).

To change the blade is not as simple as just pulling it out from its position on the Yankee Cylinder.

It goes like this;

With all three Machine crew members in position the Machineman drops the Pick-up Roll away from the wire, which breaks the flow of the paper and causes the paper to drop into a pit below the Wire. All this process has to occur, promptly and smoothly, as the pit is not huge and if it overflows the mess can take considerable effort and time to remove. With the paper now not going through the felts or over the Yankee, the First Boy can remove the old blade and with the assistance of the Second Boy can insert the new blade. Very hot, quite dark, noisy and dusty, this is not a very pleasant job and one that I hated doing on the few times I did it on training on Number 1 Machine.

With the Blade now changed the process of getting the paper back onto the Corebar begins. The Machineman presses the lever to move the Pick-up Roll back to the position where it can accept the paper. The paper then flows through the Rollers/Felts and over the Yankee where it hits the new Blade and drops into another pit. This pit from memory was bigger than the pit on Number 1 Machine and was made so because of the issues that a small pit on Number 1 Machine had caused in the past (refer chapter "Crack to the Rack"). Now the paper has to be manually fed into the After Dryers, and a small jet of water is used, that is set up to hit the Yankee at the Blade point about a foot into the side of the paper sheet. This creates a cut that allows the First Boy to grab that first foot of paper (Called the 'Tail' from memory) and toss it through the After Dryers. (It would be impossible to feed the whole 3-4 meter sheet through – and even if you could the pile of Broke would be impossible to clear). After being coaxed through the After Dryers the Tail then reaches the Corebar area, and this is where our tragic Night Shift tale re-commences.

With the Tail paper quickly mounting on the floor at the end of the After Dryers, the Corebar is dropped onto the Reel Drum which proceeds to spin the Corebar at a rate of approximately 200 metres per minute. The Reel Drum is driven by Electric motor and the Corebar is just a Heavy Metal Roll encased in Cardboard (for removal to make a Reel of Paper – imagine it as the shape of a Giant Toilet Roll) and bearings to allow it to roll on the Reel Drum (it is also over 3 metres long – in fact with the end pieces to pick it up with the Overhead Crane it would be over 4 metres long and weigh over a tonne I imagine). Upon researching to jog my memories of things I read this article;

> In 2011, the world's largest and fastest woodfree-producing paper machine was started-up at the Zhanjiang Chenming mill in China. During its first operational year, it achieved on several occasions a new world speed record. In November 2012, the recorded speed was 1,808 m/min.

Thank goodness this machine was not running at that speed as the accident would surely have been fatal.

Again with the Tail spitting out of the After Dyers and onto the ground and the Corebar spinning at full speed the Machineman would grab a chunk of this tail and pass it to the First Boy who was on the other side of a group of rolls (won't go into details on these) where he would throw it into the "Nib" of the Corebar/Reel Drum. Now the "Nib" is probably one of the most dangerous parts of the Machine for humans as it is where a lot of activity and manual interaction takes place. After going through the Nib, the paper has to catch up to the speed of the machine. While this is occurring the Second Boy is generally pulling the piling up 'Tail' away from beneath the Reel Drum area in preparation for the First Boy who would hit an air shoot leaver that would blow the Tail into the front Nib and wrap the Corebar. The Machineman would then (on the signal from his First Boy) engage the Tail Cutter Slide at the Yankee which would make the Cutter Slide go to the back of the machine, which in turn would grow the Paper Tail from One Foot wide, progressively to full Reel width.

BUT! as they were having so much trouble getting the paper to wrap into the Corebar after Blade changes this process was continually taking an excessive amount of time. The worry was always that the Pit, under the Yankee and Blade area, would overflow creating hours of extra work. It was later revealed this created anxiety in the Boys on the Machine and led to short cuts and "not so safe" practices taking place. Now back to where Snoozy, Little Legs and Simon were being told the horrible story of the injury to Ben (2nd Boy) on Red Shift:

No 2 Papermachine - The NIB is the danger point marked here. Anything that goes in here comes out the other side. The Hut pictured here at the bottom right was for Smoking and could comfortably hold four - five workers, but regularly there was eight or more when the stories were flying!

With the Blade changed and the Tail fed through the "Nib" of the Corebar/Reel Drum, two boys from the Rewinder were assisting by clearing the Tail sheet to allow the First Boy to blast (with the shoot of compressed air) the Tail into the Nib and wrap into the Corebar. But as usual this was proving to be an exhausting exercise that seemed to be going on and on. To assist the sheet going into the Nib a practice of flicking glue onto the Corebar at the point where the

Tail should wrap was engaged. This was one of those unsafe practices that was being employed by the Machine crews to expedite the process. Although not condoned by Management, they were well aware that it was occurring. How could they not with the stray glue hitting every item within a five metre radius of its intended destination, and setting hard over the days, weeks and perhaps months that this practice was being employed.

It should be explained again here that the Nib is the entry point created by the two surfaces of the Corebar and Reel Drum touching and running at speed. The exit point of this is safe but the Nib will consume anything that enters its grasp and quickly spit it out the other side. This included stray Paint Brushes that were used to dispense the glue and on this dreaded evening a number of Bens fingers as he was dragged into the Nib (while flicking the glue). With Blood shooting and his fingers passing out the other side all in attendance were horrified and obviously traumatized by the events.

Ben's blood-curdling screams were heard by the Leading Hand and Supervisor above the noise of the Machine, and they were quickly in attendance. The two Rewinder boys who were pulling out the Tail just below the accident had blood splatter on them and were then asked to retrieve the pieces of Ben's hand. One of them almost fainted when asked, while Leo, who immediately understood the importance of the task mucked in and found the three partial fingers in the paper, glue and dust. Inside the Hut the First Aid attendant, who arrived in minutes, described Ben's hand as looking like someone holding a handful of Spaghetti. Ben was rushed to Hospital and that is where they were at with the story, as no-one had any updates as to how he was at this stage.

We later that day found out (as we were on Day Shift) that they had successfully re-attached Ben's fingers but there was significant damage and his road to recovery would be a lengthy process.

Ben did physically recover, to a certain extent, but his physical capabilities in that hand was hugely reduced. The biggest issue was his mental state, as Ben was a young father who was now limited in his ability to provide for his family. He suffered horrific Nightmares that eventually led to his marriage breaking down and him suffering serious depression. He came back to work on Day shift in the 'Stores', but all who knew him concurred that he was not the same Ben.

High Interest in the Jagenberger!!

I WAS VERY FORTUNATE to be running the Jagenberg Rewinder as it did give me a relatively comfortable job that allowed me to cook up the Jagenbergers for the boys, and this allowed me to top up our family funds. Also having days off in clumps allowed me to do a second job and run my small Landscaping business. The emphasis for me to do all this was not born out of greed but need, as in the 1990's our mortgage hit a high of 17.5% and only came down to around 10% by the end of 1993. That was tough on me personally, and even though I was young it was very draining. The only shining light was a fantastic holiday that our family had to Sunny Queensland in the winter of 1992.

Landing Sunny Side Up!!

WE ALL PILED INTO our 1978 V8 HZ Kingswood and we were off. The boys were very excited as we would be visiting the fabulous theme parks that Queensland offered. We were going to all three, as Movie World had just opened and the boys were keen to see all their favourite characters in "real life". Ironically I had visited SeaWorld at about their age, where I got to feed a Seal and my mother got to feed a Dolphin from a diving board. It was not a Theme Park back then and from memory it was a couple of big swimming pools side by side on the Nerang River called Marineland. I was about five years old so it must have been the late 60's.

It was a long trip in those days (I am back in the 90's now) and we took our time, visiting a few of the major towns along the way. It was a pleasant trip until we arrived at the Riviera (our pre-booked accommodation) that we had booked for a week. As soon as we opened the door to our room the floor appeared to be moving. Heaps and heaps of Cockroaches, 'this was disgusting!' There was no way I was going to have my family stay in a place like this so I was straight back to the office demanding a refund. They were not going to give me our money back until I told them I had photos and would take them to the press (which I didn't).

They then offered me an 80% refund, which I gladly took just to get the heck out of there.

Now we had to find another place to stay with no notice, as it was now mid-afternoon and the boys were restless. We found a suitable place in Southport, that was clean and tidy but it was a bit away from the action. If the action meant the scurry of Cockroaches we were happy to be a bit away from it. We had a great night's sleep and were ready for a big day. We got ready to go out for breakfast and as we walked towards the carpark we encountered another problem "NO CAR!" We could not believe it as our holiday was turning into a disaster. We called the police who took two hours to come and they basically said they will keep an eye out for it, and that was it.

By lunchtime I was so pissed off that I decided to go for a walk and see if I could find a Car Hire mob. As my anger turned to pure determination, and I rounded a bend in the street – there it was! Our beloved HZ Holden was sitting on the side of the road two blocks away with the driver's door opened but the car was fully intact. My first thought was, those coppers must have driven past it. On closer inspection the only damage was to the door lock (which looked as though it had a screwdriver bashed into it) and the Sheepskin seat covers were missing.

I did not have my keys with me (well I had no car) and was about to run back to the unit when I noticed that the key ignition was also damaged. I grabbed it to see if I could turn it and I could. I then pushed in my Kill switch, located up under the dash, and she started first shot. If not for that Kill Switch we would most probably never have seen our beloved HZ again.

The family was over the moon when I pulled into the unit complex driveway and honked my La Cucaracha air horns. It signalled a change in fortune that led to a fantastic holiday and a desire to start a new life in a new state – Sunny Queensland!

This desire was not directed at making a new life on the Gold Coast as this place was far too commercialized for our liking. The area we fell in love with was the Bribie Island area, where we spent almost two weeks exploring. But the icing on the cake, and the one that sealed our desires was that our youngest who suffered bad Bronchial Asthma, (especially over winter) showed not a single symptom in this sub-tropical climate. (Again over Winter).

MENTALLY GONE!!

Back at work and the Jagenberg provided a good job, but I found it hard to get back into the groove. Our family plans were to one day move to Sunny Queensland, but the economic climate in Victoria especially, made it difficult to sell homes (not to mention the national Interest Rates). Life got back to normal but I had mentally shifted and I found my ability to focus on 'working - working - working' was waning.

Learning to Focus!!

IN ORDER TO TRY and reset my focus on my job after such a fabulous trip I cut back on my cooking to just the Weekends and concentrate more on improving my skills. The boys did complain a bit about not having the smell of the Jagenbergers wafting over the factory, but the truth was that sales were slowing anyway, as I think the economics of the time were biting a bit.

With this extra time on my hands I decided to take advantage of the fabulous Training programs that Bowater offered their employee's. I decided that studying Papermaking was a great way to do this as it was pitched as a way to formalize the skills that we learnt on the job. As my next job in my line of promotion was Machineman, and I had only had limited exposure to the Paper Machines, this would also help me if I made the move to that position.

Truth was that my heart was not in it and my family and I were very keen to head north, for what we saw as a brighter future. But to keep wanting this while unable to sell our home at a decent price would send me insane. I decided that we should put our Queensland plans on hold and distract myself by focusing on my career at Bowater.

The training program to formalize our on-job training was a fantastic opportunity and would qualify its participants as "Papermakers". So I signed up and started the studying.

Starting the Studying was something many did, but I would later learn (as I am writing this book) that only three guys completed the TAFE studies. Here is the note I received from one of those three Gentlemen;

> Deric Farroll wrote;
> Hi Craig, Think there was 3 of us that did the course and finish it. I know that at the start there was a lot of guys started it, all from different sections. I was in maintenance, the other 2 were in stock prep, I finished it first, Don Greymore pm3 stock prep was next to finish it. William Thomson from stock prep on pm2 completed it. There was 7 books, each with a number of modules in them. When you finally finished them we were offered an advanced section, there was 3 books and each one had a series of modules in them. The total number of modules was 36 for the whole course, each required a written up report also each one had an online test. I reckon that the 3 of us encouraged each other over the period of the course.
>
> Hope this help you

The Golden Handshake!!

FUNNY WHAT HAPPENS IN life, as now that I had resolved myself to my fate of a few more years as a Jagenberg Rewindman, an opportunity came temptingly close.

Just before the Jagenburg Rewinder was installed and Number 4 Paper Machine was built Bowater was increasing its market share and the future looked bright. But in the early 1990's things started to change and Bowater seemed to be going backwards even after its huge investment on this site.

Some of the reasons this may have occurred were;

- The economics of Australia was changing around this time with the Hawke/Keating Government de-regulation of the Australian economy.
- The Recession that ravaged the country during the 1980's
- The reduced cost of shipping and the influx of Imported Goods

Whatever the reason it 'was what it was' and the feeling around the workers on the Factory Floor was a little glum.

In late 1992 Bowater decided that it needed to trim the workforce and would be offering 10 redundancy packages to it most senior

Paper Mill workers. I think that Bowater's reasoning for this was really to keep younger workers, but this was not always the case as some of its young employees were up there in Seniority. Having to be ratified by the Union meant that they could not pick and choose who they wanted to go, and who they wanted to stay.

Now this would be a game changer for me as I had been with the company almost ten years by this stage and may get close to an offer here. The process was that Mill workers would have to put up their hand for a Golden Hand Shake and then the 10 most senior of those would be chosen.

Now with the way things were in the economy, you would think that this would be a long list. But it turns out that many of these older guys realized that if they took a Package they may not get another job elsewhere, so they chickened out. I, on the other hand saw it as a Golden Opportunity to fulfil my families dreams of moving to Queensland and a better life, especially for my youngest son with Bronchial Asthma.

But alas the same outcome looked likely as did with the inability to sell our family home at a decent price and I came in at Number 13 from memory.

Unlucky for some Number 13, and it also appeared it was for me, until a few days later when two of the first ten dropped out and decided to stay with Bowater. Sitting at Number 11 now I became optimistic that another would drop out and we would be off to Queensland.

With decision day fast approaching though Don Finder, who was much more senior to me (but still a Rewinderman) was looking like he would take the Package to Leave. This was so disappointing to me as I thought of all the 10 he was the most likely to pull out. Then with two weeks to go I made a brave move and decided to put our Family home on the market, to forge ahead with our Queensland plans. This was the first time in my life that I took a risk of this magnitude, and with the economy so flat I was very nervous. But my Grandad Joe who was my life mentor, even in his death, told me that "An Eagle Cannot Soar while Tethered" and that I should always back myself. But I was 29 years old with a large Mortgage, two Sons and a dependant Wife. "What am I Doing?" But my Grandads voice saying "Back Yourself!" played over and over in my head and I forged ahead.

Then on returning to work from an eight day break I was asked to go up to the Admin building to meet with Mr Cogers and Mr Vardy. I was shitting myself as the time had now past for the acceptance of the Golden Handshakes and it must be something else. My fears were heightened when I arrived at their Meeting Room and Des Onion was there to meet me. I said to him – 'What about my Relief' I have to let him go home? Des replied that Alan had been told to stay back for an hour while this meeting occurred. I remained extremely worried until Des told me it was about the Golden Handshake just before we entered the Meeting Room.

Switching from almost pissing my pants to sheer ecstasy, I tried desperately to contain the excitement from appearing on my face. We all sat down around the same table that I was interviewed at, some 10 years earlier, and the offer was put to me. Trying not to act too eager I asked 'What happened to Don?' To which Mr Cogers said; "He pulled out after we closed off!" (In a manner which made me think he was none too happy with Don).

At that Des stated; Well you got what you wanted Young Fella – what will it be?

Without hesitation I said "it's been nice working with you guys!" with a cheeky grin on my face. Mr Cogers said with a wry smile, "Cocky Bastard!" (He had no idea the knots that my stomach was in)

Then with that Mr Vardy asked me to come and have a chat with him as he wanted to make sure I was Ok. You may remember that

Mr Vardy was a family friend of my In-Laws and seemed genuinely concerned with my decision.

Mr Vardy and I took a walk and sat out the side of the Admin building in the shade of the lovely garden surrounds. He asked me repeatedly if I was sure I wanted this. He went on to say that at 29 I could forge a great career at Bowater as I had many working years in front of me. But I was extremely sure that I was making the right decision and knew that with the Redundancy package that I would receive, my family would now have a bright future in Queensland. I told Mr Vardy that I appreciated his concerns but I had done a lot of work setting this up and was sure that doing Shift Work for many more years was not how I wanted to forge my future. And with that he shook my hand and wished me all the best for the future.

Back on the Floor!!

WELL I STILL HAD a job to do at this stage and my focus returned to the Jagenberg and Alan, my Relief, who would be waiting for me. When I arrived I realized that I had missed a shitty job which pleased me even more. Poor Alan and Aaron were not as impressed as they had just about finished the lengthy process of setting up for running Core Board. The worst part of setting up Core Board was setting up the Slitters (cutters), all 19 of them. The Volume was not so much the problem, it was more the fact that they were 75mm apart and all blades had to be prefect and set correctly to the barrel. It was quite a process and I will not go into great detail as this will bore you (and I for that matter) but it took a long time (up to 2 hours).

Anyway Alan seemed very keen to see me. I thought that it was because he was over setting up for Core Board, but no it was that he was keen to get the Gossip! Turns out that he was one spot behind me in the Golden Handshake line and was hoping I was full of shit and had turned down the package. Alan was quite disappointed that I had taken the package. I later found out that this was because he had been with the company four years longer than I had but had transferred to the Paper Mill from Conversion after I started. But that was how it worked with the Seniority system and he knew that when he signed up for it.

We sat down together in the Hut (Aaron, Alan and I) and I went through all the details of what happened. Turns out Alan had found out three days ago that Don had pulled out and was on tenterhooks waiting for my return to see what I would do.

Start Spreading the NEWS (I'm Leaving Hooray)!!!

I WOULD WAIT UNTIL I got home this evening to tell my Family as I wanted to see the look on their faces, especially the boys who were keen to move to the place they had so much fun in. But unfortunately I was beaten to the punch by Uncle Fozzie who had phoned his wife from work, who in turn proceeded to ring my wife and congratulate her. To say I was pissed off by this would be an understatement but this is how my in-laws operated and I should have intervened to prevent the surprise being spoilt. I got home just before midnight, as I did on afternoon shift, and could not contain my excitement as I awoke the boys and gave them a big hug. I didn't go too nuts though as it was a school night. I went to bed and fell asleep quicker than I had in months as I could now relax and move forward with our plans.

I rang my mother the next morning and she proceeded to tell the whole of my side of the family including her cousins, one of whom was married to a Journalist Dan McDonnell from the Herald/Sun.

In those days if you wanted a story to be told then the Newspaper was the place to do it with the Herald-Sun being one of, if not, the biggest.

He came and interviewed us in our Healesville home, which was for sale, and it was printed in the Newspaper the next day. Queensland had become a popular escape for many Victorians and for a multitude of reasons. With most revolving around the gloomy outlook of the Victorian economy at the time. As I am writing this section it appears that Victoria is again going through a similar time, carrying a huge debt which mainly came about due to the Covid shutdowns. Perhaps we will see another "Exodus" of Victorians moving north.

Onion gone Sour!!!

THE FOLLOWING DAY I was on Day Shift and arrived at work all cheerful with my plans set in place. As I stepped up to the Clock Card Des Onion came out of the Supervisors Office and pulled me to the side. At this stage I had not yet read the article in the Newspaper as I had only just purchased a copy on the way in to work. But it was obvious that Des had read it and was none too impressed with its content.

He started getting aggressive with me, saying that I was a traitor to all the work the Union had done for me. I told him that I had not read the article yet, as I held the Newspaper up to his face in a counter aggressive manner. He told me that 'he had' and that he was sure that Management 'had also' and would not be happy.

Trying to diffuse the aggression I told him that I had said nothing to the reporter that was aimed at the Company or the Union. I went on and asked if he would give me a chance to read it so I could respond appropriately. He told me that he would meet me at my Job (The Jagenberg) at around 9-00am to discuss the matter further.

news **Review**

GOING . . .

THE MAHONS

THE way Craig and Sharon Mahon see it, their circumstances in Victoria leave them with little option but to move north.

The couple, parents of Trent, 6, and Luke, 5, expect to move to Brisbane from Healesville in about two months.

Although Craig, 30, is yet to find a job in the Queensland capital he hopes his future will be more certain there.

His current job as a paper maker on shift work has been made redundant.

The only alternative would be for Sharon, 29, to go back to work, a decision neither wants to make given their firm views about raising children.

Craig believes that even if he finds a lower-paying job in Queensland, it is likely to bring more stability and better opportunities to his family.

And if he starts his own business — possibly in landscape gardening — the demand is likely to be greater there.

"The prospects are not too good down here at the moment as far as shift work is concerned. I don't know what's happening from day to day," Craig said.

"We went up there and we really liked it. If I come off shift work here I'll have trouble finding another job in Victoria.

"But up there I can change into something else like landscaping which I've been doing here part-time. No one here wants to spend any money on things like that because they are so uncertain."

GONE . . .

Upon arriving at the Jagenberg for a chat, I ensured that I had a Coffee ready for Des (which I had made with extra sugar ☺). Time had allowed me to read the full article along with the articles of three other families that had also either made the move or were about to like our family was. By reading the entire section with the multiple reviews it was clear to me that the reporter was creating a theme and bent my story to suit that theme.

I asked Des if he had read the other articles of the other families in the story, to which he responded; “why would I want to do that – it is your story I was interested in!” I agreed with Des and said; ‘that if you read just my article then it was a bit negative in some parts, but if you read all the articles you would quickly notice what the Reporter was doing with my words’. With this Aaron called me to help as the Jagenberg decided to have one of its Barrel Wrap hissy fits and needed me urgently. As I exited the hut I asked Des if he would please do me a favour and read all the articles.

When Aaron and I had sorted the Jagenberg issue I returned to the hut and spoke again with Des, who now seemed to have a calmer look on his face. He agreed that there was a theme in the entire story and said he would take me on my word that I was not shit canning the Company and Union. He went on to say that he had been baited a bit by the boys on the floor who had cut out my story and handed it to him. Their comments were that I was selling them out after all the Union had done for me. We shook hands and as he left said; “I noticed the extra sugar!” as he laughed out loud.

The Final Countdown!!!

NOW I MUST HAVE eased the mind of Des Onion, and he in turn must have had discussions with the Company, as no more was said of the Newspaper article. In fact Des even negotiated the payment of my Pro-rata Long Service Leave, something that I was only entitled to after ten years of service. I was three or so months short of this milestone so technically they could have not paid this amount to me, along with my accumulated Sick Leave and Annual Leave.

The entire payout was $44,000 dollars. Which is not huge in today's dollars but back in 1993 a home on the North Side of Brisbane (where we settled eventually) was going for around $90,000. So the payout "WAS" significant and gave us a great start for the new journey that my family and I were about to embark on.

The Hit We Had To Accept!!!

I WAS EXTREMELY CONCERNED and stressed over the next four weeks as my job would end in six weeks and we had still not sold our family home. If we could not sell our home in a decent time-frame then we would have to start eating into the $44,000 payout to pay our Mortgage. This would in turn make the move even harder, something we were dreading.

Two weeks before I was due to finish work our real Estate Agent called and said that he had an offer that he would like to present to us. We agreed to meet with him after 4-00pm as I was on day shift and could be home by then. The agent arrived and sat with us in our dining room where he presented us with the offer. We had the home listed for $189,950 and hoped to get something in the $180,000 to $185,000 range. But sadly we were extremely disappointed when the agent said the offer was for $170,000, and then proceeded to try and convince us that this was a good offer and we should take it.

WOW! What a hard pill to swallow and the fact was that six months after we built the home, some three and a half years earlier we received an offer of $210,000 for the home. This was from a local who did not want to go through the building process and really wanted the location. Add to that we had not done any landscaping, no carports and sheds were built, and the extension of a new living room had not even been thought of yet. It just goes to show how bad the Victorian economy was at the time, but we could not let it go for that much of a hit. We counter offered at $180,000 on the proviso that we would have a 30 day settlement.

The following day the buyers lifted the offer to $175,000 and after another day of toing and froing we settled on $176,000 with a 30 day settlement. The money was less than we hoped but the timing was perfect and meant that I could finish work, have two weeks or so to pack up, and then we would be off!

The Real Estate Window Card of our last home in Victoria!

The End of An Era!!!

THE LAST DAYS AT Bowater were happy and sad for me as my future looked rosier in general but I felt that I would truly miss all the Larrikins that I called friends in this place. It is always hard to break from an environment that has kept my family and I secure and prosperous for a decade. In fact until I wrote this book I did not realize how much it formed my life and directed my future. I finished my time as a Papermaker and off I went in my HZ Holden Kingswood SL V8, past Sargent Schultz on the Gatehouse and off into a new chapter of my life.

I will miss those Larrikins!

Ending Encore!!!

ON MANY OCCASIONS I have digressed somewhat from the storyline, but really that was my intention, as without these digressions the 'Story' as well as my time at Bowater, would have been very mundane. In today's world I believe many can relate to this. I believe that Society today, in its attempt to create a more inclusive and harmonious world, has sucked the life out of our 'individuality'. This in turn frustrates us all, to the point that many cannot cope. This lack of coping then manifests itself into many forms. My time at Bowater was my induction into an amazing period of my life that I have the fondest memories of. 'Yes' Shift work is Shit and 'Yes' there were times that I hated the place, but the fond memories of the Larrikins that I had the pleasure of working with will stay with me forever!

In my Bias opinion this was the greatest period of time to be an Australian, and in my 'again bias opinion' will always be considered the mould that cast the ageless stereotype of the "True Australian Larrikin!"

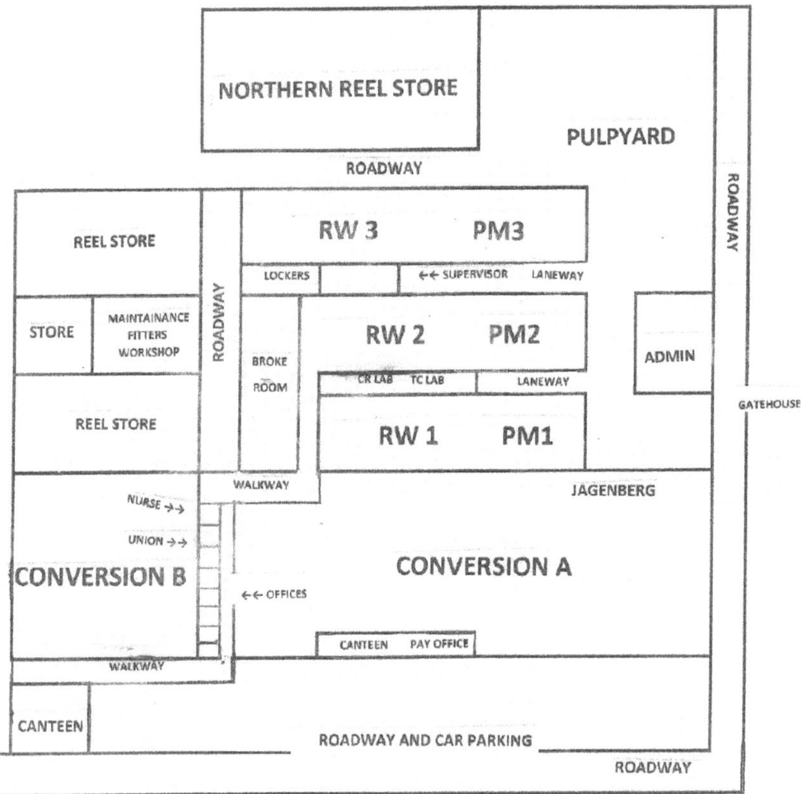

RW stands for Rewinder – PM stands for Paper Machine. To orientate you to the book the point I mustered on my first day for the Induction Tour was to the top left of this map just below the Northern Reel Store.

No 3 Mill

My beloved 1977 LX SS Torana Hatchback in Late 1981

ABOUT THE AUTHOR

Most books that I have read have this section and generally use it to tie themselves to the fibre of the book or story topic. But as a question, "About the Author?" it becomes more challenging. Let me attempt to describe myself - Craig Nelson is a complex creature who has never really fitted completely into general society as he has a total disability to conform, along with a huge desire to express himself completely and openly.

This desire gave birth to my first Book "One Simple Journey" which was a journal in the most part of my wife Tamara (Tee) and I (Cee) and our decision to quit work and travel the entire country (Australia). While never intended to be a book 'For the Masses' (my first attempt at writing), it allowed me to express myself completely and openly and helped me to understand myself a lot better.

After Travelling on ("One Simple Journey") we both got back on the treadmill and started working again. But something had changed and we viewed 'working' differently with more of a focus on a plan to leave work as early as possible to pursue the rest of our dreams. Retiring at fifty five I stepped away from a successful business to again pursue the things that really matter to me. Not having to be structured or conforming in my daily routine pumped air into my lungs, and as a result I have achieved more in retirement (funny word that) than I ever did working for someone else. It has allowed me to do the things that are important to "me!"

Writing this book "Pulp and Papermakers Fiction" is just one result of my new found time, as already I have started writing my next book "Retire with Identity" and plans sketched for another which will be a walkthrough the Real Estate Industry in the early 21st Century.

Again reflecting on About the Author as a question – the Answer is "Content!"

Milton Keynes UK
Ingram Content Group UK Ltd.
UKHW020813130524
442628UK00005B/418